BAD GIRL REPUTATION

ALSO BY ELLE KENNEDY
Good Girl Complex

BAD GIRL REPUTATION

An Avalon Bay Novel

Elle Kennedy

ST. MARTIN'S
GRIFFIN
NEW YORK

First published in the United States by St. Martin's Griffin, an imprint of St. Martin's Publishing Group

BAD GIRL REPUTATION. Copyright © 2022 by Elle Kennedy. All rights reserved. Printed in the United States of America. For information, address St. Martin's Publishing Group, 120 Broadway, New York, NY 10271.

www.stmartins.com

Designed by Steven Seighman

Library of Congress Cataloging-in-Publication Data

Names: Kennedy, Elle, author.
Title: Bad girl reputation : an Avalon Bay novel / Elle Kennedy.
Description: First edition. | New York : St. Martin's Griffin, 2022.
Identifiers: LCCN 2022013550 | ISBN 9781250796752 (trade
    paperback) | ISBN 9781250796769 (ebook)
Subjects: LCGFT: Novels.
Classification: LCC PS3611.E55857 B33 2022 | DDC 813/.6—
    dc23/eng/20220323
LC record available at https://lccn.loc.gov/2022013550

Our books may be purchased in bulk for promotional, educational, or business use. Please contact your local bookseller or the Macmillan Corporate and Premium Sales Department at 1-800-221-7945, extension 5442, or by email at MacmillanSpecialMarkets@macmillan.com.

First Edition: 2022

10 9 8 7 6 5

BAD GIRL
REPUTATION

CHAPTER 1

GENEVIEVE

Everyone even vaguely related to me is in this house. Dressed in black and huddled together in awkward conversation around cheese plates and casserole dishes. My baby pictures on the wall. In fits and starts, someone clinks a fork against a bottle of Guinness or a glass of Jameson to raise a toast and tell an inappropriate story about how Mom once rode a Jet Ski topless through the Independence Day boat parade. While my dad looks uncomfortable and stares out the window, I sit with my brothers and pretend we're familiar with these old stories about our mother, the fun-loving, life-by-the-balls-grabbing Laurie Christine West . . . when in reality we never knew her at all.

"So we were hot-boxing it to Florida in the back of an old ice-cream truck," starts Cary, one of my mother's cousins. "And somewhere south of Savannah, we hear this noise, like a rustling around, coming from the back . . ."

I cling to a bottle of water, fearing what I'll do without something in my hands. I picked a hell of a time to get sober. Everyone I've run into is trying to shove a drink in my hand because they don't know what else to say to the poor motherless girl.

I've considered it. Sliding up to my old bedroom with a bottle of anything and knocking it back until this day ends. Except I'm still regretting the last time I slipped.

But it would certainly make this entire ordeal slightly more tolerable.

Great-aunt Milly is doing circles around the house like a goldfish in a bowl. Every pass, she stops at the sofa to pat my arm and weakly squeeze my wrist and tell me I look just like my mother.

Great.

"Someone's gotta stop her," my younger brother Billy whispers beside me. "She's going to collapse. Those skinny little ankles."

She's sweet, but she's starting to creep me out. If she calls me by my mom's name, I might lose my shit.

"I tell Louis to turn down the radio," Cousin Cary continues, getting excited about his story. "Because I'm trying to figure out exactly where the noise is coming from. Thought we might be dragging something."

Mom had been sick for months before she was diagnosed with pancreatic cancer. According to Dad, she'd dealt with a constant pain in her back and abdomen that she'd ignored as the aches of getting older—and then a month later she was dead. But to me, this all started only a week ago. A call in the middle of the afternoon from my brother Jay urging me to come home, followed by another from my dad saying Mom wasn't going to be around much longer.

They'd all kept me in the dark. Because she hadn't wanted me to know.

How messed up is that?

"I'm talking about, for miles, this knocking around in there. Now, we're all pretty baked, okay? You gotta understand. Ran into this old-timer hippie freak back in Myrtle Beach who hooked us up with some kush—"

Someone coughs, grumbles under their breath.

"Let's not bore them with the details," Cousin Eddie says. Knowing glances and conspiratorial smirks travel among the cousins.

"Anyway." Cary starts up again, hushing them. "So we hear this, whatever it is. Tony's driving, and your mom," he says, gesturing his glass at us kids, "is standing in front of the freezer with a bong over her head like she's about to beat a raccoon to death or something."

My mind is far, far away from this ridiculous anecdote, jumbled and twisted with thoughts of my mother. She spent weeks lying in bed, preparing to die. Her last wish was for her only daughter to find out she was sick at the last possible moment. Even my brothers were forbidden from being at her bedside in the slow, agonizing slip into her final days. Mom preferring, as always, to suffer in silence while keeping her children at a distance. On the surface it might seem she did it for the benefit of her kids, but I suspect it was for her own sake—she wanted to avoid all those emotional, intimate moments that her impending death would no doubt trigger, the same way she avoided those moments in life.

In the end, she was relieved to have an excuse not to act like our mother.

"None of us want to open the freezer, and someone's shouting at Tony to pull over, but he's freaking out because he sees a cop a few cars behind us and, oh yeah, it occurs to us we're carrying contraband across state lines, so . . ."

And I can forgive her. Until her last breath, she was herself. Never pretending to be anything else. Since we were kids, she'd made it clear she wasn't particularly interested in us, so we never expected much. My dad and brothers, though—they should have told me about her illness. How do you keep something like that from your child, your sister? Even if I was living a hundred miles away. They should have told me, damn it. There might have been things I wanted to say to her. If I'd had the time to think about it more.

"Finally, Laurie tells me, you're gonna flip open the lid and we're gonna throw open the side door and Tony is gonna slow down enough to kick whatever it is out onto the shoulder of the road."

Chuckles break out from the crowd.

"So we count to three, I close my eyes, and I throw open the lid, expecting fur and claws to leap for my face. Instead, we see some dude in there asleep. He wandered in who knows when. Somewhere back in Myrtle Beach, maybe. Just curled up and took a nap."

This isn't how I pictured coming back to Avalon Bay. The house I grew up in crowded with mourners. Flower arrangements and sympathy cards on every table. We left the funeral hours ago, but I guess these things follow you. For days. Weeks. Never knowing when it's acceptable to say, *okay, enough, go back to your lives and let me go back to mine.* How do you even throw out a three-foot flower heart?

As Cary's story winds down, my dad taps me on the shoulder and nods toward the hallway, pulling me aside. He's wearing a suit for maybe the third time in his life, and I can't get used to it. It's just another thing that's out of sorts. Coming home to a place I don't quite recognize, as if waking up in an alternate reality where everything is familiar but not. Just a little off-center. I guess I've changed too.

"Wanted to grab you for a minute," he says as we duck away from the somber festivities. He can't keep his hands off his tie or from tugging at the collar of his shirt. Loosening it, then seemingly talking himself into straightening and tightening it again, like he feels guilty about it. "Look, I know there isn't a great time to bring this up, so I just got to ask."

"What's going on?"

"Well, I wanted to see if you might be planning to stick around for a while."

Shit.

"I don't know, Dad. I hadn't given it much thought." I didn't expect to get cornered so soon. Figured I'd have time, maybe a couple days, to see how things went and decide then. I left Avalon Bay a year ago for a reason and would have preferred to stay gone if not for the circumstances. I have a life back in Charleston. A job, an apartment. Amazon deliveries piling up at my door.

"See, I was hoping you could help with the business. Your mom managed all the office stuff, and things have kind of gone to hell on that since . . ." He stops himself. None of us know how to talk about it—her. It feels wrong no matter from which angle we try to approach it. So we trail off into silence and nod at each other to say, *yeah, I don't know either, but I understand.* "I thought, if you weren't in too much of a rush, you wouldn't mind jumping in there and making sense of it all."

I expected he might be depressed for a while and need some time to himself to cope, to get his head around it all. Maybe run off and go fishing or something. But this is . . . a lot to ask.

"What about Kellan, or Shane? Either one of them have got to know more about running that place than I do. Doesn't seem like they'd want me striding in there jumping the line."

My two oldest brothers have been working for Dad for years. In addition to a small hardware store, he also owns a stone business that caters to landscapers and people embarking on home renovations. Since I was a kid, my mom managed the inside stuff— orders, invoices, payroll—so Dad could worry about the dirty work outside.

"Kellan's the best foreman I've got, and with all these hurricane rebuilds we're doing down on the south coast, I can't afford to take him off the jobsites. And Shane spent the last year driving around on an expired license because the boy never opens his damn mail. I'd be bankrupt in a month if I let him anywhere near the books."

He's not wrong. I mean, I love my brothers, but the one time our parents had Shane babysit us, he let Jay and Billy climb onto the roof with a box of cherry bombs. The fire department showed up after the three boys started launching bombs with a slingshot at the neighbor's teenage sons in their pool. Growing up with two younger brothers and three older ones was entertaining, to say the least.

Still, I'm not getting roped into being a permanent replacement for Mom.

I bite my lip. "How long are you thinking?"

"A month, maybe two?"

Fuck.

I think it over for a moment, then sigh. "On one condition," I tell him. "You have to start looking to hire a new office manager in the next few weeks. I'll stick around until you find the right fit, but this isn't going to become a long-term arrangement. Deal?"

Dad wraps an arm around my shoulder and kisses the side of my head. "Thanks, kiddo. You're really helping me out of a jam."

I can't ever say no to him, even when I know I'm getting hosed. Ronan West might come off as a hard-ass, but he's always been a good father. Gave us enough freedom to get in trouble but was always there to bail us out. Even when he was pissed at us, we knew he cared.

"Grab your brothers, will ya? We gotta talk about a couple things."

He sends me off with foreboding and a pat on the back. Past experience has taught me that family meetings are never a positive affair. Family meetings mean more upheaval. Which is terrifying, because wasn't getting me to uproot my life to temporarily move back home already the big ask? I'm running through things in my head like breaking my lease or getting a subletter, quitting my job or pleading for a sabbatical, and my dad's still got more on the docket?

"Hey, shithead." Jay, who's sitting on the arm of the sofa in the living room, kicks my shin as I walk up. "Grab me another beer."

"Get it yourself, butt sniffer."

He's already ditched his jacket and tie, his white dress shirt unbuttoned at the top and sleeves rolled up. The others aren't much better, all of them in various states of giving up on the whole suit thing since getting back from the cemetery.

"Did you see Miss Grace? From middle school?" Billy, who's still not old enough to drink, tries to offer me a flask, but I wave it off. Jay snatches it instead. "She showed up a minute ago with Corey Doucette carrying her stupid little purse dog."

"Moustache Doucette?" I grin at the memory. In freshman year, Corey grew this creepy serial killer strip of hair on his lip and just refused to shave the nasty thing until it escalated to the threat of suspension if he didn't get rid of it. He was scaring the teachers. "Miss Grace has got to be, what, seventy?"

"I think she was seventy when I had her class in eighth grade," Shane says, shivering to himself.

"So they're, like, screwing?" Craig's face contorts in horror. His was the last class she taught before retiring. My youngest brother is now a high school graduate. "That's so messed up."

"Come on," I tell them. "Dad wants to talk to us in the den."

Once assembled, Dad starts in again on his tie and shirt collar until Jay hands him the flask and he takes a relieved swig. "So I'm just gonna come out with it: I'm putting the house up for sale."

"What the hell?" Kellan, the eldest, speaks for all of us when his outburst stunts Dad's announcement. "Where did this come from?"

"It's just me and Craig here now," Dad says, "and with him

going off to college in a couple months, it doesn't make much sense to hang on to this big, empty place. Time to downsize."

"Dad, come on," Billy interjects. "Where's Shane gonna sleep when he forgets where he lives again?"

"One time," Shane growls, punching him in the arm.

"Yeah, fuck you, one time." Billy gives him a shove. "What about when you slept on the beach because you couldn't find your car parked not even fifty yards away?"

"Will y'all knock it off? You're acting like a bunch of damn idiots. There are people still out there mourning your mother."

That shuts everyone up real quick. For just a minute or two, we'd forgotten. That's what keeps happening. We forget, and then the truck slams into us again and we're snapped back to the present, to this strange reality that doesn't feel right.

"Like I said, it's too much house for one person. My mind's made up." Dad's tone is firm. "But before I can put it on the market, we've got to fix it up a little. Put a spit shine on it."

Seems like everything's changing too fast, and I can't keep up. I barely had time to get my head around Mom being sick before we were putting her in the ground, and now I've got to pick up and move my whole life back home, only to find out home won't exist much longer either. I've got whiplash, but I'm standing still, watching everything swirl around me.

"There's no sense clearing out until Craig gets settled at school in the fall," Dad says, "so it'll be a little while yet. But there it is. Thought y'all should know sooner rather than later."

With that, he ducks out of the den. Damage done. He leaves us there with the fallout of his announcement, all of us shell-shocked and staggering.

"Shit," Shane says like he just remembered he left his keys on the beach at high tide. "You know how much porn and old weed is hidden in this house?"

"Right." Affecting a serious face, Billy smacks his hands together. "So after Dad falls asleep, we start ripping out floorboards."

As the boys argue about who gets dibs on any lost contraband they might dig up, I'm still trying to catch my breath. I guess I've never been good with change. I'm still fumbling to navigate my own transformation since leaving town.

Swallowing a sigh, I abandon my brothers and step into the hall—where my gaze snags on probably the only thing about this place that hasn't changed one bit.

My ex-boyfriend Evan Hartley.

CHAPTER 2

GENEVIEVE

The guy's got some nerve walking in here looking like that. Those haunting, dark eyes that still lurk in the deepest parts of my memory. Brown, nearly black hair I still feel between my fingers. He's as heart-stabbingly gorgeous as the pictures that still flicker behind my eyes. It's been a year since I last saw him, yet my response to him is the same. He walks into a room, and my body notices him before I do. It's a disturbance of static in the air that dances across my skin.

It's obnoxious, is what it is. And that my body has the audacity to react to him, *now*, at my mother's funeral, is even more disturbing.

Evan stands with his twin brother Cooper, scanning the room until he notices me. The guys are identical except for occasional variances in their haircuts, but most people tell them apart by their tattoos. Cooper's got two full sleeves, while most of Evan's ink is on his back. Me, I know it from his eyes. Whether they're gleaming with mischief or flickering with joy, need, frustration . . . I always know when it's Evan's eyes on me.

Our gazes meet. He nods. I nod back, my pulse quickening. Literally three seconds later, Evan and I convene down the hall where there are no witnesses.

It's strange how familiar we are with some people, no matter how much time has passed. Memories of the two of us wash over me like a balmy breeze. Walking through this house with him like we're back in high school. Sneaking in and out at all hours. Stumbling with hands against the wall to stay upright. Laughing in hysterical whispers to not wake up the whole house.

"Hey," he says, holding out his arms in a hesitant offer, which I accept because it feels more awkward not to.

He always did give good hugs.

I force myself not to linger in his arms, not to inhale his scent. His body is warm and muscular and as familiar to me as my own. I know every inch of that tall, delicious frame.

I take a hasty step backward.

"Yeah, so, I heard. Obviously. Wanted to pay my respects." Evan is bashful, almost coy, with his hands in his pockets and his head bowed to look at me under thick lashes. I can't imagine the pep talk it took to get him here.

"Thanks."

"And, well, yeah." From one pocket, he pulls out a blue Blow Pop. "I got you this."

I haven't cried once since finding out Mom was sick. Yet accepting this stupid token from Evan makes my throat tighten and my eyes sting.

I'm suddenly transported back to the first time a Blow Pop ever exchanged hands between us. Another funeral. Another dead parent. It was after Evan's dad, Walt, died in a car accident. Drunk driving, because that's the kind of reckless, self-destructive man Walt Hartley had been. Fortunately, nobody else was hurt, but Walt's life ended on the dark road that night when he'd lost control and smashed into a tree.

I was twelve at the time and had no clue what to bring to a wake. My parents brought flowers, but Evan was a kid like me.

What was he going to do with flowers? All I knew was that my best friend and the boy I'd always had a huge crush on was hurting badly, and all I had to my name was one measly dollar. The fanciest thing I could afford at the general store was a lollipop.

Evan had cried when I clasped the Blow Pop in his shaking hand and quietly sat beside him on the back deck of his house. He'd whispered, "Thanks, Gen," and then we sat there in silence for more than an hour, staring at the waves lapping at the shore.

"Shut up," I mutter to myself, clenching the lollipop in my palm. "You're so dumb." Despite my words, we both know I'm deeply affected.

Evan cracks a knowing smile and smooths one hand over his tie, straightening it. He cleans up nice, but not too nice. Something about a suit on this guy still feels dangerous.

"You're lucky I found you first," I tell him once I can speak again. "Not sure my brothers would be as friendly."

With an unconcerned smirk, he shrugs. "Kellan hits like a girl."

Typical. "I'll make sure to tell him you said so."

Some wandering cousins glimpse us around the corner and look as though they might find a reason to come talk to me, so I grab Evan by the lapel and shove him toward the laundry room. I press myself up against the doorframe, then check to make sure the coast is clear.

"I can't get hijacked into another conversation about how much I remind people of my mom," I groan. "Like, dude, the last time you saw me, I still wasn't eating solid food."

Evan adjusts his tie again. "They think they're helping."

"Well, they're not."

Everyone wants to tell me what a great lady Mom was and how important family was to her. It's almost creepy, hearing people talk about a woman who bears no resemblance to the person I knew.

"How you holding up?" he asks roughly. "Like, really?"

I shrug in return. Because that's the question, isn't it? I've been asked it a dozen different ways over the past couple days, and I still don't have a proper answer. Or at least, not the one people want to hear.

"I'm not sure I feel anything. I don't know. Maybe I'm still in shock or something. You always expect these things to happen in a split second, or over months and months. This, though? It was like just the wrong amount of warning. I came home, and a week later she was dead."

"I get that," he says. "Barely time to get your bearings before it's over."

"I haven't known which way is up for days." I bite my lip. "I'm starting to wonder if there's something wrong with me?"

He fixes me with a disbelieving scowl. "It's death, Fred. There's nothing wrong with you."

I snort a laugh at his nickname for me. Been so long since I've heard it, I'd almost forgotten what it sounded like. There was a time when I answered to it more than my own name.

"Seriously, though. I keep waiting for the grief to hit, but it doesn't come."

"It's hard to find a lot of emotion for a person who didn't have a lot for you. Even if it's your mom." He pauses. "Maybe especially moms."

"True."

Evan gets it. He always has. One of the things we have in common is an unorthodox relationship with our mothers. In that there isn't much relationship to speak of. While his mom is an impermanent idea in his life—absent except for the few times a year she breezes into town to sleep off a bender or ask for money— mine was absent in spirit if not in body. Mine was so cold and detached, even in my earliest memories, that she hardly seemed to exist at all. I grew up jealous of the flower beds she tended in the front yard.

"I'm almost relieved she's gone." A lump rises in my throat. "No, more than almost. That's terrible to say, I know that. But it's like . . . now I can stop trying, you know? Trying and then feeling like crap when it doesn't change."

My whole life I made efforts to connect with her. To figure out why my mother didn't seem to like me much. I'd never gotten an answer. Maybe now I can stop asking.

"It's not terrible," Evan says. "Some people make shit parents. It's not our fault they don't know how to love us."

Except for Craig—Mom certainly knew how to love him. After five failed attempts, she'd finally gotten the recipe right with him. Her one perfect son she could pour a lifetime of mothering into. I love my little brother, but he and I might as well have been raised by two different people. He's the only one of us walking around here with red, swollen eyes.

"Can I tell you something?" Evan says with a grin that makes me suspicious. "But you have to promise not to hit me."

"Yeah, I can't do that."

He laughs to himself and licks his lips. An involuntary habit that always drove me crazy, because I know what that mouth is capable of.

"I missed you," he confesses. "Am I an asshole if I'm sort of glad someone died?"

I punch him in the shoulder, to which he feigns injury. He doesn't mean it. Not really. But in a weird way I appreciate the sentiment, if only because it gives me permission to smile for a second or two. To breathe.

I toy with the thin silver bracelet circling my wrist. Not quite meeting his eyes. "I missed you too. A little."

"A little?" He's mocking me.

"Just a little."

"Mmm-mmm. So you thought about me, what, once, twice a day when you were gone?"

"More like once or twice *total*."

He chuckles.

Truthfully, after I left the Bay I spent months doing my best to push away the thoughts of him when they insisted their way forward. Refusing the images that came when I closed my eyes at night or went on a date. Eventually it got easier. I'd almost managed to forget him. Almost.

And now here he is, and it's like not a second has passed. We still have this bubble of energy building between us. It's evident in the way he angles his body toward mine, the way my hand lingers on his arm longer than necessary. How it hurts not to touch him.

"Don't do that," I order when I notice his expression. I'm caught in his eyes. Snagged, like catching my shirt on a door handle, only it's a memory tripping up my brain.

"Do what?"

"You know what."

Evan's lips lift at the corner. Just a twitch. Because he knows the way he looks at me.

"You look good, Gen." He's doing it again. The dare in his eyes, the implications in his gaze. "Time away agreed with you."

The little shit. It isn't fair. I hate him, even as my fingers make contact with his chest and slide down the front of his shirt.

No, what I hate is how easily he can have me.

"We shouldn't do this," I murmur.

We're tucked away but still visible to anyone should they get the urge to glance in our direction. Evan's hand skims the hem of my dress. He pushes up under the fabric and softly drags his fingertips along the curve of my ass.

"No," he breathes against my ear. "We shouldn't."

So, of course, we do.

We slip into the bathroom next to the laundry room, locking the door behind us. My breath lodges in my throat when he lifts me up on the vanity.

"This is a terrible idea," I tell him as he grips my waist and I brace myself against the sink.

"I know." And then he covers my mouth with his.

The kiss is urgent and hungry. Lord, I missed this. I missed his kisses and the greedy thrust of his tongue, how wild and unbridled he is. Our mouths devour each other, almost too roughly, and still I can't have enough of him.

The anticipation and frantic need is too much. I fumble with the buttons of his shirt, pulling it open to drag my nails down his chest until the pain makes him pin my arms behind my back. It's hot and raw. Maybe a little angry. All the unfinished business working itself out. I close my eyes and hold on for the ride, losing myself in the kiss, the taste of him. He kisses me harder, deeper, until I'm mindless with need.

I can't stand it anymore.

I force my arms free to unbuckle his belt. Evan watches me. Watches my eyes. My lips.

"I've missed this," he whispers.

So have I, but I can't bring myself to say it out loud.

I gasp when his hand travels between my thighs. My own hand is trembling as I slip it inside his boxers and—

"Everything okay in there?" A voice. Then a knock. My entire extended family is on the other side of the door.

I freeze.

"Fine," Evan calls back, his fingertips a scant inch from where I was just aching for him.

Now, I'm sliding off the vanity, pushing his hand off me, withdrawing mine from his boxers. Before my flats even connect with the tiled floor, I already hate myself. Barely in the same room with him for ten minutes, and I lose all self-control.

I almost had sex with Evan Hartley at my mother's funeral reception, for fuck's sake. If we hadn't been interrupted, I have no doubt I would've let him take me right then and there. That's a new low, even for me.

Damn it.

I'd spent the last year training myself to at least approximate a normal functioning adult. To not surrender to every destructive instinct the second it pops into my head, to exercise some damn restraint. And then Evan Hartley licks his lips and I'm open for business.

Really, Gen?

As I'm fixing my hair in the mirror, I see him watching me with a question on his tongue.

Finally he voices it. "You okay?"

"I can't believe we almost did that," I mumble, shame lining my throat. Then, I find my composure and steel up my defenses. I lift my head. "Just so we're clear, this isn't going to be a thing."

"The hell does that mean?" His affronted gaze meets mine in the reflection.

"It means I have to be in town for a bit for my dad, but while I'm here, we're not going to be seeing each other."

"Seriously?" When he reads my resolved expression, his sours. "What the hell, Gen? You stick your tongue down my throat and then tell me to get lost? That's pretty shitty."

Turning to face him, I shrug with feigned indifference. He wants me to fight him because he knows there's a lot of emotion here, and the more he drags it out of me, the better his chances. But I'm not going there again, not this time. This was a lapse in judgment. Temporary insanity. I'm better now. Head on straight. Got it all out of my system.

"You know we can't stay away from each other," he tells me, growing more frustrated at my decision. "We spent our whole relationship trying. Doesn't work."

He's not wrong. Until the day I finally left town, we were on and off since freshman year of high school. A constant push-and-pull of loving and fighting. Sometimes I'm the moth, other times the flame.

What I eventually figured out, though, is that the only way to win is not to play.

Unlocking the door, I pause to offer a brief look over my shoulder. "There's a first time for everything."

CHAPTER 3

EVAN

This is what I get for trying to be a nice guy. She needed to forget for a little while—that's cool. I'll never, ever complain about kissing Genevieve. But she could've at least played nice afterward. *Let's get together later and have a drink, catch up.* Blowing me off altogether is harsh even for her.

Gen has always had sharp edges. Hell, it's one of the things that draws me to her. But she's never looked at me with such dead disinterest. Like I was nobody to her.

Brutal.

As we leave the West house and walk toward Cooper's truck, he gives me a look of suspicion. Beyond appearances, we're entirely different people. If we weren't brothers, we probably wouldn't even be friends. But we are brothers—even worse, twins—which means we can read each other's minds with one measly look.

"You're kidding me," he says, sighing with what has become a near-permanent state of judgment plastered on his face. For months now, he's been on my case about every little thing.

"Leave it." Honestly, I'm not in the mood to hear it.

He pulls away from the curb among the long line of cars parked on the street for the reception. "Unbelievable. You hooked up with her." He slides a side-eye at me, which I ignore. "Jesus

Christ. You were gone for ten minutes. What, you were like, I'm so sorry for your loss, here, have my penis?"

"Fuck off, Coop." When he phrases it like that, it does sound kind of bad.

Kind of?

Fine. Alright. Maybe nearly having sex at her mother's funeral reception wasn't the brightest of ideas, but . . . but I missed her, damn it. Seeing Gen again, after more than a year apart, was like a punch to the gut. My need to touch her, kiss her, had bordered on desperation.

Maybe that makes me a weak bastard, but there you have it.

"I think you've done enough of that for the both of us."

I grit my teeth and force my gaze out the window. The thing about Cooper—when our dad died and then our mom basically abandoned us as kids, he somehow got it in his head that I wanted him to become both. A constantly nagging, grumpy bastard who's always disappointed in me. For a little while, things got better after he settled down with his girlfriend Mackenzie, who managed to yank the stick out of his ass. But now it seems like finally being in his first stable relationship has got him back to thinking he's qualified to pass judgment on my life.

"It wasn't like that," I tell him. Because I can feel him fuming at me. "Some people cry when they're grieving. Gen's not a crier."

He half shakes his head, twisting his hands on the steering wheel while his jaw works on grinding down his molars, like I can't hear what he's thinking.

"Don't give yourself an aneurysm, bro. Just spit it out."

"She's barely been in town a week and already you're in it up to your neck. I told you it was a bad idea going over there."

I would never give Cooper the satisfaction, but he's right.

Genevieve shows up and I lose my damn mind. It's always been that way with us. We're two mostly harmless chemicals that when mixed become an explosive combination, leveling a city block with salt water.

"You act like we robbed a liquor store. Relax. All we did was kiss."

Cooper's disapproval pours off him. "Today it's just a kiss. Tomorrow is another story."

And? It's not as if we're hurting anybody. I frown at him. "Dude, what does it matter to you?"

He and Genevieve used to be cool. Even friends. I get that maybe he holds a grudge about how she left town, but it's not like she did it to him. Anyway, it's been a year. If I'm not still making a thing of it, why should he?

At a stoplight, he turns to meet my eyes. "Look, you're my brother and I love you, but you're an ass when she's around. These last few months you've really gotten your shit together. Don't throw all that away on a chick who's never going to stop being a mess."

Something about it—I don't know, the contempt in his voice, the condescension—sticks right in my craw. Cooper can be a real self-righteous prick when he wants to be.

"It's not like I'm dating her again, okay? Don't be so dramatic."

We pull up to our house, the two-story, low-country cottage-style on the beach that's been in our family for three generations. The place was all but falling apart before we started making reno-vations over the past several months. It's taken most of our savings and more of our time, but it's coming along.

"Yeah, you keep telling yourself that." Cooper shuts off the engine with an exasperated breath. "Same old pattern: takes off whenever she wants, suddenly pops back in, and you're ready to bake cookies together. Sound like any other woman you know?" With that, he hops out of the truck and slams the door shut.

Well, that was uncalled for.

Of the two of us, Cooper has held the hardest grudge against our mother, to the point he's resented me for not needing to hate her as much as he does. In her latest episode, though, I backed him up. Told her she wasn't welcome to hang around anymore, not after what she did to him. Shelley Hartley had finally crossed one line too many.

But I guess taking Cooper's side wasn't enough to get him to ease up on me. Everyone's full of low blows today.

At dinner later, Cooper still hasn't let the Genevieve thing go. Not in his nature.

It's damn irritating. I'm trying to eat my damned spaghetti, and this asshole is still laying into me while he tells Mackenzie, who's been living with us for the past few months, about how I basically screwed my ex on top of the still-warm casket of her dead mother.

"Evan says he'll just be a minute, then leaves me by myself in that house to give our condolences to her dad and five brothers, who pretty much think it's Evan's fault she ran out of town a year ago," Cooper grumbles, stabbing a meatball with his fork. "They're asking where he is; meanwhile, he's got Mr. West's baby girl bent over the bathtub or whatever."

"We just kissed," I say in exasperation.

"Coop, come on," Mac says, wincing away from her fork, which is coiled with pasta and hanging mid-air. "I'm trying to eat."

"Yeah, have some tact, jackass," I chide.

When they're not looking, I slip a piece of meatball to Daisy, the golden retriever puppy at my feet. Cooper and Mac rescued her off the jetty last year and she's nearly doubled in size since then. At first I wasn't thrilled with the idea of taking care of this creature Cooper's new girlfriend had dumped on us, but then she spent a night curled up at the end of my bed having puppy dreams, and I broke like a cheap toy. Dog's had me wrapped around her paw ever since. She's the only girl I can trust not to take off on me. Luckily, Coop and Mac worked out, so we didn't have to fight a custody battle.

It's funny how life works out sometimes. Last year, Cooper and I hatched an admittedly mean-spirited plot to sabotage Mac's relationship with her boyfriend at the time. In our defense, the guy was a douchebag. Then Cooper had to spoil all the fun and catch feelings for the rich college girl. I couldn't stand her at first, but it turned out I'd read Mackenzie Cabot all wrong. I was at least man enough to admit I'd misjudged her. Cooper, on the other hand, can't keep his thoughts to himself so far as Gen's concerned. Typical.

"So what's the real story with you two?" Mac asks, curiosity flickering in her dark-green eyes.

The real story? How do I even begin to answer that? Genevieve and I have history. Lots of it. Some of it great. Some, not so good. Things have always been complicated with us.

"We got together freshman year of high school," I tell Mac. "She was basically my best friend. Always good for a laugh and down for anything."

My mind is suddenly flooded with images of us messing around on dirt bikes at two in the morning with a fifth of tequila between us. Surfing the swells as a hurricane moved in, then riding out the storm in the back of her brother's Jeep. Gen and I constantly dared each other's limits of adventure, getting into a few scrapes with death or mutilation that we had no right escaping unscathed. There was no adult in the relationship, so there was never a point when someone said stop. We were always chasing the rush.

And Gen was a rush. Fearless and undaunted. Unapologetically herself, and to hell what anyone had to say about it. She made me crazy; more than once I broke my hand wrestling some asshole cornering her in a bar. Yeah, maybe I was possessive, but no more than she was. She'd drag a chick out by her hair for looking at me the wrong way. Most of it had something to do with the off-and-on part—getting jealous, fighting, and turning around to make the other one jealous. It was a little messed up, but it was our language. I was hers and she was mine. We were addicted to make-up sex.

The quiet moments were just as addictive. Lying on a beach blanket at our favorite spot in the Bay, her head in the crook of my neck, my arm slung around her as we looked up at the stars. Whispering our darkest secrets to each other and knowing there'd never be any judgment on the other end. Hell, aside from Cooper, she's the only one to ever see me cry.

"There was a lot of breaking up and making up," I admit. "But that was our thing. And then last year, she was suddenly gone. One day she just picked up and left town. Didn't say a word to anyone."

My heart squeezes painfully at the memory. I thought it was a joke at first. That Gen had taken off with her girlfriends and wanted me to freak out and drive to Florida or something to track her down, then fight a little and bang it out. Until the girls promised me they hadn't heard a peep from her.

"I found out later she'd settled down in Charleston and started a new life. Just like that." I swallow the bitterness that clogs my throat.

Mac contemplates me for a moment. We've grown fairly close since she started living here, so I know when she's trying to formulate a nice way to tell me I'm a disaster. Not like it's anything I don't know.

"Go ahead, princess. Say what's on your mind."

She puts her fork down and pushes her plate away. "Sounds like a toxic situation for both of you. Maybe Gen was right to end it for good. It might be better you two stay away from each other."

At that, Cooper slides me a glare because there is almost nothing he loves more than an I-told-you-so.

"I said the same thing to Cooper about you," I remind her. "And now look at you guys."

"For fuck's sake." Cooper throws his utensils on his plate, and his chair squeaks against the wooden floor. "You can't compare the two. Not even close. Genevieve is a mess. The best thing she ever did for you was stop taking your calls. Let it go, dude. She's not here for you."

"Yeah, you must be loving this," I say, wiping my mouth with my napkin before tossing it on the table. "Because this is payback, right?"

He sighs, rubbing his eyes like I'm some dog refusing to be house-trained. Condescending prick. "I'm trying to look out for you because you're too dick-blinded to see where this will end. Where you two always end up."

"You know," I say, getting up from the table. "Maybe you should stop projecting all your hang-ups onto me. Genevieve isn't Shelley. Stop trying to punish me because you're mad your mommy left you."

I regret the words even as they leave my mouth, but I don't turn back as Daisy follows me to the kitchen door and we head for the beach. Truth is, no one knows better than me all the messed-up shit Gen and I have been through. How inescapable we are. But that's just it. Now that she's back, I can't ignore her.

This thing between us, this pull—it won't let me.

CHAPTER 4

GENEVIEVE

I regret this already. My first day in the office at Dad's stone business is worse than I imagined. For weeks, maybe months, the guys walked in here to leave invoices in a haphazard pile on the desk in front of an empty chair. Mail was tossed in a tray without so much as looking at who it was from. There's still a mug of sludge that used to be coffee sitting on top of the filing cabinet. Opened sugar packets the ants have long since scavenged are sitting in the trash can.

And Shane isn't helping. While I sit at the computer trying to discern Mom's file-naming system to track down some kind of record of paid and outstanding accounts, my second-oldest brother is down a TikTok hole on his phone.

"Hey, fuckhead," I say, snapping my fingers. "There are like six invoices here with your name on them. Are these paid or still pending?"

He doesn't bother raising his head from his screen. "How should I know?"

"Because they're your jobsites."

"That's not my department."

Shane doesn't see me shake my hands in the air as I'm imagining throttling him. Asshole.

"There are three emails here from Jerry about a patio for his restaurant. You need to get on the phone with him and set up an appointment to do a walk-through and give him an estimate."

"I've got shit to do," he says, barely muttering the words as his attention stays focused on the tiny glowing box in his hands. It's like he's five years old.

I launch a paper clip at him with a rubber band. Nails him right in the middle of his forehead.

"Shit, Gen. What the hell?"

That got his attention.

"This." I push the invoices across the desk and write down Jerry's phone number. "Since you've already got your phone out, make the call."

Utterly disgusted with my tone, he sneers at me. "You realize you're basically Dad's secretary."

Shane is sincerely testing my love for him and desire to let him live. I have four other brothers. Not like I'll really miss one.

"You don't get to boss me around," he gripes.

"Dad made me office manager until he finds someone else." I get up from the desk to put the papers in his hand and shove him out of the office. "So as far as you're concerned, I am your god now. Get used to it." Then I slam the door on him.

I knew this would happen. Growing up in a house with six kids, all of us were always jockeying for position. We all have an autonomy complex, everyone trying to exert their independence while getting shit on from the upper rungs of the age ladder. It's worse now that I'm the twenty-two-year-old middle kid telling the big brothers what's what. Still, Dad was right—this place is a wreck. If I don't get it all sorted in a hurry, he'll be broke in no time.

Later, after work, I meet up with my brother Billy for a drink at Ronda's, a local dive for the retired swingers crowd that spends their days driving up and down Avalon Bay in golf carts and trading keys in a fishbowl over a game of poker. The rising May temperatures in the Bay means the return of wall-to-wall tourists and rich pricks clogging the boardwalk, so the rest of us have to find more creative places to hang out.

As Billy smiles at the leathery-faced bartender for a beer—nobody in this town cards the locals—I order a coffee. It's unseasonably sweltering outside, even at sunset, and my clothes are sticking to my skin like papier-mâché, but I can always drink a cup of hot, unleaded caffeine. It's how you know you're from the South.

"Saw you and Jay bringing in some boxes last night," Billy says. "That the last of it?"

"Yeah, I'm leaving most of my stuff in storage back in Charleston. Doesn't make much sense to haul my furniture down here just to move it all back up in a few months."

"You're still set on going back?"

I nod. "I'll have to find a different place, though."

My landlord was a total jerk about breaking my lease a couple months early, so I'll still be paying him while I'm here living in my childhood bedroom. Leaving my job didn't go much better. My boss at the real estate agency all but laughed at me when I mentioned taking a leave of absence. I hope Dad's planning on paying me well. He might be a grieving widower, but I don't work for free.

"So guess who walked into the hardware store the other day?" Billy says with a look that tells me to brace myself. "Deputy Dogshit came in hassling me about the sidewalk sign. Something about town ordinances and blocking pedestrian traffic."

My nails bite into the weathered bar top. Even after a year, the mention of Deputy Rusty Randall still coaxes a special kind of anger.

"That sign's been there for, what," Billy says, "twenty years at least."

As long as I can remember, definitely. It's a staple of the sidewalk, our wooden A-frame sign with the cartoon handyman announcing, *YES, WE'RE OPEN!* and waving a pipe wrench. The other side features a chalkboard with the week's sale or new products. When I was little and loved following Dad to work, he used to yell at me from inside that I better not be drawing on the sign. I'd hastily erase my artwork and begin transferring it to the concrete, doing my best to force traffic around my masterpieces and just about biting the ankles off tourists who stomped their Sperrys through my sidewalk gallery.

"The guy wouldn't leave until I brought the sign inside," Billy grumbles. "He stood there for fifteen minutes while I pretended to help some customers and haggled with him about his bullshit ordinance. I was about to call Dad to talk some sense into him, but he went for his cuffs like he was about to arrest me, so I said, screw it. I waited a few minutes after he left and then put it back out."

"Asshole," I mutter into my coffee. "You know he gets off on it."

"I'm surprised he didn't tail you into town. Half expected him to be sitting outside the house in the middle of the night."

I wouldn't have put it past him. About a year ago, Deputy Randall became my cautionary tale. That night was my rock bottom, the moment I realized I couldn't go on living like I was. Drinking too much, partying every night, letting my demons get the best of me. I had to do something about it—get my life back—before it was too late. So I made a plan, and a couple months later, I packed up everything I needed and set off for Charleston. Billy was the only person I told about that night with Rusty. Even though he's two years younger than me, he's always been my closest confidant.

"I still think about her," I tell my brother. The guilt churning in my gut at the thought of Kayla and her children is still potent after all this time. I'd heard a while back she'd left Rusty and taken the kids. "I feel like I should find her. Apologize."

Though the idea of facing her, and how she might react, is enough to send me into an anxiety spiral. It's become a new feeling for me since that night. There was a time when nothing scared me. The stuff that left other people biting their nails rolled right off my shoulders. Now, I look back on my wilder days and cringe. Some of those days were not so long ago.

"Do what you want," Billy says, taking a deep swig of his beer as if to wash the lingering topic out of his mouth. "But you have nothing to apologize for. The guy's a jackass and a creep. He's lucky we didn't find him down a dark dirt road somewhere."

I'd sworn Billy to secrecy; otherwise, he definitely would've run and told Dad or our brothers what had happened. I'm glad he kept it quiet. No sense in all of them winding up in prison for beating the pulp out of a cop. Then Randall would win.

"I'm going to run into him eventually," I say, more to myself.

"Well, if you've got to skip town in a hurry, I still have about eighty bucks stashed in my old bed frame at Dad's house." Billy grins at me, which does go a long way to unwinding the knot in my chest. He's good like that.

As we're closing out the tab, I get a text from my best friend Heidi.

Heidi: *Bonfire on the beach tonight.*
Me: *Where?*
Heidi: *The usual.*

Meaning Evan and Cooper's house. The place is loaded with emotional landmines.

Me: *I don't know if that's a good idea.*
Heidi: *Come on. A couple drinks then you can bail.*

Heidi: *Don't make me come get you.*
Heidi: *See you there.*
Me: *Fine. Bitch.*

I stifle a sigh, as my tired brain tries to work through yet another pitfall to consider. Settling back into town, I was excited to reconnect with old friends and spend more time with others, but trying to dodge Evan makes that more complicated. I can't very well draw a line down the center of town. And no part of me wants the summer to devolve into tests of loyalty and calling dibs on our tight web of friends, ties crossing and overlapping. It isn't fair to either of us. Because as much as I know nothing good comes from letting Evan back in, I have no intentions to hurt him. This is my punishment, not his.

CHAPTER 5

EVAN

All the freaks come out at night. Under a full moon, we're the hidden images of ourselves, revealed in silver light. It's the Bay turned wild with inhibition and mischief, everybody hot and bothered and aching for a good time. Any excuse for a party.

On the beach, dozens of our friends, and more than a few random tagalongs, surround a bonfire. Our house is set back just beyond the dunes and grassy tree-dotted lawn, its outline evident only in the orange porch lights. It's a good time, kicking back with a few beers, smoking a bowl. A couple people with guitars haggle over song requests while a nearby group plays strip glow frisbee. Whatever it takes to get laid these days, I guess.

"So this clone is wasted, right," Jordy, an old high school friend of ours, says to those of us gathered around the fire, sitting on a driftwood log while he rolls a joint. Dude could do this shit with his eyes closed and it'd still be the tightest, neatest roll you've ever seen. "And the guy stumbles into our table. Like knocks right into us. He keeps calling me Parker."

We laugh, because it's such a clone name. Those collar-wearing pansy-ass Richie Riches who go to Garnet College are nothing if not predictable. Can't hold their liquor and making it everyone else's problem.

"For like twenty minutes he's talking to us, holding on to the table to keep from splattering on the floor. No idea what the hell he's babbling about. Then suddenly he's like, *hey, come on, bros, after-party at my house.*"

"No," Mackenzie says, eyes flashing wide and dread in her voice. "You did not." She's keeping Cooper in a better mood tonight, sitting in his lap with her tits shoved up in his face. Got him well occupied, which is a relief. I was getting sick of his tantrums.

Jordy shrugs. "I mean, he insisted. So the four us, right, are pretty much having to carry this guy out of the bar. Then he hands me his keys and says, *you drive, it's the blue one.* I press the button on the fob, and this Maserati SUV flashes its lights at me. Like no way, right? That's a hundred-thousand-dollar car. I'm pretty sure I stepped in piss at some point in that dirty bar bathroom, but sure, guy."

"Just tell me he still has his kidneys," I say with a grin.

"Yeah, yeah. We didn't chop him or the car for parts." Jordy waves his hand, then lights the joint. "Anyway. So the guy goes, *Car, take me home.* And the thing is like, *okay, Christopher, here's your route home.* At that point I'm thinking, well, shit. So I rev that baby up and start driving. About a half hour later we get to his stupid-huge mansion down the coast. I'm talking iron gate and topiaries and shit. So we make it there alive and the dude's like, *hey, want to see something cool?*"

Always the famous last words. Like the time our buddy Wyatt tried the knife trick from *Aliens* and had to get thirty-seven stiches and have a tendon reattached. Come to think of it, that was one of the last times Genevieve and I hung out. Which, until all the blood, was a pretty good time. Can't say for sure how we ended up on the sixty-five-foot Hatteras sportfishing boat out in the middle of the bay, only that we had a nightmare of a time getting it to the dock and somehow still managed to come ashore about ten miles from where we were aiming. Navigating gets a hell of a lot harder in the dark after a few Fireballs.

I can't believe I'd almost forgotten about that night. But I guess I've done a lot of forgetting over the last year. Or tried to, at least. For a while, I expected Gen would show up as if nothing had happened. Like she overslept for six months. Then seven, eight months—a year gone, and I'd finally trained myself to stop thinking about her every time this thing or that reminded me of another time when. So of course, just when I've almost got her out of my system, she's back. A fresh, unfiltered shot straight into my bloodstream when I was damn near clean. Now all I taste are her lips. I feel her nails down my back every night while I'm lying in bed. I wake up hearing her voice. It's infuriating.

"This crazy bastard thinks he's Hawkeye or some shit," Jordy says, passing the joint around the circle. "Running around with a bow, shooting flaming arrows all over his backyard. I'm like, *nah, white boy, I've seen this movie.* The guys and I are gonna bail but, oh, right, we drove this dude's car and we're stuck out here behind an iron gate."

I can't help glancing toward the house. I keep expecting Gen to come walking out of the shadows. I feel Mackenzie giving me the eye and realize she's caught me looking. Or rather, caught me *hoping.* Because I know Heidi or one of the girls will have invited Gen, and if she doesn't come, it's because she'd rather hide out at her dad's place than chance seeing me again. The notion seriously grates.

"We have to make a run for it because this dude is out of his mind, and we're climbing through these damn hedges and getting all cut up. I've got Danny on my shoulder to heave him up over the fence. Juan is trying to get an Uber but the reception sucks, so the app isn't loading. We're hauling ass, hearing all kinds of commotion behind us, while I'm thinking, one of these rich folks are going to think that house is burning down and call the cops on us. Sure enough, about ten minutes later, we're heading back toward the main road and a car comes up real slow behind us."

I hear a voice and look over my shoulder. It's Gen, standing a few yards away with Heidi and some of the girls. She's wearing a long-sleeve shirt falling off one shoulder and barely revealing a tiny pair of shorts hugging her ass like they're painted on. Long black hair cascades down her back. Kill me.

Gen's got this way about her. Confident and cool but with this edge of absolute batshit terror, like at any moment she could blow a kiss and drag a knife through your parachute, then push you out of a plane. There's nothing sexier than the way her blue eyes smile when she's got mayhem on her mind.

"Then the car stops. Man, my chest is pounding. A guy sticks his head out the window and shouts at us: *Get in, assholes. Drunk Lannister is on the loose and it's the Battle of the Blackwater out there.*"

The group erupts in laughter. The fire flashes as someone coughs up a mouthful of beer. I note Gen is pointedly not looking in this direction.

Jordy gets the joint back and takes a hit. "Turns out Luke went home with some clone chick down the street and was outside when they saw this dude shooting off these arrows, which caught at least two boats on fire at their docks. Neighbors were running out of their houses firing back flares. Like, sheer madness."

Cooper catches me watching Gen. Without a word, I hear him scolding me. Then he shakes his head, which may as well be a dare. He might be settled down, but I still intend to have a good time. And I know Gen. Maybe she was on some cold turkey kick before, but now that she's back, there's no point in either of us pretending we know how to stay away from each other. It's chemistry.

Wandering away from the bonfire, I approach her. I'm half

hard already, thinking about the last time I saw her. Legs wrapped around me. Teeth digging into my shoulder. My skin still bears the marks she left behind. Just the sight of her has me wanting to take her to bed and make up for time lost.

She feels me coming before I open my mouth, casting her gaze over her shoulder. There's the briefest flicker of recognition—the shared spark of lust and longing—before her expression turns impassive.

"What are you drinking?" I say as what I figure is an easy way in.

"I'm not."

It's awkward right from the off. All the familiarity of our conversation back at her house—gone. To the point that even Heidi and Steph wince with embarrassment.

"What do you want?" I ask, ignoring her attitude. If that'd ever worked on me, we wouldn't have kept getting back together. "I'll run up to the house and make you something."

"I'm good, thanks." Gen stares off at the waves climbing up the sand.

I stifle a sigh. "Can we talk? Take a walk with me."

She pulls her hair over her shoulder in a move I recognize right away. It's her fuck-off flip. The I've-already-stopped-hearing-you hair toss. Like we're strangers.

"Yeah, no," she says, voice flat and all but unrecognizable. "I'm not even sticking around. Just stopped by to say hey."

But not to me.

"So it's like that?" I try to curb the bite in my tone and fail. "You come back here and pretend you don't know me?"

"Okay," Heidi interjects with a bored roll of her eyes. "Thanks for stopping by, but this is a penis-free zone tonight. Run along, Evan."

"Fuck off, Heidi." She's always been a shit-stirrer.

"Yep, happy to." At that, she and Steph drag Gen closer to the bonfire and leave me standing there like an idiot.

Cool. Whatever. I don't need this aggravation. Genevieve wants to play games, fine. I grab a beer from the cooler and notice a group of girls stroll up to the party looking like they stumbled out of Daddy's Bentley. They're all dressed in the same sort of little ruffle tops and short skirts—straight off the clone assembly line. Definitely Garnet students, and my money's on sorority sisters. Gen's complete opposites in every way. They stand around looking lost and confused for a minute, until one of them homes in on me.

She tries her best to look chill while slipping in the sand to stride over. With too much lip gloss, she smiles at me. "Can I get a drink?"

I happily pop the cap off a beer for her and grab a few more for her friends. The best part about rich girls coming to slum it out here with the townies is they're easily amused. Tell them a few embellished stories about near-death exploits and running from the cops, and they eat that shit up. It scratches their sticking-it-to-the-parents itch, allowing them to live dangerously from a safe, vicarious distance, and gives them something to tell their friends about. Normally, feeling like I'm an attraction at a zoo would piss me off, but tonight I'm not the one with the sour face.

As the chicks let their hands linger on my arms while they laugh at my jokes and peel up my shirt after I tell them I have tattoos, Gen is staring daggers from her spot near the fire. Hitting me with a glare that says, *really, them?* And I don't give her the satisfaction of a response, because if she wants to pretend I'm dead to her, then I'm cold all over.

"I've got one too," the bravest of the girls informs me. She's cute, in a cookie-cutter clone sort of way. Nice rack, at least. "Got it on spring break last year in Mexico. Want to see?"

Before I can answer, she pulls her skirt up to flash the inside of her thigh at me. Her tat is a jellyfish, looking like it's gliding up into her lacy panties. I don't know how that's supposed to be sexy. But Gen watches me look, and that's kind of hot.

"Did it hurt?" I ask her, meeting Gen's eyes over the girl's shoulder.

"A little. But I like the pain."

"Yeah, I get that." It's almost too easy. This chick is practically begging me to take her back to the house. "It's pain that teaches us what pleasure is. Or how would we even know the difference?"

Eventually, her friends give up trying to share me and wander off to find their own one-night stands, and it doesn't take long before she kisses me and I'm copping a handful of her ass. It's a familiar routine, one I've indulged in plenty of times this past year. Forgetting myself in a hungry tongue and eager body meant forgetting about Gen for a while, not having to remember the cold truth that she'd left me without a word.

But right now, she's the only thing on my mind. When I come up for air, I spot Gen biting her lip at me like she'd slit my throat if there weren't so many witnesses. Ha. Too damn bad. She started it.

"Motherfucker!"

I blink, and suddenly there's some polo-wearing douchebag crowding my sightline. His face is red with anger, making him look like a pissed-off lobster. He calls the girl Ashlyn, who scrambles away from me with a guilty look about a second before the dude sucker punches me. It isn't a great shot and barely naps my head sideways.

"Well, that was rude," I remark, readjusting my jaw. I've taken so many hits in my life, I barely feel it anymore.

"You stay the hell away from her!" He's all hopped up on his macho bullshit, and he's got his buddies behind him.

I look over at Ashlyn, but she's not at my side anymore. She's huddled with her friends five yards away, refusing to meet my eyes. The smug gleam on her face as she watches Mr. Polo tells me I was more than frivolous entertainment for her tonight. I was payback.

"Easy, there," I tell the guy. A few heads turn, then several more as the party becomes aware of the confrontation. "Your sister and I were just getting acquainted."

"That's my girlfriend, asshole."

"You're sleeping with your sister? That's fucked up, dude."

His second punch is stronger. The taste of blood fills my mouth as I lick at the gash in my lip. I spit a wad of red mucous in the sand.

"Come on, pretty boy," I taunt, smiling with red, wet teeth. My arms tingle with expectant energy. "You can do better than that. She even showed me her tattoo."

He comes at me again, but this time I dodge the shot and send him to the ground with blood pouring out of his nose. We wrestle, sand sticking to the blood streaking down our shirts. We exchange blows, rolling around until some of his buddies and mine finally jump in to tear us apart. My friends tell the clones to get lost. They're outnumbered, after all. Still, as pretty boy and his group are retreating, I can't help feeling interrupted, my muscles not nearly tired and the adrenaline still running hot.

"Come again any time," I shout after them.

Then I turn around to a wave of salt water splashing me in the face.

When I wipe my eyes, Gen's standing there with an empty red cup. I smirk at her. "Thanks, I was thirsty."

"You're an idiot."

"He hit me first." My lip stings and my hand is sore, but I'm otherwise unscathed. I reach for her, but she steps away.

"You haven't changed a bit." At that, she tosses the cup at my feet and leaves with Heidi and Steph, her look of dismissive disgust landing harder than any blow I endured from the party crasher.

I haven't changed a bit? Why *should* I change? I'm the same person she's always known. Only difference is she disappeared for a year and came back with a superiority complex. Pretending to be someone she's not. Because I felt it, the other day at her house. The real Genevieve. This new chick is an act, and not a very good one. I don't know who she thinks she's impressing, but I'm not about to feel bad about being honest. At least one of us is.

"What was that?" Cooper follows me up to the house as I reach the back deck.

"I don't want to hear it," I say, pulling open the sliding glass door to the kitchen.

"Hey." He grabs my shoulder. "Everyone was having a good time until you had to start some shit."

"I didn't start anything." This is so typical. Some random dude messes with me, and Cooper makes it my fault. "He decided to throw down with me."

"Yeah. It's always the other guy. But somehow they always pick you. Why is that?"

"Just lucky, I guess." I try to walk away again but Cooper gets in my path and shoves my chest.

"You need to get your shit together. We're not kids anymore. Picking fights because you've got some chip on your shoulder has gotten real old, Evan."

"Just once, it'd be nice if you took my side."

"Then stop being on the wrong side."

Fuck this. I push him aside and go upstairs to take a shower. Cooper has always refused to see my side of anything. He's too busy being a judgmental prick. Must be all warm and cozy in his Good Twin delusion, but I'm sick of it.

Waiting for the water to heat up, I stare at my reflection in the mirror and experience a jolt of shock. My lip's a bit swollen, but not too bad. No, it's the ravaged look in my eyes that startles me. It matches the broken, battered feeling I've been struggling to ignore since my best friend skipped town on me, but I hope like hell I wasn't wearing that expression back there with Gen. She knows she stuck a knife in me when she bailed, but I'll be damned if she sees the damage it wrought.

CHAPTER 6

GENEVIEVE

It's dark outside by the time I shut off the computer in the office Friday night. I hadn't intended to work so late—everyone else had long since gone home—but I was in a spreadsheet trance and just kept going until Heidi texted to remind me that I'd agreed to meet up later with the girls. It's taken me the better part of two weeks, but I've finally managed to get a handle on the invoice tracking system. By next week, I should be caught up on all the outstanding accounts just in time to make payroll. I had to give myself a Google crash course on the software, but thankfully Mom had it set up to automate most of the process. Last thing I need is a bunch of angry employees when their paychecks are screwed up. While part of me is worried that doing too good a job might make me indispensable, I'm hoping that efficiency will help motivate Dad to allow someone else to take over soon.

As I'm locking up the building, a familiar pickup truck pulls into the parking lot. My shoulders tense when Cooper steps out and approaches me with the determination of a man with something on his mind.

"Hey, Coop."

He's identical to his brother, with dark hair and daunting brown eyes. Tall and fit, both arms covered in tattoos. And yet, strangely, I've never been attracted to Cooper. Evan caught my eye, and even in the dark I could tell them apart, as if there was some distinct aura about each of them.

"We need to talk," he tells me with an angry edge to his voice.

"Okay." His abrupt tone puts me off, raising my defenses. I grew up the middle child with five brothers. Absolutely no one gets to come in hot at me. So I plaster on a placating smile. "What's the problem?"

"Stay the hell away from Evan." At least he's direct.

I knew it was a bad idea showing up at the bonfire the other night. Every instinct said going anywhere near Evan wouldn't end well, but I'd convinced myself if I kept my distance, didn't engage, it wouldn't be so bad. Clearly it was too close.

"Maybe you should be having this conversation with him, Coop."

"I'm having it with you," he bites back, and for a second I'm unnerved. I've never gotten over the uncanny feeling of arguing with Evan's face but Cooper's words. I've known them since we were kids, but when you're as close as Evan and I were, it's hard to reconcile these feelings of intimacy that belong to a completely different yet similar person. "He was doing fine until you came back. Now you're not even here a few weeks and he's beating the tar out of some college prick because you've got his head all fucked up again."

"That's not fair. We've barely even spoken."

"And look at the damage it's done."

"I'm not Evan's keeper," I remind him, uncomfortable with the animosity wafting off him. "Whatever your brother's up to, I'm not responsible for his behavior."

"No, you're just the reason for it." Cooper is all but unrecognizable. He used to be the nice one. The reasonable one. Well, as reasonable as a Hartley twin can be. Cornering me in a parking lot isn't like him.

"Where's this coming from? I thought we were cool. We used to be friends." The three of us had been a trio of trouble once upon a time.

"Fuck off," he says, scoffing. It startles me. He might as well have spit in my face. "You tore my brother's heart out and took off without even a goodbye. What kind of cold-ass person does that? You have any idea what that did to him? No, Gen. We're not friends. You lost that privilege. Nobody hurts Evan."

I don't know what to say to that. I stand there, mouth dry and mind blank, watching this person I've known practically my whole life look at me like I'm scum. Guilt burns at my throat, because I know he's partially right. What I did *was* cold. No warning, no goodbye. I may as well have taken a match to my history with Evan and set it on fire. But it hadn't occurred to me Cooper would give a shit that I'd left his brother. If anything, I figured he'd be relieved.

Apparently I was wrong.

"I mean it, Gen. Leave him alone." With a last glare of contempt, he gets in his truck and drives away.

Later, at Joe's Beachfront Bar, I'm still distracted by the encounter with Cooper. Amid the crappy music and scents of perfume and body spray wrestling in the salt air blowing in from the open patio, I keep rehashing the interaction. It was unsettling, the way he sought me out to basically say stay away or else. If I didn't know Cooper, I'd have good reason to feel intimidated. As it is, though, I do know him. And his brother. So the more I spin the conversation over in my head, the more pissed off I get that he had the nerve to come and, what, tell me off? As if Evan weren't a grown man with more than a few malfunctions of his very own that have nothing to do with me. Coop wants to play the protector? Fine, whatever. But despite my lingering guilt over my abrupt departure, learning that Evan's still going around causing trouble only strengthens my conviction that leaving had been the right thing to do. Evan's had plenty of time to straighten himself out. If he hasn't, that's on him.

"Hey." Heidi, who's seated across from me at the high-top table, snaps her fingers in my face, waking me from my bitter stewing. Of all the girls in our group, I'm closest with Heidi, who's probably the most like me. With her platinum bob and razor-sharp tongue, Heidi's a total badass, a.k.a. my kind of girl. She also knows me far too well.

"You alive in there?" she adds, eyeing me with suspicion.

I answer with a half-hearted smile, ordering myself to be more present. Although we texted often when I was gone, I haven't hung out with my friends in ages.

"Sorry," I say sheepishly. I stab at the ice in my virgin cocktail with a straw. Nights like this, I could use a real drink.

"You sure you don't want something stronger?" Alana asks, temptingly holding out her glass of tequila with just the lightest mist of lime and simple syrup.

"Leave her alone." Steph, ever the defender of the weak, throws herself between me and peer pressure. "You know if she has a drink the convent won't take her back."

Okay, so she isn't all that nice.

"Yes, Sister Genevieve," Heidi says with a sarcastic smirk, speaking slowly like I'm an exchange student or something. An attempt at a crack on how long I've been away. "It must be overwhelming with all these lights and loud music. Do you remember music?"

"I moved to Charleston," I tell her, throwing up my middle finger. "Not Amish country."

"Right." Alana takes another sip of her drink, and the salty-sweet smell really does make me thirsty. "The notorious dry city of Charleston."

"Yeah, no, that's funny," I say to their teasing. "You're hilarious."

They don't get it. Not really. And I don't blame them. These girls have been my best friends since we were kids, so to them there's never been anything wrong with me. But there was. An uncontrollable destructive streak that drove my every decision when I was drinking. I wasn't making good decisions. Couldn't find the middle ground between moderation and obliteration. Other than a regrettable lapse last month on a trip to Florida where I woke up in a stranger's bed, I've kept pretty well to sobriety. Not without effort, though.

"Then here's to Gen." Heidi raises her glass. "Who may have forgotten how to have a good time, but we'll take her back anyway."

Heidi's always been good for a backhanded compliment. It's her love language. If she's not insulting you at least a little, you might as well be dead to her. I appreciate that about her, because there's never any confusion about where she stands. It's an honest way to live.

But she throws me for a loop by softening her tone again. "Welcome home, Gen. I really did miss you." Then, as if realizing she'd actually—gasp—revealed a sliver of emotion, she scowls at me, adding, "Don't ever leave us again, bitch."

I hide a smile. "I'll try not to."

"Welcome home," Steph and Alana echo, raising their glasses.

"So fill me in," I say, because I'd love to talk about literally anything else. Between the funeral and moving back home, all anyone does is ask me how I'm doing. I'm sick of myself. "What else is going on?"

"Alana's banging Tate," Steph spits out with too much enthusiasm, as if the declaration has been nervously pacing in the wings all night, waiting for its entrance. While Heidi and Alana are notoriously tight-lipped, Steph's a huge gossip and has been since we were kids. She gets off on the drama, so long as it doesn't involve her.

"Jesus, Steph." Alana throws a cardboard coaster at her. "Say it a little louder."

"What? It's true." Steph sips her drink with an unrepentant sparkle in her eyes.

"How'd that happen?" I ask curiously. Our friend Tate gets around, to put it mildly. Even among the more promiscuous in our wider circle of friends, he's notorious. He's not usually the type Alana goes for. She's . . . well, particular, is a way of putting it.

Alana shrugs in response. "Darndest thing. I was stumbling around in the dark one night and, whaddya know, I tripped and fell on his dick."

Interesting. Tis the season for summer hookups. Good for her, I guess.

Heidi rolls her eyes, unamused with Alana's evasiveness. "More like hooking up since last fall."

I raise an eyebrow. Since last fall? I'd never known either of them to be interested in long term. "So is this a thing, or . . . ?"

She gives another noncommittal head tilt that fails to convince. "An irregular occurrence of one-night stands. Of the extremely sporadic sort."

"Then there's Wyatt," Steph adds like she's sitting on a secret, all dumb smiles and arched eyebrows.

"Wyatt?" I echo in surprise. This revelation is even more baffling than the Tate one. "What about Ren?"

"You know how they've been doing the on-again/off-again dance for like three years? Dumping each other every other week? Well, it finally backfired," Heidi reveals with a smirk. "She dumped him over something stupid, and he moved on."

Wow. I definitely didn't see that coming. Lauren and Wyatt were similar to me and Evan in that way, constantly breaking up and making up, but I never expected them to end it for good.

"And you moved in on him?" I demand, turning to Alana. "Ren's our friend—isn't that against girl code?"

"I didn't move in on him." Alana huffs at the suggestion. "We're not hooking up, no matter what this one thinks—" She glares at Steph. "For some ludicrous reason, he's decided he has a thing for me." She flips her copper-colored hair over one shoulder, looking annoyed. "I'm trying to shut it down, okay?"

Taking pity on her, I swiftly change the subject. "Catch me up on Cooper and the new girl," I tell Heidi. It wasn't so long ago Heidi was doing the "will they, won't they" dance with Coop. In their case, however, the friends with benefits arrangement blew up in her face. "What's her deal?"

"Mackenzie," she replies, without the hint of irritation that had at one point tinged her occasional texts to complain about Cooper and his new rich girlfriend. "Garnet dropout. Basically walked out on her parents and let them cut her off."

"It was a whole thing," Steph agrees. "Oh, and she bought the old boardwalk hotel. The Beacon. She's been restoring it to reopen soon."

Damn. She *is* loaded. Must be nice. Me, I'd settle for having any kind of direction about what I'm doing with my life. Filling out spreadsheets and chasing down my brothers for invoices isn't exactly my lifelong dream. And as much as I appreciate everything my dad's built to support us, the family business feels more like a trap than an opportunity. It isn't me. Though hell if I know what is.

"She's actually kind of cool," Heidi says, albeit grudgingly. "I wasn't a fan at first. But they're good together, and Coop's usually in a better mood since she's been around, so that's something."

Could've fooled me. Whatever this girl's effect on him, it isn't foolproof.

"What's that look?" Alana asks.

"He sort of accosted me when I was leaving work."

"He what?" Heidi's evident alarm snaps her upright.

It sounds stupid to say out loud. Cooper's got a reputation for being a bit of a hellion, but he's easily the tamer of the Hartley twins. Scolding me in a parking lot still feels wildly out of character for him. Then again, where his brother's concerned, he's always had a short fuse. Evan has that effect on people.

"Yeah, I don't know," I tell them. "He all but threatened me to stay away from Evan. Said he doesn't consider me a friend anymore after the way I hurt his brother."

"Harsh," Steph says with sympathy.

"I guess he has a point about that part." I pretend to be unbothered, shrugging. "But he also blamed me for Evan being out of control, which isn't exactly fair. Evan's a grown man. He's responsible for his own actions."

Alana looks away like she's got something to say.

I narrow my eyes. "What is it?"

"No, nothing." She shakes her head, but there's clearly more she's reluctant to elaborate on. When the three of us press her with silence, she finally relents. "It's just, I mean Evan went and got the shit kicked out of him to make you jealous. Seems like the kind of thing Cooper would notice and disapprove of."

"So you're taking his side, then? It's all my fault?"

"No. All I'm saying is, the way Cooper thinks, he's going to look at that and you showing up as a bad omen of things to come. Let's be honest, he's always been terrible at keeping Evan in line. He probably thinks if he can scare you off, it'll make everything easier."

"That's a crappy thing to do," Steph says.

"Hey, I'm just guessing." Alana finishes her drink and drops her glass on the table. "Another round?"

Everyone nods, and she and Steph leave for a pit stop at the restroom before putting in an order for round two.

After draining the last of her drink, Heidi eyes me warily and makes an uneasy entreaty. "So, listen. This is awkward, but, um, you know Jay and I are sort of dating."

My eyes widen. "Jay as in my brother Jay?"

"Yeah."

"Um. No. I did not."

"Yeah, well, it's new-ish. Honestly, he'd been chasing me for a date since the fall, but I wasn't sure it was a good idea. He finally broke me down a couple months ago. I wanted to make sure you're cool with it. I don't want things to be weird with us."

What's weird is seeing Heidi squirm. Hardly anything penetrates her don't-mess-with-me exterior or puts her on the defensive. She'd spook a bull shark. So it's cute, I guess, that she wants to ask my permission to date my older brother.

"You want my blessing, is that it?" I tease, sucking air from the bottom of my glass of mostly ice melt while I make her wait. "Yeah, it's fine. This town is so small it was only a matter of time before one of you ended up with a West brother. I'm just surprised it's Jay."

Jay's the sweetest of my brothers. Well, after Craig, anyway, but Craig doesn't count because he literally just graduated high school. Jay is twenty-four and doesn't have a mean bone in his softie body. He's almost the complete opposite of Heidi, who's all sharp edges.

"Trust me, I'm equally surprised," she says dryly, running a hand through her blonde bob. "I swear, I've never gone out with anyone so damn nice. Like, what's his problem?"

I burst out laughing. "Right?"

"The other night we were on our way to the drive-in and he pulled over to help a little old lady cross the street. Who the fuck does that?"

"Please don't tell me you screwed my brother at the drive-in."

"Okay, I won't tell you."

"Oh God. I walked right into that one, huh?"

"Uh, hi there, Genevieve," a male voice interrupts.

Heidi and I turn as a cheerfully nervous guy arrives at our table, dressed in a short-sleeved button-down shirt and khaki pants. He's cute, in a Boy Scout sort of way, with brown hair and freckles. If it weren't for a vague feeling I recognize him, I'd say he was a tourist who got lost and stumbled away from the boardwalk.

"I'm Harrison Gates," he says. "We went to high school together."

"Oh, sure, right." The name barely nudges my memory, but now that he's placed his face for me, he does seem familiar. "How's it going?"

"Good." He directs a smile at Heidi as well, but his gaze remains focused on me. "I don't mean to bother you. I just wanted to offer my condolences about your mom."

"Thank you," I tell him sincerely. Whatever my mixed feelings about her death, the nice part about coming home to a small town is that people do generally give a damn. Even people who would have sooner run me over with their car a few years ago have come up to say a few kind words. It's what you do. "I appreciate that."

"Yeah." His smile grows larger and somewhat less anxious as his posture relaxes. "And, you know, I wanted to say welcome back."

Heidi gives me a look that appears to be a warning to bail, but I don't understand her alarm. Harrison seems nice enough.

"So what are you up to these days?" I ask, because it seems rude not to talk to the guy for a minute, at least.

"Well, I just joined the Avalon Bay Sheriff's Department, if you can believe it. Still sounds weird to say it out loud."

"Really? Huh. You seem too nice to be a cop."

He laughs. "I hear that a lot, actually."

Even before the incident last year, I'd had plenty of unfortunate run-ins with the local police. When we were kids, it seemed they had nothing better to do than to follow us around town harassing us. It was a sport for them. The school bullies but with guns and badges. That asshole Rusty Randall being the biggest bully of them all.

"Watch out with this one, Rookie. She's more trouble than she's worth."

As if he heard me cursing him in my head, a uniformed Deputy Randall saunters up and slaps a hand on Harrison's shoulder.

My entire body instantly goes ice-cold.

Heidi snaps a comeback at him that I don't really hear above the deafening fury screaming through my skull. My teeth dig into the inside of my cheek to keep me from spouting off at the mouth.

"If you don't mind," Randall says to Harrison, "I need a moment of her time."

He's gained weight since I last saw him. Lost a lot more hair. Where he used to hide his true self behind a friendly smile and a wave, now his face is contorted in a permanent scowl of resentment and malice.

"You know what, we're a little busy here," Heidi says, cocking her head at him in a way that begs a fight. "But if you'd like to make an appointment, maybe we'll get back to you."

"Was that your car I saw parked across the street?" he asks me in a mocking tone. "Maybe I ought to run the tag for unpaid tickets." Even Harrison seems uncomfortable at Randall's threat, eyeing me with confusion. "What do you say, Genevieve?"

"It's fine," I interject before this gets out of hand. Heidi's looking like she's about to flip a table. And poor Harrison. He really has no idea what he's stepped in. "Let's talk, Deputy Randall."

What more can he really do to me, after all?

CHAPTER 7

GENEVIEVE

I'd always had a bad feeling about Rusty Randall. When I used to babysit his four kids back in high school, he would say things—little offhanded comments that made me uncomfortable. But I never said anything back, preferring the money and figuring I only ever had to see him for a few minutes coming and going, so it wasn't a big deal. Until that night last year.

Some friends and I had gone out to a bar on the outskirts of town. We knew it was a cop hangout, but after a couple hours of pre-partying, Alana had gotten in her head it would be a hoot. In hindsight, it was not one of her better ideas. We were knocking back tequila shots and rum runners when Randall slid up to our table. He was buying our drinks, which was fine. Then he started getting handsy. Which wasn't.

Now, outside Joe's, Deputy Randall leans against the cruiser parked at the curb. I don't know what it is about cops resting their hands on their equipment belts, fingers always flirting with their weapons, that incites an instinctual rage in me. My nails dig into the flesh of my palms as I brace myself for what comes next. I'm careful to stay in the light of a streetlamp where people from the bar's entrance are still visible.

"So here's how it is," Randall says, talking down his nose at me. "You're not welcome back here. Long as you're in town, you stay the hell away from me and my family."

Not his family anymore, the way I heard it. But I bite back the snarky remark, along with the rush of scorn that rises in my throat. He has no right to speak to me in that tone of disgust, not after the way *he* behaved last year.

We were admittedly wasted that night back then, the girls and me, while Rusty kept trying to talk me into going out to his car with him and fooling around in the parking lot. I was gentle, at first. Laughing it off and making my way around the room to avoid him. Clinging to the girls because there was safety in numbers. Until he cornered me against the jukebox, tried to slather his mouth on mine, and jammed his hand up my shirt. I shoved him away and told him, loud enough for the whole bar to hear, to fuck off. Thankfully, he'd left, albeit cranky and dissatisfied.

That could have been the end of it. I could have gone back to my friends and let it go. Certainly wasn't the first time I'd been hit on by an overaggressive older man. But something about the encounter had stung me right to the bone. I was pissed. Fuming. Absolutely irate. Long after he'd gone, I sat there stewing over the encounter and all the ways I should have stuck my foot in his groin and rammed the heel of my palm into his throat. I kept throwing down shots. Eventually Steph and Alana left, and it was just me and my friend Trina, who's probably the only person in our old circle of friends who had me beat for wild instincts. She wasn't ready to let what Randall did go and said neither should I. What he did was wrong, and it was my responsibility to not let him get away with it.

In front of me now, Randall stands up straight, bearing down on me. I back up onto the sidewalk, glancing around for my best exit. Frankly, I have no idea what this man is capable of, so I assume everything.

"Look," I say. "I own that I acted crazy by showing up at your house the way I did. But that doesn't change the fact that you felt me up in a bar after I spent the whole night trying to get away from you. Far as I'm concerned, it's you who needs a reminder to keep his distance. I'm not the one looking for a confrontation."

"You better keep your head down, girl," he warns, growling at me with a wet, phlegmy voice full of impotent anger. He's getting off on the power trip. "None of that partying bullshit. I catch you with drugs, you're gonna find yourself in the back of this car. So much as sniff trouble around you, you're going to jail. Hear me?"

He's aching for a reason, the slightest provocation to nail me. Too bad for him, I left that Genevieve behind a long time ago. From the corner of my eye, I spot Heidi and the girls standing at the entrance to the bar, waiting for me.

"We done here?" I ask, keeping my chin up. I'd walk into traffic before giving Randall the satisfaction of knowing his threats affect me. "Good."

I walk off. When the girls ask, I just tell them to watch their backs. Wherever we are this summer, whatever we do, it's a sure thing he'll be watching. Biding his time.

I'm not about to play his game.

Later, at home, I lie in bed still rigid with anger. There's tension tugging at the muscles in my neck. A throbbing pressure pushing against my eyeballs. I can't be still. So that's how, at nearly midnight, I find myself sitting on the floor at my closet, surrounded by boxes, yearbooks, and photo albums, taking a walk down memory lane. An ill-advised walk, because the first picture in the first album I open? One of me and Evan. We're eighteen, maybe nineteen, standing on the beach at sunset. Evan has both arms wrapped around me from behind, one hand holding a bottle of beer. I'm in a red bikini, resting my head against his broad, shirtless chest. We're both smiling happily.

I bite my lip, trying hard to fend off the memories attempting to bat their way into my brain. But they barrel through my mental defenses. I remember that day on the beach. We watched the sunset with our friends, then took off alone, walking in the warm sand toward Evan's house where we locked ourselves in his bedroom and didn't come out till the next afternoon.

Another picture, this one at some party at Steph's house, and this time we're sixteen years old. I know it's sixteen because those awful blonde highlights in my hair had been a birthday present from Heidi. I look ridiculous. But you wouldn't know it from the way Evan is staring at me. I don't know who took the photo, but they managed to capture in his expression what I can only describe as adoration. I look equally smitten.

I find myself smiling at our young, besotted selves. It wasn't long after that party that he told me he loved me for the first time. We were hanging out in my backyard floating on our backs in the pool, engaged in a pretty serious conversation about how much we wished our mothers gave a shit about us, when he suddenly cut me off mid-sentence and said, "Hey, Genevieve? I love you."

And I'd been so startled to hear him utter my full name and not *Fred*, the dumb nickname whose origins I don't even remember, that I sank like a stone. I didn't even register the second part of that statement until I came up to the surface, eyes stinging, coughing up water.

His indignant expression had greeted me. "Seriously? I tell you I love you and you try to drown yourself? What the hell?"

Which made me laugh so hard I peed myself a little and then stupidly *confessed* to peeing a little, at which point he swam to the ladder and heaved his wet body out of the pool. He'd thrown his hands up in exasperation and growled, "Forget I said anything!"

Laughter tickles my throat. I'm half a second away from texting him to ask if he remembers that day when I realize I'm supposed to be keeping my distance.

My phone buzzes beside me.

A glance at it triggers an anguished groan. How does he do it? How does he always know when I'm thinking about him?

Evan: *I'm sorry about the other night.*
Evan: *I was an idiot.*

I sit there staring at the texts until I realize all the tension I'd been feeling over my run-in with Randall, all the anger and shame, has dissipated. My shoulders are limp, the ten-ton boulder on my chest finally removed. Even my headache has subsided. I hate that he can still do that too.

Me: *Yes you were.*
Evan: *I think I've still got sand in my eye, if that makes you feel better.*
Me: *A little.*

There's a long delay, nearly a full minute before I see him typing again. The little gray bubbles appear, then disappear, then reappear.

Evan: *Missed you.*

Already I feel the tug, those old ties pulling me back to a place I swore I wouldn't go again. Backsliding would be so easy. Making a promise to myself and actually keeping it this time is much harder.

It isn't his fault—Evan didn't make me this way. For once, though, I'm choosing me.

Me: *Missed you too. But that doesn't change anything. I meant what I said.*

Then I shut off my phone before he can respond.

Although it brings an unbearable ache to my chest, I force myself to look through the rest of the albums and piles of loose photos. Our entire relationship plays out in scenes preserved in single perfect moments.

You tore my brother's heart out and took off without even a good-bye. What kind of cold-ass person does that? You have any idea what that did to him?

Cooper's words, his accusations, buzz around in my head, making my heart squeeze painfully. He's right—I didn't say goodbye to Evan. But that's because I couldn't. If I had, I know he would have succeeded in convincing me to stay. I've never been able to say no to Evan. So I left without alerting him. Without looking back.

It's past one a.m. when I finally shove the photos in their boxes and slide them to the back of the closet under clothes and old shoes.

Only dead things pine for the past. Sad things. I might be sad, but I'm not dead. And I intend to live while I still can.

CHAPTER 8

EVAN

Cooper and Mac are already sitting down in the kitchen with Uncle Levi when I walk through the door on Sunday night. The plans for Mac's hotel are spread out on the table. She has her laptop open, hunched over the keyboard while gnawing on a pen. Daisy is the only one to acknowledge me, running up to climb my leg as I kick off my shoes.

"Hey, pretty girl," I coo at the excited puppy.

"You're late," Cooper informs me.

"I stopped to pick up dinner." I drop the bags of Chinese takeout on the counter. My brother doesn't even turn his head from the blueprints. "No, don't sweat it. My pleasure."

"Thank you," Mac says over her shoulder. "No egg in the fried rice, right?"

"Yes, I remembered." For fuck's sake, it's like I'm the damn help around here.

"Leave that," Levi says. "Come here. We need to talk about next week."

Levi is our dad's brother. He took us in after Dad died in a drunk driving accident when we were little and raised us when our mom couldn't be bothered to care. Our uncle's the only real family Cooper and I have left, and although it was difficult to bond with him growing up—he's the gruff, quiet type whose idea of spending quality time together is sitting silently in the same room—the three of us have gotten closer lately.

He's been running his own construction business for years. And after the recent hurricanes that ravaged Avalon Bay, he's been flush with more renovation and demolition work than he can handle. Since Levi made Cooper and I partners in the business not too long ago, we've got a hell of a lot more on our plates too.

Our biggest and most pressing gig is The Beacon, the old landmark hotel on the boardwalk that Mac bought several months ago. The hotel had been gutted from the storm and sat abandoned for a couple years until Mac impulsively decided to fix it up. Her family is disgustingly wealthy, but she'd purchased The Beacon with her own money—I only recently found out that she'd made millions running her own websites that post cheesy relationship stuff.

"Got a call from Ronan West," Levi is saying. "He needs some renovations on his house before he puts it up for sale. So that means we need to split one of you to run a crew out there."

"Let one of the guys do it," Cooper says, copping an attitude at the mention of Gen's dad. Because Coop's a damn child. "I don't want things slipping at the hotel because we leave someone else in charge over there."

We're in the final stages of the renovation at Mac's hotel, which is supposed to have a soft opening a few months from now in September. The idea being: She'll bring in a select guest list to feel the place out and build up a reputation for the spa through the winter season, then hold the grand opening in the spring.

"Ronan's a friend," Levi counters. "I can't send some knuckle-head to him. I want to know he's taken care of right."

"I'll do it," I offer.

"Of course." Cooper says with an exasperated sigh. "I don't think that's a good idea."

"No one asked you." Starved, I edge away from the table to grab one of the boxes of lo mein and dig in.

"We've got a good handle on the hotel." Mac eyes my lo mein, then gets her box of fried rice and hops up on the counter to eat. "Shouldn't be a problem."

Cooper shoots her a look for contradicting him, but she just shrugs. Maybe the best part of having Mac around is that she loves to wind my brother up. Which usually means taking my side in an argument.

"You're a glutton for punishment." Cooper shakes his head at me.

Maybe I am, but he doesn't understand Gen like I do. Sure, we've had our toxic moments, the fights, the reckless nights. But there were great times as well. Together, we're fusion. Perfect energy. Right now she thinks there's some righteous atonement in keeping our distance, but that's only because she's let herself forget what it's like when we're at our best.

I simply have to remind her. But to do that, I need to get close to her.

"Hey." Levi demands my attention. "You sure you can keep it professional? I don't want you acting like a fool over there while you're on the job. We might be Hartley and Sons now, but that's still my name on the business card."

"Don't worry," I promise through a mouthful of noodles. "I got this."

Cooper sighs.

On Monday afternoon, Levi and I pull up to the West house. Ronan had dropped off a key at Levi's this morning so we could let ourselves in to have a look around. The purpose of today's visit is to walk the property and come up with a task list of anything that needs replacing, fixing, painting. Ronan's left it up to Levi to give him his opinion and a price quote for what he thinks it will take to get the best offer when it goes on the market. After twenty-some years and six kids, the rambling two-story house has definitely seen better days.

It is a little odd being back here under the circumstances. Even weirder to be walking through the front door after all those times Gen and I got caught sneaking in or out through her window. And don't get me started on all the pool parties we threw when Gen's parents were away.

My uncle and I conduct a sweep of the interior first, scribbling on our clipboards as we point out various issues that jump out at us. We scope out the exterior next, looking at the siding that needs replacing and deciding the wobbly wooden fence around the back-yard probably warrants a PVC upgrade. Looks better and is easier to maintain. After some more clipboard notes, we let ourselves through the gate to check out the pool and—holy sweet Jesus.

I come up short at the sight of Gen tanning on one of the lounge chairs.

Topless.

Kill me.

"I thought they stopped making pornos like this in the nine-ties," I drawl, getting an irritated grumble in response from Levi.

Totally unbothered, Gen rolls onto her side, looking like a swimsuit model with her long legs and oiled skin glowing under the sun. Those astounding, perky breasts are pointing right at me. Not as though I'd forgotten what they look like, but the sight of her in just tiny bikini bottoms and sunglasses gets me reminiscing about old times.

"You don't knock anymore?" Gen says, then reaches for a glass of water.

"Did I ever?" My gaze keeps flitting back to her perfect rack.

It's taking all my wits to remember my uncle is standing next to me.

"Your, uh, dad asked us over to give him a quote for the renovation," Levi answers, staring uncomfortably at the ground. "He didn't say anyone would be here."

I stifle a laugh. "Come on, Gen, put those things away. You're gonna give the poor man a stroke."

"Aw, Levi's not interested in anything I've got, anyway." She sits up, reaching for her bikini top. "How's Tim doing?" she asks Levi.

He grunts out a, "Yeah, good," while still diligently averting his eyes. My uncle doesn't talk much about his long-time partner, who works from home as an editor for academic journals. Levi prefers to keep their personal life private. It wasn't always easy for him being a gay man in this town, and I think he finds it simpler to let most people believe what they want. Even among his friends that know, they don't ask about it. As a couple, he and Tim don't tend to go out much on account of the latter being sort of a recluse. They like things quiet, those two. It suits them, I suppose.

"What are you doing home?" I ask Gen. I heard her dad had her working at the stone yard.

"We're open on Sundays," she says, covering her chest with her forearm as she untangles the strings of her top. "So we get Mondays off. You guys need anything from me?"

Levi finds his voice while dutifully looking at his clipboard. "Is Ronan going to want any landscaping back here?"

Gen shrugs. "No idea."

Relieved, he takes the excuse to go inside and call Ronan, leaving me alone with Gen.

After a moment of noticeable reluctance, she shifts in her chair. "Tie me up?" Holding her top to her chest, she turns her back to me.

"Or . . . we could leave it off."

"Evan."

"You're no fun." I sit at the edge of her lounger and reach for her bikini strings. I've had worse jobs.

"Does this happen to you a lot? Catching cougars and rich college girls in various states of undress?" Her tone is dry.

"This is exactly how every one of these projects start," I say solemnly, tying the thin strings of her bikini. "First time I've had a hard-on in front of my uncle, though, so that's a whole new level of family trauma."

"You could have warned me," she accuses, turning to face me once she's adjusted herself. "Dropping in without notice was sneaky on your part."

"I didn't know you'd be here," I remind her. "I was planning to help myself to some underwear and be on my way."

Gen just sighs.

"You know, this whole topless scheme of yours—"

"Scheme? I didn't know you were coming," she protests.

I ignore that. "Reminds me of that field trip senior year," I finish, not even pretending I'm not watching the little beads of condensation that fall off her water glass and travel down her chest as she takes a sip.

"What field trip?"

"Don't play dumb. You know exactly what I'm talking about." That trip was pretty damn unforgettable.

Her lips curve slightly before flattening in a tight line. "How about we don't go there?" she says with another sigh.

"Go where?" I blink innocently. "The aquarium?"

"Evan."

"It was raining that day. You were mad at me because you said I was flirting with Jessica in math class, so you showed up the next day for the field trip in a white tank top with no bra to throw yourself at Andy What's-his-face. So we get off the bus in the rain, and then everyone's catching an eyeful of your twins."

There's a long beat, during which I can see her resolve crumbling.

"You stole me a T-shirt from the gift shop," she says grudgingly.

I hide a smile of satisfaction. So easy to get her to join me on this trip down memory lane. "Because I would have had to break Andy Fuck Face's nose for staring at your tits the whole trip."

Again, she pauses. Then, "Maybe I thought it was hot when you got jealous."

My smile breaks free. "Speaking of jealous . . ."

Her expression goes cloudy. "What?"

"I saw the murder in your eyes at the bonfire the other night." When she doesn't take the bait, I toss out another lure. "You know, when I was talking to that college chick."

"Talking?" she echoes darkly. A familiar hint of murder glints in her eyes before her lips quickly curl in annoyance—directed at herself.

I know Genevieve, and right now she's kicking herself for showing weakness. So, as expected, she deflects.

"You're referring to the girl whose boyfriend beat you up?" Gen flashes a saccharine smile. "The one who only pretended she wanted to get with you to make her man jealous?"

"One, you're not allowed to look that gleeful at the idea of someone beating me up. Two, I didn't get beat up—that dude's crew had to carry him away, in case you didn't notice. And three, if I'd wanted to get with her, I would've gotten with her."

"Uh-huh. Because from where I was standing, it looked like you tried to shoot your shot and she left with her boyfriend."

"Tried? I wasn't trying." I tip my head in challenge. "Genevieve. Baby. We both know I have no trouble convincing women to take their clothes off."

"And he's modest too."

I wink at her. "Modesty is for guys who don't get laid."

I'm gratified to see her swallow. Christ. I want to fuck her. It's been so long. *Too* long. Doesn't matter how many girls I hooked up with in Gen's absence. No one compares to her. No one gets me as hot, makes me as crazy.

"Well, since seduction comes so easy for you, why don't you skedaddle and go find someone who wants to be seduced?" With a bitchy flick of her eyebrows, Gen picks up her water and takes another sip.

I snort. "Stop pretending like you don't want to rip my clothes off and fuck me in that pool."

"I don't." Her tone is confident, but I don't miss the flare of heat in her eyes.

"No?" I say, licking my suddenly dry lips.

"No," she repeats, but her confidence is slipping.

"Really? Not even a teeny, tiny part of you is tempted?"

Her throat dips as she gulps again. I see her hand trembling slightly as she puts down her glass.

I lean closer, breathing deeply. The salty, sweet scent of tanning oil is rich in the humid air. I want to rip her top off with my teeth and wrap her hair between my fingers. She tries to act like she's so above it all, but I can see her pulse thrumming on the side of her neck, and I know she feels the same insatiable need.

"Meet me later," I say without forethought but then commit to the idea. "Our spot. Tonight."

She's impassive behind those silver reflective sunglasses. But when she bites her lip and hesitates to answer, I know she's considering it. She wants to say yes. It'd be so easy. Because we've never had to try to be together, it's just natural. Our tides always flowing in the same direction.

Then she pulls away. She stands and wraps a towel around her waist. The impenetrable wall goes up and I'm locked on the other side.

"Sorry," she says with a dismissive shrug. "I can't. I have a date."

CHAPTER 9

GENEVIEVE

Three hours after my encounter with Evan, I'm still kicking myself. In a moment of triumphant stupidity, my mouth ran away from me, and now I've got to materialize a date for tonight out of thin air. After the lie popped out of my foolhardy mouth, Evan was naturally pissed, though he was doing his best to act like it was no big deal. Sometimes he forgets I know him too well. All his tics and tells. So, while pretending he wasn't fuming inside, he'd quizzed me on the where and when, which compounded one lie with another, and then another. I managed to dodge on the question of who by insisting Evan wouldn't know the guy, but I wouldn't put it past him to check up on me, so therein lies the rub.

By eight o'clock tonight, I need to come up with a man to take me out.

Since I'm not about to hop on Tinder for a fake date to dissuade my ex, I throw up the SOS in our group chat, then end up at Steph and Alana's place to get the brain trust together on this one. Heidi's at work, which is probably a good thing because her advice in the chat thread was utterly useless. *Tell stupid lies, win stupid prizes*, she'd texted in her typical no-nonsense way.

Ugh. I mean . . . she's not wrong.

"So you emotionally masturbated to teasing Evan with your boobs and then swerved him," Alana says to my explanation of events. We're sitting on their back porch while I try visualizing my sweet tea with vodka in it. "I mean, not to take his side, but I'd call that mixed signals."

"I don't think I'm telling it right. He walked in on me."

Steph regards me in amusement. "Yeah. But you kinda liked it."

"It's fine if you did," Alana tells me, reclining on the porch swing while she sways back and forth. "Everybody's got a kink."

"It's not a kink."

Although, now that she's named it, I suppose she isn't so far-off. Evan and I have always had this tension between us. Pushing and pulling. Making each other jealous and manipulating a response. It's all part of the bad habits I'm trying to break. Yet, in doing so, I'm repeating the steps. New tune, same old dance.

"It's the bad-boy dick magic," Alana says in her flat intonation, devoid of humor. "Makes us crazy. It isn't our fault the screwed-up ones are the best in bed."

I mean, she has a point. And when it comes to Evan Hartley, it's the most random stuff that gets me all messed up. The little things that trigger memories and invite involuntary responses. My body has been programmed to certain stimuli. It's instinct. Second nature. He licks his lips and I start imagining his face between my legs. Today, it was the way his hair smelled.

And it certainly didn't help that he taunted me about pool sex and then asked me to meet him at our spot later.

I only came up with the date excuse because I was so close to accepting his invitation. Because what would be the harm in a little consensual sex between friends, right? No harm at all . . . until a little sex leads to a lot of sex, and then we're spending every waking minute together, starting trouble and picking fights because every bit of adventure and conflict wrings a few more drops of adrenaline out of each other.

"I can't help myself around him. He's an addiction. I try to stay aloof, but then he smiles and flirts and coaxes me into flirting back," I find myself confessing. "But if I don't break the habit, I'll never get a fresh start."

"So we break the cycle," Alana decides. "We just have to find someone who is everything that Evan isn't. Shock the system, so to speak."

"Well, that pretty much eliminates everyone we know." Scratching off the list of names that are either his friends or people I can't stand, there are hardly any people left in this town who aren't related to me. Trolling college bars for a random Garnet dweeb isn't my idea of a good time either.

"What about that guy from the other night?" Steph asks. "The one who approached you and Heidi."

"Who, Harrison?" She can't be serious.

"No, that's good." Alana sits up. Her face lights as the scheme assembles behind her eyes. She's the queen of schemes, this one. "That's really good."

Steph nods. "The way Heidi told it, it sounded like the guy had a crush on you."

"But he's . . ." It even tastes bad on my tongue. "A *cop*. And he wears khakis. Tourists wear khakis."

"Exactly," Alana says, nodding her head as she sees all the pieces come together. She lands her determined gaze on me. "The Anti-Evan. He's perfect."

"It's one date," Steph reminds me. "Gets Evan off your back, and there are worse ways to spend a night than getting a free meal out of a guy who has zero chance of trying to get laid."

There is that. And she's right; Harrison was plenty nice. As far as dates go, this one comes with bare minimum expectations and is super low risk. The worst part, I guess, will be running out of things to talk about and realizing right away that we have absolutely nothing in common. But we'll just part awkwardly at the end of the night and never have to see each other again. Simple. And if Evan shows up, he takes one look at Harrison, decides to feel sorry for me, and walks away laughing. I can handle that if it keeps Evan at bay.

"Alright," I agree. "Operation Boy Scout is a go."

Since I don't know anyone who would have a cop's number in their phone, and there is no chance that I call a police station just to, like, chat, it takes some creative social media sleuthing to slide into Harrison's DMs. His Instagram is adorably if not pathetically bland. But I remind myself, this makes him a completely harmless suitor and reinforces the message that I am reforming. No more bad boys.

> Me: *It was nice seeing you the other night.*
> Me: *Sorry we got interrupted. Dinner tonight?*

It's a bold opening, but I'm a woman on a mission. And a deadline. Thankfully, Harrison responds within a few minutes.

> Harrison: *This is a surprise. Yeah, that'd be great.*
> Harrison: *Should I pick you up around 7?*
> Me: *Sure. But leave the cruiser at home.*
> Harrison: *Copy. See you then.*

There. That wasn't so hard.

What I've come to realize over the last year of my makeover is that change is a choice we make every day, a thousand times a day. We choose to do this one thing better. Then the next. And the next. And the one after that. So maybe duping a nice guy into a fake date in order to let my ex down gently isn't exactly putting me up for sainthood—but baby steps. The point is, the old me wouldn't have been caught dead in the same room as Harrison. And who knows, maybe we walk away from this as friends.

CHAPTER 10

EVAN

She does this shit on purpose. She likes to know she still has the power to mess with my head, dangling the possibilities in front of my face just to yank the carrot away at the last moment. What I'm more concerned about is the guy. This fucking guy who thought it'd be a good idea to run up on Genevieve right under my nose. Dude better have his affairs in order.

Needless to say, I'm buzzing when I get back to my house after work. But I don't make it three steps through the door before Cooper pounces on me.

"Hey," he calls from the living room, where he and Mac are sitting on the couch watching TV, "did you get in touch with Steve about the pipe fittings?"

"What?" I kick off my shoes and throw my keys at the side table with too much force. "No, I was out at Gen's house with Levi."

"And after that you were supposed to stop by the office to call Steve about the order for the hotel. We need those fittings tomorrow so we can replace the plumbing on the second floor."

"So you do it." I stalk into the kitchen and grab a beer from the fridge. Daisy rushes up to wag her tail at my feet, more hyper than usual.

"I think she wants to go out," Mac says. "Mind taking her for a walk?"

"You stuck to the couch or something?"

"Whoa." Cooper jumps to his feet, apparently still capable of using his legs. "What's with the attitude?"

"I just walked in the damn door and you two can't wait ten seconds before jumping down my throat." I flick the bottle cap into the trash and snap my fingers at Daisy, which sends her whimpering back to Mac. "Meanwhile, you both have done what today, exactly? Instead of bitching about stuff not getting done, why not get off your asses and do it yourself?"

Having exactly no interest in this conversation, I head outside to the garage.

What gets me is Gen doesn't date. The thought of her putting on a pretty dress and doing her makeup to sit nicely at dinner is laughable. She'd sooner gnaw off her own arm than make small talk over appetizers. So what is this, some elaborate attempt to convince me she's changed? Bullshit. Gen's the type of girl who steals a motorcycle from outside a biker bar just to take a joyride. She does not, under any circumstances, let a guy pull her chair out.

Maybe she does now.

The nagging voice in my head pokes a hole in my conviction. What if pretty dresses and sit-down dinners are her thing now? Is it so far-fetched? Maybe the girl I knew last year isn't the same one who—

I banish the thought. Because, no. Just no. I know Genevieve West like the back of my hand. I know what excites her. I know what makes her smile, and I know what brings tears to her eyes. I know her every mood, and I know the deepest fucking parts of her soul. Maybe she's got herself fooled, but not me.

As my head turns itself over, I strip off my shirt, toss it aside, and start hitting the heavy bag hanging from the ceiling in the corner of the garage. Dust explodes off the surface with every strike of my fists. Great billowing plumes of fine gray powder. The first few hits shock my nerves, slap the noise from my mind. The sharp, shooting pain radiates through my hands, then my arms, elbows, and shoulders, until the pain dulls and I barely feel it anymore. But I still feel her. Everywhere. All the time and growing more insistent.

She *left* me. Me, who'd slept all night in a chair by her hospital bed that time she got a concussion after falling off a tree during a climbing race with two of her brothers. Me, who'd let her cry in my arms every time her mom missed an important event in Gen's life.

She just left without telling me.

No. Worse—without asking me to come with her.

"You're not going to have any skin left if you don't tape those up." Cooper sneaks up on me. He positions himself behind the bag to hold it in place while I mostly ignore him to concentrate on my aim. Small clusters of blood have already appeared on the synthetic leather. I don't care.

When I don't respond, he presses on.

"Come on. What's going on? Something happen?"

"If you're going to talk, you can leave." I punch through the bag. Past it. Driving my fists harder with every swing. The distraction dissipates with every repetition, and as my nerves become desensitized to the impact, my brain finds the effects wearing off too.

"So it's about Gen." There's a sigh of equal parts disapproval and disappointment, as if I came home with a D on my report card. It's exhausting having a brother who thinks he's my dad. "When are you going to let that go? She ghosted you, dude. What more is there to say?"

"Remember how much you appreciated my input on Mac last year?" I remind him. Because I learned my lesson. When I was all up in his business about crossing over to the dark side to catch feelings for a rich chick, he told me no small number of times to get bent. And he was right. "Well, same."

"I'm just trying to look out for you," he says, like somehow I've missed the point. Then, sensing I'm quickly losing my tolerance for him, Cooper changes tacks. "Come on, let's get out of here. Go out. Take your mind off everything."

"Pass." What I figured out a long time ago is there's nothing that bleaches thoughts of Genevieve out of my head. She's woven into the fabric. I can't rip her out without tearing myself apart.

I catch Cooper's eyes for a second between hits to the bag. There's unhappiness in them. But it isn't up to me to make him feel better, and I don't take responsibility for trying. "You can go now, Coop."

With a clenched jaw, he stalks out of the garage.

Not long after he's gone, I give up on the bag. My knuckles are bloody; bits of flesh hang off in kernels. It's gross as fuck.

When my phone buzzes in my pocket, I entertain a moment of dim-witted anticipation expecting it to be Gen, then curse to myself when I see it's my mother.

Shelley: *Hey baby. Just checking in to see how you're doing.*

Yep, my mother is not in my contacts list under *MOM*, but Shelley. Which speaks volumes.

She's been messaging me in an attempt to resurrect our relationship after Cooper briefly had her arrested for stealing several grand from him a few months back. He's had it with her shit for a long time, but that was the last insult for him. The final betrayal.

I haven't told Cooper about the texts yet, because as far as he's concerned, she's dead to him. Admitting I've been in contact would have him downright furious.

Not that I'm so forgiving either. Not anymore, at least. For years, I was willing to give her the benefit of the doubt, even when I knew she couldn't be trusted. That every visit was simply a precursor to another broken promise and another exit without a goodbye. I just don't know how to ignore her.

Sighing, I shoot a quick text back.

Me: *All good here. You?*
Shelley: *I'm in Charleston. Was hoping maybe you'd come visit?*

I stare at the screen for a long moment. For weeks, she has been insisting she's reformed. New leaf and all that. Her last message said she wants a chance at reconciliation, but the amount of chances this woman has gotten from us is comical at this point. There were times Cooper and I needed a mother when we were kids. Now, we get along just fine without one. Hell, we get along *better*. Life's much less stressful without a person that blows into town every few months or years to spin some bullshit about a big opportunity and getting her life together, and all she needs is a place to stay and a few bucks, yada yada. Until we wake up one morning and she's gone again. The coffee can above the fridge empty. Cooper's room ransacked. Or whatever new low Shelley decides to sink to.

When I don't respond right away, another message pops up.

Shelley: *Please? We could start off easy. Coffee? A walk? Whatever you want.*

My hesitation earns me another message.

Shelley: *I miss my sons, Evan. Please.*

I grit my teeth. Thing is, I didn't pack for a guilt trip. She can't play the mom card after years of negligence.

Her next message names a time and place. Because she knows I'm the soft one when it comes to her, and I always have been. She wouldn't dare come at Cooper like this. Which is all the more conniving and unfair.

Still, even understanding all this, a part of me wants to believe her, to give her a chance to prove she can be a decent person. If to no one else, then to us.

Me: *I'll think about it and get back to you.*

But reconciliation is a stretch goal. Coop is intent on taking this grudge to the grave. I'm sure he'd be happier if he never had to think about her again. For me, well, if I'm honest with myself, I guess I'm still raw about the whole thing. Last time she was here, she put on a good act, her best performance yet. She had me most of the way to believing she'd stick around and give it a try. Be a real mom. As much as she could be to two grown men who barely know her.

Needless to say, it blew up in my face with Coop getting in another *I told you so.*

And since I'm not in the mood for a repeat when I sit down for dinner later, I keep the news of Shelley being in Charleston to myself. She's the least of my concerns, anyway. The thoughts of Gen on her date scream much, much louder in my head.

While Mac is passing me the mashed potatoes, I'm imagining Gen laughing over salads and appetizers with some asshole. Cooper's talking shop, but I'm picturing this dude sizing up how to get Gen back to his place tonight. He's thinking about what she looks like naked, and will some steak and lobster buy him a blowjob on a first date?

My jaw's so tight I can barely eat.

Then, as we're clearing the table, a bug crawls in my ear asking, *what if Gen actually likes this bastard?* What if she's falling for his bullshit, eating his game with a spoon? Maybe she wore some sexy outfit with the intentions of leaving it on his bedroom floor. Maybe later tonight, she'll be dragging her nails down his back.

I nearly put my fist through the wall, curling both hands over the countertop as I help Mac load the dishwasher.

And what happens if Gen and this guy get together for real? It's one thing if she dated someone in Charleston, because I wouldn't have to see it. But she's home now. If she finds a new guy, I'll be forced to watch them walk around, rubbing it in my face while I'm at work, fixing up her dad's house? Walking in on them in the kitchen suddenly trying to act chill with that flush on her face that says she just had his fingers inside her? Oh, hell no. I'd end up taking a hammer to his hand.

"We're going for a walk on the beach with Daisy," Mac says, neatly folding the dishcloth and placing it next to the sink. "Wanna come?"

"Nah. I'm good."

I'm not good. I'm not good in the slightest.

The moment Cooper and Mac exit onto the back deck, I grab my keys and head to the front door.

In no time at all, I'm riding into town on my motorcycle to see for myself. Damned if I'm going to be made the cuck.

CHAPTER 11

GENEVIEVE

"I think I screwed up," I whisper to Harrison as the waiter in a white dress shirt and black vest lays the linen napkin in my lap. There are already three sets of glasses on the table and we haven't even ordered anything yet. When the waiter offered us still or sparkling water, I asked for the free kind. "I had no idea this place was so fancy."

Or expensive. It only opened recently, and I noticed it as I passed by the other day. When I was concocting this diversion for Evan earlier, it just popped into my head. Now, I'm wearing my best summer dress, even put on makeup and did my hair, and yet I still feel underdressed.

For his part, Harrison does a decent job of passing as one of the yacht club guys that wash into Avalon Bay for the season. Button-down shirt and those damn khakis with a belt that matches his shoes. It works for him, though.

"I don't mind." Harrison pushes some glasses out of the way to make room for his menu. "I don't eat out much. It's nice to have an excuse."

"Okay, but I'll obviously split the check."

With a Disney Channel smile, Harrison shakes his head. "I can't let you do that."

"No, seriously. I wouldn't have suggested this place if I'd known. Please."

He sets the menu aside and meets my eyes with stern conviction. It ages him ten years. "If you keep trying to shove money in my pocket, I'm bound to get offended." Then he winks at me, those boyish freckles blossoming on his cheeks, and I realize he's putting me on.

"That's your cop face, isn't it?"

"I've been working on it in the mirror," he confirms, leaning in with his voice hushed. "How am I doing?"

"I'd say you've got it down pat."

Harrison sips his water as though he's just remembered that first dates are supposed to make us nervous. "There was a little old lady the other day I pulled over for running a stop sign. I made the mistake of asking if she'd not seen the sign, which I guess she took to mean I thought her vision was the trouble, and so this woman gets on the phone to the sheriff telling him some high school kid's stolen a cruiser and a uniform and is out terrorizing the community."

I burst out laughing.

"Anyway. I've been told I better figure my way to looking more the part," he finishes.

The waiter returns to take our drink order, and would we care for a bottle of wine? I wave off the wine list when Harrison offers it to me. My experience is generally limited to the five major food groups: whiskey, vodka, tequila, rum, and gin.

"Hang on, I got this," Harrison says, getting excited as he scans the list. "I watched a wine documentary on Netflix once."

A smile springs free. "Nerd."

He shrugs, but with a satisfied smirk that says he's quite proud of himself. "We'll have two glasses of the 2016 pinot grigio, please. Thank you."

The waiter nods his approval. I consider speaking up to refuse, but what's the harm in one glass of wine? It's not like I'm pounding shots or downing cocktails. I won't even get a buzz on a stingy pour. Besides, I don't want to dive headlong into the details of my reputation recovery before we've even ordered food. Not a great conversation starter. I think of it like an accessory to complete my ensemble of mature adult Gen.

"I think that went well," I tell him.

"I was nervous there for a minute, but I think I pulled it out in the end," he agrees with a laugh.

Honestly, as far as fake first dates go, this one's off to a better start than I had any right to expect. We ended up meeting at the restaurant instead of him picking me up, and part of me worried he might walk up holding flowers or something. As he'd kissed my cheek in greeting, he admitted he'd considered bringing a bouquet but realized I wasn't the type, and it'd probably embarrass both of us. He was right, and the fact that he figured that out put him in an entirely new perspective. Now, the vibe is chill and we're getting along. None of those uncomfortable silences and darting glances to avoid eye contact, while we both struggle to devise an exit strategy. Dare I say, I'm having a good time. Strange as that is.

The old me wouldn't have been caught dead in this place. Which I suppose is the point. I'm stepping out of the long shadow my past has cast over my life. Harrison is certainly living up to his part of this plot. A bit shy and reserved in comparison, but sweet and funny in a nineties family sitcom sort of way. And although I can't muster up any sexual attraction to him, perhaps that's a good thing. Evan and I were all but defined by our rabid sexual chemistry. It ruled us.

But if I'm going to be serious about this good girl turn, maybe I need a good boy to match.

"Anyway," he says once we've ordered our meals, after going off on a tangent about why he can't eat mussels anymore. "I feel like I'm being rude, doing all the talking. I tend to ramble sometimes."

"No, you're fine," I assure him. I'd much rather not have the conversation focus on me. "Tell me, what's the weirdest call you've gone out on?"

Harrison ponders, staring into his glass of wine while spinning it in little circles on the table by the base. "Well, there was this one. Second week on the job. I've still got a babysitter, this guy Mitchum, who, if you picture a disgruntled math teacher with a gun, is pretty much spot-on. From the second we meet, his personality is he wants me dead."

I snort out a too-loud laugh that disturbs the tables nearby and has me hiding behind my napkin.

"I'm serious," Harrison insists. "I don't know what it was, but I walked into the boss's office before my first shift, and Mitchum was standing there looking at me like I'd knocked up his daughter."

I can't imagine anyone being put off by Harrison's first impression. Then again, I've never been too fond of the cops in this town, so maybe that's all the explanation there needs to be.

"We get called out to this house in Belfield," he continues. "Dispatch says a couple of neighbors are having some kind of dispute. So we arrive on scene to find two older fellas jawing at each other in the front yard. Mitchum and I separate them to get their stories and figure out real quick they both started hitting the bottle early that day. They were arguing over a mower or a mailbox, depending on which one of them tells it. Nothing especially interesting, but they've both got rifles they're waving around, and somebody let a few shots off."

I'm trying to anticipate where this story is headed when Harrison shakes his head at me, as if to say, don't even try.

"Mitchum asks the one guy, *why don't you put the gun away?* He tells us he only got his gun because his neighbor got his own. And the other neighbor says he only got his gun after the other guy put the gator on his roof."

"What?" I bark out another disturbing noise that disrupts the entire restaurant, though now I'm too preoccupied to feel contrite. "Like a real alligator?"

"This fella's been trying to shoot the thing down, if you can believe that. Pumping rounds into his own roof, the walls, wherever. We can't be sure they're even all accounted for—thank goodness we never got any reports of stray bullets."

"How'd he get it up there in the first place?" I demand.

"Turns out the guy works for the phone company. He's out driving to a job when he finds this gator in the middle of the road. On his lunch break he decides to drive the cherry picker home and drop that poor animal up there, though I can't for the life of me imagine the mechanics of that situation. Turns out they'd had a run-in that morning which precipitated the retaliation."

"I almost have to admire the guy," I admit. "I've never had a grudge that warranted a biblical plague. I guess I need to find a better class of nemesis."

"But get this. Mitchum, sweet guy that he is, tells me I have to climb up there and get the gator down."

"No way."

"Now remember, it's my first shift on the street, and if this guy goes back to the station and says I can't hack it, I could be banished behind a desk for good. So I don't have much of a choice. Still, I ask, *shouldn't we get animal control out there instead?* And he tells me, *sorry, kid, the dog catchers only work on the ground.*"

"Wow." I'm honestly stunned. Not that I didn't know cops were bastards, but that's some cold shit right there. Talk about friendly fire. "What'd you do?"

"The short version," he says with the haunted stare of a man who's seen things, "involves a ladder, a ribeye, some rope, and about four hours to get that thing down."

"Damn, Harrison, you're my hero. Here's to protecting and serving," I say, clinking my wineglass with his.

We make it halfway through our entrées before he tires of dominating the conversation and once again tries to turn it on me. This time, the topic being my mother.

"I'm sorry again," he says. "This must still be a difficult time. With moving back and all."

His consolatory tone reminds me that I'm still putting on an act, playing a part I've written of the person I should be: the grieving daughter, still mourning her dear mother. Wallpapering a better story over our absent relationship, because it sounds good.

Which is something I've never had to do with Evan.

Fuck. Despite my best efforts, thoughts of him creep in through the seams. He's the only person who understands my darkest thoughts, who doesn't judge or try to dissect me. He understands that the empty place where everyone else holds their mothers in their hearts doesn't make me a bad person. For all our failings, Evan never needed me to be anyone but myself.

"Ooh, that looks good."

Speak of the fucking devil.

Completely blindsiding us, Evan suddenly drops a chair at our table and sits down between Harrison and me.

He grabs a scallop off my plate and pops it in his mouth. His daring gaze flicks to me with a self-satisfied grin. "Hey."

Unbelievable.

My jaw doesn't know whether to drop or tighten, so it alternates between the two disparate movements, I'm sure making me appear unhinged. "You're out of your mind," I growl.

"Brought you something." He places a green Blow Pop on

the table, then appraises me with almost lewd interest. "You look nice."

"Nope. Not doing this. Go home, Evan."

"What?" he says with mock innocence. He licks lemon-butter sauce from his fingers. "You've made your point. I came to spring you from this stuck-up nightmare."

He stands out among the other diners, wearing a black T-shirt and black jeans, hair wind-tossed, and all of him smelling like motorcycle exhaust.

"Come on." Harrison, to his credit, takes the interruption in stride. A bit confused as he questions me with his eyes, but maintaining a polite smile. "We're having a nice time. Let the lady finish her dinner in peace. I'm sure whatever you two have to talk about can wait until later."

"Oh, shit." Laughing, Evan cocks his head at me. "This guy's serious? Where'd you find him? I mean, damn, Gen, you're basically dating our seventh-grade science teacher."

That wipes the friendly smile from Harrison's face.

"Evan, stop it." I grab his arm. "You're not funny."

"Alright, I've asked you nicely," Harrison says. He stands up and I'm reminded of all the times cops chased me and Evan out of convenience store parking lots and abandoned buildings. "Now I'm telling you. Leave."

"It's fine," I warn Harrison. "I've got it."

Still holding Evan's arm, I tighten my grip. There's no way I'm letting him start a brawl in the middle of this restaurant and get his ass thrown in jail for breaking a cop's nose.

"Please, Evan," I say flatly. "Just go."

He ignores the request. "Remember when this place was a clothing store?" Evan leans in closer, brushing his fingers over my hand on his arm, which I snatch away from his touch. "Did you tell him about the time we did it in the dressing room while the church ladies were just outside the door trying on their Sunday hats?"

"Screw you." My voice shakes with anger, cold and brittle, the words barely passing through my lips as my throat constricts. I'd slap him if I didn't know for certain it would only encourage his sabotage. The more emotion Evan can pull from me, the more proof he has to continue his pursuit.

Pushing back from the table to stand, I catch a brief glimpse of Harrison's sympathetic gaze before I turn away and leave.

I hit the railing that separates the boardwalk from the beach below like a car slamming into an embankment. I might have kept on walking into the ocean, blind with rage, if it hadn't stopped me. I want to throw something. Launch a brick through a storefront window to hear it shatter. Take a baseball bat to a china shop. Anything to get this restless static out of my arms, the thick, stone-hard ball of fury throbbing in my chest.

When I hear footsteps behind me, my fist tightens. A hand touches my arm and I'm mid-swing when I turn to see Harrison with his hands up, braced for impact.

"Oh gosh, I'm sorry." I drop my hands. "I thought you were Evan."

Harrison laughs nervously and flashes a relieved smile. "No worries. This is what all those de-escalation courses are for at the academy."

It's sweet, his commitment to deflecting everything with a joke and a heaping, sugary spoonful of optimism. I don't have that stuff in me.

"Really, though. I'm sorry for everything back there. That was so embarrassing. I'd make some excuse for him, but Evan's kind of a jerk on his best days." I lean over the railing, resting my arms on the splintered wood. "And here all you did was say hi in a bar to be nice. Bet you didn't expect all this drama, huh? Got more than you bargained for."

"Nah, I knew there was a chance I'd have a pissed-off Hartley on my ass if I went out with you."

I lift a brow. "Oh really?"

"We went to the same high school," he reminds me, his voice wry but gentle. "Everyone had a front-row seat to the Genevieve and Evan show."

Embarrassment heats my cheeks, and I avert my eyes. Somehow, knowing Harrison witnessed our high school antics is even more humiliating than having Evan crash this date.

"Hey. Don't look away like that. Everyone has baggage." He comes to lean against the railing beside me. "We've all got a past. Things we'd rather people not judge us for. How can anyone grow if we only let them be who they were yesterday, right?"

I glance over in surprise. "That's an unusual outlook for a cop."

"Yeah, I get that a lot."

We stand there for a while, just listening to the waves and watching the way the lights of the boardwalk float on the water. I'm about to pack it in, pick up my dignity off the ground and head home, when Harrison makes another suggestion.

"You want to take a walk?" As though he's spent this whole time mustering the courage, he offers his hand. "I don't think I'm ready to go home. Besides, we didn't make it to dessert. I bet the ice-cream place might still be open."

My first instinct is to say no. Just go home and nurse my anger. Then I remember what Alana said. If I'm going to walk a different path, I have to start making different choices. And I suppose that starts with giving Harrison a chance to change my mind.

"That sounds nice," I say.

We stroll down the boardwalk toward Two Scoops, where he

buys us a couple of ice-cream cones. We keep walking, passing families and other couples. Teenagers running around, making out in the shadows. It's a balmy night with a warm breeze of salt air that offers the slightest relief from the heat. Harrison holds my hand, and while I let him, it feels wrong. Unnatural. Nothing like the feeling of anticipation and longing that comes with touching that person you can't wait to kiss, the one who sets your nerves racing, gets your fingertips excited.

Eventually, we end up in front of the old hotel. Last time I saw this place, it was gaping open, walls collapsed, with furniture and debris pouring out. The Beacon had been all but eviscerated in the hurricane. Now, it's like it never happened. Practically brand new, with its sparkling white façade and green trim, shiny new windows, and a roof without any holes in it.

Now that Cooper's girlfriend owns this place, I'll probably never be allowed to step foot inside.

"It's remarkable what they've managed to do with the place," Harrison says, admiring the renovation. "I heard it's supposed to open in the fall."

"I loved this place when I was a kid. For my sixteenth birthday, my dad brought me and my friends in for a spa day. Got our nails done, facials and stuff." I grin at the memory. "They gave us robes and slippers, water with cucumbers in it. All that fancy stuff. It probably sounds stupid, but I remember thinking this was the most beautiful place. All the dark wood and brass, the paintings on the walls, the antique furniture. It was how I imagined palaces must look on the inside. But, you know, kids are stupid, so . . ." I shrug.

"No, it's not stupid," Harrison assures me. "We had my grandparents' anniversary dinner here years back. They served all this really pretty-looking food—real rich-people stuff, because my family wanted to give them a special party—and my grandad got so mad, kept yelling at the waiter to just bring him some meatloaf. I swear," Harrison laughs, "he left that party like it was the worst night of his life. Meanwhile, the family spent a small fortune to cater the thing."

We trade a few more stories, and eventually he escorts me back to my car parked outside the restaurant. While much of my irritation with the ordeal from earlier has dissipated, nothing makes this part of the night any less awkward.

"Thank you," I say. "For dinner, but really for being so nice. You didn't have to be."

"Believe it or not, I had a great time." His earnest expression tells me he actually means that.

"How are you even like this?" I demand, befuddled by him. "So positive and upbeat all the time. I've never met anyone like you."

Harrison shrugs. "Seems like a lot of work being any other way." Like the true gentleman he is, he opens my door for me. Then, with a tentative gesture, he offers me a hug. It's a relief, honestly, not to do the whole dance around a kiss. "I'd like to call you, if that's okay."

I don't get a chance to contemplate the possibility of a second date.

"Step away from the car," a voice shouts.

Frowning, I turn around in time to spot Deputy Randall crossing the street. He's got a mean way about him. A look that intends to do harm.

"Put the keys on the ground," he commands.

For fuck's sake. I shield my eyes as he approaches with a flashlight shining in my face. "It's my car. I'm not stealing it."

"I can't allow you to drive impaired," Randall says, resting a hand on his utility belt.

"Impaired?" I look at Harrison, seeking confirmation I'm not hallucinating this. Because Randall cannot be serious. "What are you talking about?"

"Rusty," Harrison says timidly, "I think you've made a mistake here."

"I clearly observed the young lady standing in an unsteady manner and leaning on the door for support."

"Bullshit," I spit at him. "I barely touched a glass of wine over an hour ago. This is harassment."

"I gotta say, Rusty, I've been with her all night." Harrison is soft-spoken and polite, presenting a nonthreatening contradiction to Randall's nonsense assertions. "She's telling the truth."

"Told you before, kid," Randall says with an almost gleefully cruel sneer. "This ain't one you want to waste your time on. If she's awake, she's either drugged out or drunk, making a sloppy embarrassment of herself all over town." He huffs out a sarcastic laugh. "If drunk and disorderlies were frequent flyer miles, she could book a trip around the world. Ain't that right, Genevieve?"

"Fuck you. Asshole." I know I'll regret the words even as they're coming out of my mouth, but I don't bother clamping my lips shut. It feels good to let it out, ineffectual as it is. A brief fantasy of snagging his pepper spray flickers through my mind.

The faintest twitch of a smirk tugs at the corner of Randall's mouth. Then, forehead creased, he orders me to come stand behind the car and take a field sobriety test.

My jaw snaps open in shock.

"You can't be serious," protests Harrison, who's clearly starting to understand what an utter dickweed Randall is.

"No." I cross my arms and consider just driving away. Daring Randall to stop me. Those old instincts of mayhem and defiance roar back with a vengeance. "This is ludicrous. We both know I'm not drunk."

"If you fail to comply with a lawful order, you will be under arrest," he informs me. Randall is practically drooling at the prospect of putting me in handcuffs.

I turn to Harrison, who, though plainly alarmed, admits with a shrug there's nothing he can do about it. Seriously? What the hell's the point of dating a cop if he can't get you out of a trumped-up traffic stop with a disgruntled egomaniac?

What truly pisses me off, however, what really tears the nails from the bed, is knowing Randall gets off on this. He loves applying his authority to humiliate me. Busting a nut with his power trip.

Not wanting to make a scene, I stalk toward the rear bumper and appraise Randall with a cool look. "What would you like me to do? *Officer.*"

A smile stretches across his face. "You can start by reciting the alphabet. Backwards."

If he thinks this weakens me, he's sorely mistaken.

That which doesn't kill me makes my anger stronger.

CHAPTER 12

EVAN

For some reason, I saw that encounter going better in my head. I thought it'd be charming, in our kind of demented way. At the very least, make her laugh. Because as much as she'd given me a hard time back in the day, she always ate that stuff up, getting me jealous and riled until I snapped and stormed in to throw her over my shoulder. Then we'd fuck it out and be cool again.

This time, not so much.

I rake both hands through my hair and stare out at the dark water beyond the long pier. After Gen stormed out of the restaurant and her dipshit date gave me some unconvincing advice to leave her alone, I walked out here to get some air, get my head on straight. But so far, all I've succeeded in doing is wallowing over how much I miss Gen.

With a tired exhalation, I shove my hands in my pockets and leave the pier. Coming up the steps to the boardwalk, where my bike is parked along the curb, I'm not quite sure what I'm looking at until I hear Gen's voice across the street telling a cop with his flashlight pointed at her to suck her dick.

My eyebrows soar in confusion, then knit in displeasure. The cop's got her on the street behind a car, with her arms spread, touching her finger to her nose. Meanwhile, her dweeb date is there doing nothing while she begrudgingly walks a straight line and recites the alphabet, muttering obscenities along the way. Even from a distance I can feel the humiliation in Gen's expression. The way her eyes stare into the distance.

I'm halfway to running over there before I stop myself. Damn it. The last thing I need right now is to go to jail for bouncing a cop's face off the pavement. I wouldn't make it out of a cell alive. Besides, Cooper's already up my ass about fighting—getting locked up would give him a lifetime *I told you so* account that I'm not about to pay into. So I stand there, hugging the railing, fists clenched.

I recognize Rusty Randall, though I don't know him well. Just that he's got a reputation as a creep with a not-so-secret drinking problem of his own. To her credit, however, Gen takes it like a champ, never the type to let anyone see her rattled.

Still, it turns my stomach to watch this degrading episode. Dozens of people stare at her as they pass. She was stone-cold sober when I saw her an hour ago. And by how easily she's navigating the test, I'd say it's clear she didn't pop into a bar to pound a bunch of shots after she left the restaurant. Which means Randall is only being a dick because he can.

Finally, after a brief conversation, she's allowed to get in her car. I'm gratified to note she barely glances at her polo-clad date as she leaves.

I quickly get on my bike to follow her, making sure to keep my distance. I just want to make sure she gets home okay. After a while, though, I realize we aren't headed to her house. We leave the lights of town behind, headed north along the coast where the population thins out and the stars appear overhead. Soon we're winding down a two-lane road through the black wooded landscape where the moon over the bay appears in brief glimpses through the trees.

Eventually, she pulls onto the dirt shoulder near a narrow

footpath you can only find if you know it's there, even in day-light. She gets out of her car, grabs a blanket from the trunk, and proceeds through the trees. I wait a few minutes before following her. At the end of the path, where the trees give way to the sandy beach, I find her sitting on a driftwood log.

Her head lifts when she hears me approach. "You suck at tail-ing people," she says.

I take that as an invitation to sit. "I stopped trying to be sly about it after I realized where you were headed."

"I didn't come here to meet you." With the blanket wrapped around her shoulders, she buries her toes in the cool sand. "This is just where I come to think. Or it was."

That she chose this place hits me right in the chest. Because it's our spot. Always has been. It was our emergency rendezvous after running from the cops, the make-out spot when we were grounded and sneaking out of the house. Our secret hideout. Not even Cooper knows I come here.

"I saw what happened back there," I tell her. She's not much more than a black outline against the night. It's so dark out here, moonlight gets swallowed before it hits the ground. The stars, though, are really something. "What was that all about?"

"Nothing. Just some asshole giving me a hard time."

"That was Randall, right? Didn't you used to babysit for him?" He wasn't a super nice guy or anything, but I remember once or twice he let her slide on this or that in high school when other cops had it in for us pretty bad. It was sort of a transactional un-derstanding.

"Yeah, well, things change." Her voice is tight and sour.

She doesn't elaborate just yet, and I don't push. Thing I learned a long time ago: Gen will talk when she wants to. She's a locked box—nothing gets in or out unless she wants it to. A person could spend a lifetime trying to pick her open.

So I wait, silent, listening. Until minutes pass and she lets out a sigh.

"Not long before I left town, I blew up Randall's family."

I slant my head. "How'd you manage that?"

In a voice heavy with fatigue, she explains how he assaulted her in a bar after he failed to coax her to do him in the parking lot. My fists clench so hard my knuckles crack. I want to hit something. Tear it to shreds. But I don't dare move because I want to hear everything she has to say.

"When I got home after we closed down the bar, that's all I could think about. Vengeance. I was raging," Gen continues. "The Randall house was only a few blocks away, so I got it in my head to walk my ass over there at three in the morning. Next thing I know, I'm banging on the door with my hair sweaty and makeup melting off my face. His wife Kayla answered the door all bleary-eyed and confused. I forced my way past her to start shouting in the middle of her living room until Rusty came downstairs."

I don't miss the deep crease of shame that digs into her forehead. I have to stop myself from reaching out and taking her hand.

"I told her how her sleazeball husband tried to coerce me into sex then assaulted me in a bar. How everyone in town but her knew he was sleeping around behind her back. He denied it all, of course. Said I'd come on to him. The jilted, jealous girl." Gen laughs humorlessly. "I was a screaming lunatic who probably looked like I'd just washed in with the tide. Meanwhile, her four kids were peering out from the hallway, terrified. Kayla had no reason to believe me, so she told me to get the hell out of her house."

I wish I'd known, wish I'd been there for her. I could have stopped this entire ordeal dead in its tracks. Kept her from leaving. Now, I'm not sure what's worse. Wondering this whole time what made her leave, or understanding now that if I'd just been there, we wouldn't have lost the last year of our lives together.

"The next morning, I woke up with a monster hangover and a perfect memory of what I'd done. Every terrible moment of my total meltdown. It would've been less mortifying to set his cruiser on fire. At least then I'd still have had my self-respect. I couldn't bear the shame and regret. Not for that skeezy douchebag, but for storming into that poor woman's house and traumatizing her kids. Kayla didn't deserve that. She was a kind woman who'd always been nice to me. Her only fault was being married to an asshole and not knowing any better."

"I'd have killed him," I tell her, now seriously regretting I didn't take my shot when he had her on the boardwalk. "Beat him within an inch of his life and dragged him out to sea behind a boat."

The urge to hop on my bike and find Randall is almost irresistible. In seconds, a montage of brutal fantasies spin through my head. Knocking every tooth out of his skull. Snapping his fingers like matchsticks. Putting his nut sack under the rear tire of my motorcycle. And that's all for starters. Because absolutely no one lays a goddamn hand on my Genevieve.

I hate what he's done to her. Not just that night, or this latest power trip, but the way she's resigned herself to defeat, the exhaustion in her voice. It rips me up inside and I can't stand it. Because there's nothing I can do. Short of kicking his ass and spending the next twenty years in prison, I don't know how to fix it.

"I wish you'd told me," I say quietly.

"I—" She stops for a beat. "I didn't tell anyone," she finishes.

Yet I have a suspicion she'd been about to say something else.

"It's a big part of the reason why I left," she admits. "Not only him, but his wife and those kids. I couldn't stomach walking around town knowing people would hear about what happened, how I made a first-rate ass of myself and ruined that family."

"Oh, screw that." I shake my head emphatically. "To hell with him. You did his wife a favor. And better those kids find out sooner than later that their dad's a bastard. Trust me, the prick had it coming." I've got no sympathy for him, and neither should she.

A half-hearted *yeah* is all she mutters in response. And all I want is to make this better for her. Take away the garbage that's clogging up her head. Help her breathe again. Then it occurs to me, I haven't been much help tonight. Her evening had gone to hell before Randall even got there, and that's on me.

"I'm sorry," I say roughly. "For crashing your date. I wasn't thinking clearly."

"You don't say."

"I'm not sure I ever am when it comes to you. Truth is, my head hasn't been right for about a year now."

"I can't be responsible for your happiness, Evan. I can barely account for myself."

"That's not what I'm saying. When you left, my whole life changed. It would be like if Cooper suddenly disappeared. A huge piece of me broke off and was just gone." I scrub a hand over my face. "So much of me was wrapped up in us. And then you came back, and it's got me all twisted up inside. Because you're here, but you're not really back. Not like it was. I don't know how to fit everything into place the way it was before, so I'm just walking around all out of sorts."

Agony lodges in my throat. For as long as I can remember, I've been a goner for this girl. Turning myself inside out to keep her attention. Always terrified that one day she'd realize I was a loser who wasn't worth her time, figure out she's always had the option to do better. Last year, I thought she'd reached that conclusion, but it turns out I was the idiot thinking her leaving had anything to do with my dumb ass.

"I'm not trying to hurt you," she says softly.

Silence falls over us. Not strained or uncomfortable, because it's never that way with me and Gen, even when we want to murder each other.

"I remember the first time I knew I wanted to kiss you," I finally say, not quite sure where the sentiment even came from. But the memory is clearer than day. It was the summer before eighth grade. I'd been making a fool of myself for weeks trying to impress her, make her laugh. I didn't know yet that's how crushes start. When the balance tips from friendship to attraction. "A few weeks before we started eighth grade. We were all out there diving off the old pier."

She gives a quiet laugh. "God, that thing was a death trap."

It really was, that decrepit wooden pier half sunken into the waves and falling apart. Victim of a hurricane years prior, infested with rusty nails and splinters. At some point, high school kids had hauled a metal ladder out to the part of the pier that was still standing and tied it to a pylon with bungee cords. It was a sort of rite of passage to swim out through the crashing waves, climb the rickety thing, and leap off the top railing. Then all you had to do was not let the waves throw you back against the pylons covered in barnacles that would tear the flesh off your bones.

"There was that ninth-grader—Jared or Jackson or somebody. He'd been flirting with you all afternoon, doing flips off the pier like he was so damn cool. And being all obnoxious about it too. Like, *hey, look at me, I'm such a badass*. So you dared him to jump to one of the pylons from the pier. It was maybe a ten-foot leap to a one-foot target, and right below were all sorts of torn-up, jagged pieces sticking up out of the water. With the waves just absolutely thrashing below us." I grin. "Suddenly he wasn't so loud anymore. Starts making excuses and shit. And while everyone's ragging on him for chickening out, you take a running start and go flying through the air. I was looking at Cooper for the split second like, oh fuck, we're gonna have to jump in after you and drag you back to shore when you break your neck or get impaled on something. But then you nailed it. Perfect landing. Coolest thing I'd ever seen."

She laughs to herself, remembering. "I got stung by a jellyfish after I jumped down. But I had to be chill about it, you know. Didn't want to look like a dumbass for jumping out there in the first place."

"Yeah, probably a good idea. You would've had ten pervert boys whipping their tiny dicks out to pee on your leg." We both shudder in disgust at that dodged bullet.

"You didn't kiss me that day, though," she points out. "Why not?"

"Because you're fucking scary."

"Oh." She laughs, elbowing my arm good-naturedly.

"I mean, I know we'd been friends for years by then, but when you figure out you have a crush on someone, it's like you're starting from scratch. I didn't know how to approach you."

"You figured it out."

She shifts beside me, and I sense the change in the air between us. Something happens. Without her saying a word, I feel her decide to not be mad at me anymore.

"Didn't have a choice," I admit. "I was going to claw out of my skin if I didn't find out what your lips felt like."

"Maybe you should have." The blanket drops from around her shoulders. She turns to look at me. "Eaten yourself alive. Spared us both the trouble."

"Believe me, there's no version of this"—I gesture between us—"where we don't get together, Fred. One way or another. I can tell you that for certain."

"And to hell with the collateral damage."

"Yes." Without hesitation.

"While it all burns around us."

"I like it that way." Because nothing else matters when she's mine. Nothing. She's everything and all of it.

"There's something wrong with us," she murmurs, closing the space between us until I feel her arm brush mine and her hair sweep across my shoulder in the breeze. "It shouldn't feel like this."

"How should it feel?" I haven't the slightest idea what that means, but I wouldn't change the way I feel about her for anything.

"I don't know. But not this intense."

I can't resist the urge any longer. I reach out to tentatively brush her hair behind her ear, then thread my fingers through the long, soft strands at the back of her neck when she tilts her head into my touch.

"Do you want me to leave?" I ask hoarsely.

"I want you to kiss me."

"You know what'll happen if I do, Gen."

Heat flares in her eyes, those vivid blue depths that never fail to draw me in. "Yeah? What'll happen?" she asks, the slight curve of her lips telling me she already knows the answer but wants to hear me say it.

"I'll kiss you." I drag my thumb along the nape of her neck. "And then . . . then you'll ask me to fuck you."

Her breath hitches. "And then what?" Her voice is shaky.

"You know what." I gulp through the sudden onslaught of pure, carnal lust. "I can never say no to you."

"I know the feeling," she says, and then her lips touch mine and from there I'm no longer in control. We become this autonomous thing with a mind of its own. Like blacking out. She bites my lip with a soft moan, grabbing a fistful of my T-shirt. I'm rock hard and ready to be inside her, but I don't want this to end.

"Let me taste you," I whisper against her mouth.

Lying back on the log, the blanket beneath her, she parts her legs for me, granting me the access I desperately crave. Not even trying to be polite about it, I pull down her lacy panties, shove them in my pocket, and throw her leg over my shoulder.

"I've missed this," I say with a happy groan.

God, and I have. I missed the way she pulls my hair when I suck her clit, arching her back to grind against my face as I drag my tongue over her delicate flesh. I missed her soft sighs of pleasure. Her fingers tangled in my hair.

I push her knees up to her chest, spreading her open, as she trembles against my mouth. She's quiet, all but holding her breath. At least until I work two fingers inside her. Then she moans uncontrollably, and it's almost unfair how fast she comes. I want to make it last for her, but I'm also greedy to make her shake for me.

I don't even expect her to fuck me. I'd be happy to go down on her every day and twice on Sunday just to go home and yank it to the memory. But afterward Gen throws the blanket on the sand and starts unzipping my jeans. She takes my cock in her hand and strokes me, slow and firm. We don't speak. As if we're both afraid words will shatter the darkness, the seclusion that makes this all possible. Out here, alone and in secret, is it even real? We can be anyone, do anything. If no one knows, it never happened.

She sits me on the blanket, both of us still clothed. She knows I've got a condom in my pocket because I almost always do, so she takes it, rips it open and slides it on me before sliding herself down on my dick. So wet and tight. Her hips rock back and forth, taking me deep, summoning a ragged breath from my lungs. I drag down the zipper of her dress and unhook her bra to grab two handfuls of her breasts. Squeezing. Sucking her nipples while she rides me. Burying my face in her warm skin.

It's fucking perfection.

Small noises start to escape her lips. Sighs that become louder, more desperate. Then she loses all control of her voice, moaning against my ear.

"Harder," she begs me. "Please, Evan. Harder."

I grab her ass, holding her above me while I thrust into her. She bites my shoulder. I don't know why that always does it, but seconds later I come, hard, shaking as I hold her tight to my chest. Every time with Gen is the best sex I've ever had. Raw and unfiltered, the most honest we know how to be.

If only that feeling could last forever.

CHAPTER 13

GENEVIEVE

I forget to be afraid of myself, of what I become inside Evan's orbit. It's so much work, worrying, constantly guarding my own worst instincts, thinking and then unthinking every decision. I forget to hate myself and instead let my dress fall to the sand. I walk naked out into the waves while Evan pulls his shirt off, watching me from the shore. I remember how it feels to have his eyes on me. Knowing me, searing me into his mind. I remember the power in it, the excitement in what I do to him by just standing here.

Up to my waist in the water, I turn around to watch him wade in after me—and remember he has the same power. I'm transfixed by the lines of his muscles and broad shoulders. The way he grabs a handful of water and runs it through his hair. A shudder runs through me at the magnificent sight.

"Yeah, so, it's been fun," he says glibly. "But I gotta run."

"Oh yeah? Somewhere to be?"

"Yeah, I got a date, actually. In fact, I'm already running late. Gonna have to stop at the store for more condoms."

"Right, sure," I say, dragging my hands through the water to keep myself steady against the tide. "Anyone I know?"

"Doubt it. She's a meter maid."

"Hot." I bite back a laugh. "Just your type. I know how wild you go for civic authority."

"You know, it's the polyester, if I'm honest. Tacky uniforms get my dick hard."

"So if I told you I became a UPS girl in Charleston—"

"I'd destroy that."

"Promises, promises."

Grabbing my waist, he lifts me and I wrap my legs around his hips. I hang on to him with my hands clasped behind his neck as he keeps us firm against the push and pull of the waves.

Evan squeezes my ass in both hands. "Please, Gen, dare me to bend you over. I'm begging you."

To that I smack a handful of salt water at him. "Animal."

He shakes the water from his face, flipping his hair out of his eyes. "Woof."

We're good like this. That's the thing. It'd be easy to walk away if he were a bastard who treated me badly and was only nice when he wanted to get laid. But it's not like that at all. He's my best friend. Or was.

"So, go on," Evan says gruffly. "Tell me about Charleston. What kind of trouble were you getting into?"

"You're going to be disappointed." This past year was decidedly drab, but that's what it was meant to be. A complete social detox. "There's not much to tell, really. I got a job working for a real estate office. Secretary slash assistant slash miscellaneous. If you can believe that."

"That must have been a hell of a job interview." A wave comes at us sideways and tosses us toward shore. Evan sets me on my feet but keeps those strong hands on my hips.

"Why's that?"

His eyes sparkle in the moonlight. "Well, I assume under relevant experience, you listed the Goldenrod Estates."

The mention of that place brings to mind all sorts of mischief. A few years ago, Goldenrod Estates was a housing development still under construction just south of Avalon Bay. Another gated community for people with more money than taste, all those gaudy McMansions sitting on top of each other. But when the hurricane came through and tore down half the town, construction halted as every company rushed to snap up all the restoration and repair work they could get. The places were abandoned for months, leaving kids like us to roam free through the empty, open homes.

"That was a good summer," I admit. One of our fonder memories.

"The empty pool party."

"Oh, shit. Yes. Like fifty people crammed in a huge concrete hole."

"Then Billy comes running up and says the cops are coming."

The night in question flashes through my mind. I remember my brother's frantic entrance, how we'd shut off the music and turned out the flashlights. All of us holding our breath, crouched down in the dark.

"And your dumb ass decides to be the hero," I say, more in amusement than accusation. "Climbs out of the pool and runs across the street."

"You didn't have to follow me."

"Well, yeah." I sway with the current, letting my toes drag in the sand as the force of the tide pushes and pulls. "But I wasn't letting you go to jail alone."

The memories keep surfacing. Evan and I got up on the roof of a house across the street, watching the red and blue lights grow brighter against the walls of the unfinished houses as cars drew closer. Half a dozen cruisers, at least. Then, hoping to distract the cops from our friends, we began waving our flashlights, shouting at the officers to get their attention. We leapt off the roof, pounding pavement and darting through houses as we ran from the cops, eventually losing them in the woods.

God, we were invincible together. Untouchable. With Evan, I was never bored a minute in my life. Both of us were constantly feeding the high, looking for the next shot of adrenaline as we pressed the limits of our own capacity for trouble.

"There a guy?" he asks suddenly. "Back in Charleston?"

"What if there was?" But there wasn't, not really. Just a series of unimpressive dates and short-lived relationships that mostly passed the time. It's tough when you're comparing every guy you meet to the one you ran away from.

"No reason," he says, shrugging.

"Just want to talk to him, right? Just a chat."

Evan smirks. "Something like that."

I can't help that his jealousy excites me. It's stupid and petty, I know, but in our bizarre way, it's how we show we care.

"What about you? Any girls?"

"A few."

I frown at his vague tone. Feeling the claws trying to come out, I force myself to retract them. Force myself not to picture Evan with another woman. His mouth on someone who isn't me. His hands exploring curves that aren't mine.

But I fail. The images swarm my brain and a low growl escapes my throat.

Evan laughs mockingly. "Just want to talk to them, right?" he mimics. "Just a chat?"

"No. I want to burn their houses down for touching you."

"Damn, Fred, why do you always go right to arson?"

I snicker. "What can I say? I run hot."

"Damn right." His hands glide up my stomach to cup my bare breasts. He squeezes, winking at me.

I shiver when his fingertips dance over my nipples, which pucker tightly. Evan notices the response, and a faint smile tugs at his lips. He's so good-looking it's almost unfair. My gaze sweeps from his chiseled features to the defined muscles of his bare chest. His sculpted arms. Flat abdomen. Those big, callused hands that had just pinned me down while his hungry mouth feasted between my legs.

"You're killing me, Gen." Evan growls the words at whatever he sees playing out on my face. His fingers bite into my flesh. "Don't do that unless you mean it."

"Do what?"

"You know what." Holding onto my waist, he walks us backward toward shore. "You're having fuck-me daydreams. I'm pretty much there, if you want to go again."

"I didn't say that."

He presses himself against me, letting me feel him hard against my leg. "You're a tease, you know that?"

"I do." We reach dry sand. Standing there, we stare at each other, until a tiny smile tickles my lips. "You like it."

Then I kiss his neck. His shoulder. Down his chest until I'm on my knees with his erection in my grip, stroking him. Evan runs both hands into his hair and drops his head back, breathing heavy.

When I don't do anything, he peers down at me, his dark eyes burning with need. "Are you just going to sit there, or are you going to suck it?"

"Haven't decided yet." I lick my lips, and he lets out a tortured groan.

"Tease," he says again, trying to thrust forward.

I tighten my grip in warning, but that just makes his eyes gleam brighter.

"More," he begs.

"More what?" I use my index finger to draw teeny circles around the tip of his cock, prolonging his torture.

"More everything," Evan chokes out.

His hips snap forward again, seeking contact, relief. Laughing at his desperation, I slide my tongue up his shaft and then take him in my mouth.

He moans loud enough to wake the dead.

There are things about Evan I've missed more than others. Getting wasted, blacking out, waking up in a random closet of some random warehouse wearing clothes that weren't my own—I could live without some of those memories. But how he makes me feel when we're alone? How he gives himself over to me, trusts me completely—I love this version of us. The good us.

I relish in the soft groans that vibrate in his chest and the tension tightening his muscles. The way his hands drop to his hips, then to my hair, as he resists the urge to thrust hard and fast, because one time I gently bit him in warning and now he lives in fear of me—just a little. It's our game. I'm on my knees but he's the one at my mercy. I make him feel only what I give him. The pleasure and anticipation. Slowing to prolong the experience, rushing to pull him to the edge of frustration. Until finally, he breaks.

"Gen, *please*."

So I let him come, pumping him until he reaches his release. Then, totally spent, he slinks to the ground and tugs me to lie with him on the blanket.

We're quiet for a while. Surrounded by the comforting darkness, surrounded by only the sound of the breeze rustling the palm trees and the waves rushing up the sand.

"Did I tell you my mom texted me?" Evan says suddenly.

It's not at all where I expect his mind to go, and I hesitate to entertain the subject. Not because it bothers me in any particular way, but I know it tends to upset him.

"She wants me to meet her in Charleston. Make amends or whatever."

"Does Cooper know?"

"Nope." Evan stretches to clasp his hands behind his head, prone under the stars. His beautiful profile is strained when I turn to peek at him. "Last time she was in town, she stole his life savings."

"Oh jeez. That's rough."

"He got most of it back, but . . . yup. Needless to say, he's not rolling out the welcome mat for her anytime soon."

"Do you want to see her?" I ask carefully.

Shelley is a sore spot for Evan and his brother, and always has been. Whereas I was relieved to finally be freed from the standoff of my failed relationship with my mom, I've spent years watching Evan get his hopes up that one day his mother will come to her senses and love him, then have them utterly devastated. I don't share his faith.

"I don't want to be made a fool of again," he confesses. He sounds bleak, exhausted. "I know how I look. Cooper thinks I'm an idiot, that I don't get it. I do, though. I understand what he does, but I can't help that I don't want to miss the one time she might mean it. Maybe that sounds stupid."

"It doesn't," I assure him. Naïve, maybe. Wishful, yes. Both qualities I've never put much stock in. But not stupid.

"It'd be different if it weren't just Coop and me, I think. If our dad was still around." He glances at me with a sad smile. "I mean if he wasn't an asshole. And if we had a bunch of brothers and sisters."

"My mom had too many damn kids," I interject. "Trust me, that didn't make her a better person. I guess having my brothers around helped me to not feel so lonely in that house, but nothing fixes it when you know your mom doesn't give a damn about you."

It's strange how saying those words out loud—saying my mother didn't give a damn about me—brings comfort rather than heartache. I told myself a long time ago I didn't need her love or approval or attention. That I wouldn't waste my breath on someone who couldn't be bothered. And I kept telling myself that until I believed it, entirely and without hesitation. Now that she's dead, I don't miss the wasted years or regret all the times I saved myself the grief of trying. The best gift we give ourselves is respecting our needs first. Because no one else will.

"You wouldn't want a big family?" Evan asks. "Your own, someday?"

I pause in thought, considering all the times one of my brothers walked into the bathroom to take a dump while I was in the shower. The times I came home to one of them in my bed with a girl because another one locked them out of their own room. And then on the flipside: my older brothers all piling in the car to teach me to drive because my dad by then couldn't take the stress of it. Teaching me to play pool and shoot darts. How to drink and throw a punch. They're a bunch of stinking, disgusting brutes. But they're my brutes.

"Yeah, I guess I do." Although I don't particularly want to think about *making* that big family—when I imagine what the six of us must have done to my mother's vag, I blame her a little less for her casual animosity toward us. "Not anytime soon, though."

"I do," he says. "Want a big family, I mean. I'd even be the stay-at-home dad. Do the diapers and make lunches and all that."

"Right." I snort out a laugh at the image of Evan standing in the front yard with two arms full of tiny naked children while the house burns behind him. "Find yourself a sugar momma whose uterus isn't entirely shriveled to sawdust yet."

He shrugs. "What the hell else am I doing, you know? Let's be honest, I tripped and fell into the business with Levi. I didn't really do much to earn that, except mostly show up on time to work. Cooper's got the plans and ambition. Getting his furniture business going and whatnot. So why not be the guy who stays home with the kids?"

"I really wouldn't have figured you for the type." Evan's never been interested in what's expected of him—in all the ways society tells us to get a job, get married, have kids, and die with a mortgage we can't afford and generational credit card debt. "Guess I thought you always had a plan to hop on your bike one day and set out on the open road or whatever cliché shit."

"That's a vacation, not a life. I love the small-town beach life. Where everyone knows everyone. It's a good place to raise a family."

Yet there's uncertainty lingering in his voice. "But?"

"But what the hell do I know about being a father, right? Given my role models, I'd probably permanently scar my kids too."

I sit up to meet Evan's eyes. In his flippant dismissals I hear his pain, the years of trauma buried under bravado. Beating himself up for what's been done to him because there's no one else around to take the blame.

"You'd be a good dad," I say softly.

Another shrug. "Eh. Maybe I wouldn't entirely ruin them."

"You'd have to be more than just the fun dad, though," I remind him as he tugs me back down. I rest my head on his chest and drape my leg over his hip. "Learn discipline. Can't have your kids ending up like us."

"The horror." He kisses the top of my head.

Even after we've closed our eyes, we still mutter about this or that late into the night, until our words become further apart and eventually we drift to sleep. Naked under the stars.

CHAPTER 14

GENEVIEVE

The sun creeps in slowly at first, then all at once, an explosion of light prying my eyelids open. I wake up with sand in my butt, and I can't even blame a hangover. Because it's him. It's always him.

Still naked on the ground from the night before, I haul myself up to fish for my clothes. I find my phone half buried and my underwear hanging out of the pocket of Evan's jeans. There are a dozen missed calls and texts from my dad and Shane asking where the hell I am. I'm more than an hour late for work, and judging by their increasingly worried messages, they're about ready to send out a search party and start calling hospitals.

Evan is still asleep on the blanket. I've got hell waiting for me at the shop, but still I can't tear my gaze away from him. The long lines of his body, tan and strong. Memories of last night skitter across my limbs like a flurry of tiny sparks. I'd do it all again, pick up right where we left off and to hell with responsibilities and obligations.

And that's the problem.

He rolls over, exposing his back, and I realize for the first time what was too dark to see last night. On his lower back, just above his right hip and tucked in among his other tattoos, there's an illustration of a small beach cove with two distinctive palm trees bent from hurricanes and crisscrossing each other. Identical to the ones behind me. It's our spot. Our one perfect place on earth.

Which only makes this harder.

Evan stirs as I'm wrapping my hair in a bun and digging my keys out of the sand. "Hey," he mumbles, adorably drowsy.

"I'm late," I tell him.

He jerks upright with a concerned expression. "What's wrong?"

It's only when I rub my eyes that I realize my vision's blurry with tears. I inhale deeply, exhaling a feeble sputter of air that makes me feel a bit wobbly. "This was a mistake."

"Wait. Hold on." He grabs his pants and shakes them out to start getting dressed, a hurried panic evident in his movements. "What's happened?"

"I told you we couldn't do this." I ease backwards, blinking away the moisture in my eyes. All I want to do is run. Get away from him as fast as I can, because every second I linger in his presence weakens my resolve.

"Gen, hey. Stop." He grabs my hands to still me. "Talk to me for a second."

"We can't keep doing this." I implore him to understand what I already know is beyond his reasoning. "We're no good for each other."

"But where's this coming from? Last night—"

"I have people who are counting on me." Desperation clogs my throat. "My dad, my brothers. We're all working on keeping the business afloat. I can't blow them off to hide out with you all night." I gulp down a massive lump of sadness. "As long as we're around each other, I can't trust myself."

"What's the big deal?" He turns his back in frustration, tugging at his hair. "We had a good time and no one got hurt."

"We're both late for work because we stayed up all night fucking like teenagers whose parents are out of town. When are we going to grow up, Evan?"

He rounds on me, dark eyes blazing with frustration. "What is so wrong about wanting to be with you? Why do you want to punish us for this?" he demands, gesturing between us. "Why are you punishing yourself for caring about me?"

"I've just decided to start caring about myself more. That means being responsible for the first time in my life. I can't do that when every time I see you I forget anything else exists. That's why I didn't say goodbye to you before I left. Because I knew—" I stop before the rest of that sentiment can escape.

"You knew what?"

I hesitate, remembering the pain I'd seen on his face last night when he'd confessed how much my leaving had affected him. *A huge piece of me broke off and was just gone.* I'd hurt him badly, a hell of a lot more than I'd realized. And hurting Evan makes me sick to my stomach. I don't like doing it, and I don't want to do it now, but . . . I'm not sure I have a choice.

"You said last night that you wish I'd told you about the showdown with Randall," I finally say.

"Yeah . . ." His tone is wary.

"Well, I tried. I didn't sleep a wink that night. I stayed up all night thinking about what I'd done, stewing in my humiliation. It wasn't a total rock-bottom moment, but it was definitely a wake-up call. It was obvious the partying had become a problem and was starting to cloud my judgment. There's no way I ever would've showed up on Kayla Randall's doorstep in the middle of the night if I'd been sober."

I shake my head in disgust. At myself, not him. Although,

I certainly hadn't been impressed with him either, the morning after my unhinged visit to the Randall house.

"I knew you were out with the guys that night and would probably sleep in, so I waited around all morning for you to call or text," I tell him. "And when you didn't, I finally drove over to your place so I could tell you what happened with the Randalls."

A frown touches his lips. "I don't remember you coming over."

"Because you were still passed out," I say flatly. "It was one in the afternoon, and I walked into your house to find you snoring on the couch, empty bottles and full ashtrays all over the coffee table. There was spilled beer on the floor, all sticky under my shoes, and someone must've dropped a joint on the armchair at some point, because there'd been a hole burned into it." I sigh softly, shaking my head again. "I didn't bother waking you. I just turned around and went home. And started packing."

Now he looks startled. "You left town because I was hung-over after a night with the boys?" There's a defensive edge to his voice.

"No. Not entirely." I try not to groan. "It was just another wake-up call, okay? I realized I'd never be able to change my ways if we were together. But I knew that if I told you I wanted to leave, you would convince me to stay." There's a bitter taste in my mouth, but I know it's not Evan's fault. It's mine. "I can't say no to you. We both know that."

"And I can't say no to you," he says simply. He exhales a ragged breath. "You should've just talked to me, Gen. Hell, I would've gone with you. You know that."

"Yes. I knew that too. But you're a bad influence on me." At his wounded look, I add, "It's a two-way street. I was an equally bad influence on you. I was worried that if we left the Bay together, we'd just bring those bad habits to wherever we ended up. And I was done with those habits. I'm done with them now."

Gathering my shoes, I steel myself for what comes next. After all this time away, it hasn't gotten any easier. "You ought to think about getting your shit together too. We aren't kids anymore, Evan. If you don't make a change, you're going to wake up one day and realize you've become the thing you hate most."

"I'm not my parents," he grits out between clenched teeth.

"Everything's a choice."

I hesitate for a beat. Then I step forward and kiss him on the cheek. When his gaze softens, I step out of his reach before he can change my mind. Because I *do* care about him. I care about him way too fucking much.

But I can't take responsibility for his life when I'm barely capable of running mine.

After stopping by the house to change clothes, I finally make it into work, where my dad's waiting for me in the office. I know it's bad when he's sitting in Mom's chair. Well, my chair now. Dad hardly ever comes into the office and absolutely never sits down, preferring to be out at the jobsites and meeting with clients. The man hasn't stopped moving since the day he first went to work for his dad when he was eleven.

"Let's talk," he says, nodding at a chair in front of the desk. "Where've you been?"

"I'm sorry I'm late. I was out and overslept. Won't happen again."

"Uh-huh." He sips his coffee, chair tipped back against the wall. "You know, I was sitting here waiting for you, and I got to thinking. And it occurred to me I never really disciplined you as a kid."

Talk about an understatement. Although Dad was never the overly strict type, I probably got it the easiest, being the only daughter in a house full of boys. It's one of the reasons we got along so well.

"And maybe I need to take some responsibility for how that turned out," he says slowly. Pensive. "All the partying and getting in trouble . . . I didn't do you any favors letting you carry on like that."

"I'm pretty sure I would have done what I wanted either way," I admit.

He answers with a knowing grin.

"At least this way I didn't grow up hating you."

"Yeah, well, teenagers are supposed to hate their parents at least a little, at some point or another."

Maybe that's true, but I prefer it this way, knowing the alternative. "I am trying to do better," I tell him, hoping he can see the sincerity on my face. "This was a slip, but I promise I won't make it a habit. I want you to know you can count on me. I understand how important it is to chip in around here right now."

He sits forward. "We can both do better, kiddo. Truth is, you've been great around here. Got the place running smooth. Customers love you. Everybody's always going on about what a charming young woman you turned out to be."

I grin. "I clean up nice when I want to."

"So." Dad gets up and comes around the desk. "I'll get out of your hair. Consider this your first official reprimand, kiddo." He pats me on the head and strolls out.

Oddly, I think I kind of enjoyed that, talking with my father like adults. I appreciate that he respected me enough to tell me I messed up without beating me over the head about one mistake. And I'm thrilled that he thinks I'm doing well here. When I agreed to run the office, I was terrified I'd screw it up, drive the whole thing into the ground, and leave Dad bankrupt and broken. Instead, it turns out I might actually be *good* at this stuff.

For once, I'm not a total disaster.

CHAPTER 15

EVAN

I used to enjoy being alone on a jobsite, hanging drywall or pouring in a driveway. Give me a list and eight hours, and I'd have that shit knocked out no problem. I always work faster by myself, especially when I don't have to listen to some asshole's radio or him telling me about his sick pet fish or whatever. Today is different. I've been at the West house all morning installing new kitchen cabinets, but it's taking me twice as long as it should. These cabinet doors don't want to level out. I keep dropping stuff. At one point, I damn near ran a drill over my finger.

It's been days of unanswered texts since Gen ran off from our spot. My calls are going straight to voicemail. It's maddening. She just drops all those truth bombs and accusations in my lap and then ghosts me? She barely gave me a chance to respond.

Then again, what the hell could I even say? Apparently, I hadn't been that off-base when I blamed myself for running her out of town. Randall set the ball in motion, but I kicked the damn thing in the net. Goal! Gen's gone!

I was a wake-up call for her. Christ. My hungover, passed-out self drove the girl I love more than anything else in this world right out of my life.

Damned if that doesn't rip apart my insides.

I fight the pain tightening my throat, my hand once again squeezing the drill a little too hard. Fuck. I'm going to get myself killed on this job if I don't start focusing.

But no, I refuse to take *all* the blame. Since when did I become the root of all her problems? Seems like a convenient excuse to avoid dealing with her own baggage. I might have been a delinquent for most of my life, but at least I'm not trying to lay that blame on everyone else.

"Hey, man." Gen's youngest brother Craig strolls into the kitchen wearing a T-shirt and a pair of basketball shorts. He gives me a nod as he grabs a soda from the fridge. "Thirsty?"

I'd love a beer, but I accept the soda anyway. "Thanks." I might as well take a break, seeing as how I've entirely lost track of what I was doing anyway.

"How's it going in here?" he asks after scanning the dust-covered disaster that is the half-demolished kitchen. He takes a seat at the kitchen table that now sits under a drop cloth and my toolboxes.

"Slow," I reply honestly. "But I'll get it done." *Or Levi will have my ass.* "You ready to get the hell out of here?"

Craig shrugs, sipping his soda. "I guess. It's weird thinking this won't be our house the next time I come home from college."

He falls quiet, examining the writing on the side of his can. He was always a quiet kid. Four years younger than Gen and a total mama's boy, which, despite making her resentful, also made Gen especially protective of him.

I lean against the counter. "What are you up to this summer? Any big plans?"

He evades the question, staring down at the table for a beat. Then his attention wanders the room, his shoulders hunched like a kid in the back of the classroom who doesn't want to get called on. "You'll think it's dumb," he finally answers.

"What is it?" I say. "Spit it out."

Reluctant, he sighs. "Jay and I signed up to do the Big Brothers program. Mentoring kids and whatever. So, yeah."

Why am I not surprised? Those two were always the Boy Scouts of the family. While Gen and her two oldest brothers were out raising hell and being a bad influence on Billy, Jay and Craig were doing their homework and cleaning their rooms. I guess when you have six kids, some of them are bound to turn out straight-edge.

"That's cool," I tell him. "You like it so far?"

He nods shyly. "It feels good, like, when my Little Brother looks forward to hanging out. He doesn't have a lot of friends, so when we get to go do stuff, it's a big deal for him."

Craig's the right type for that sort of thing. A little dorky and soft, but a nice kid. And, most importantly, smart and responsible. Leave me with a kid for ten minutes and they would probably catch fire somehow. Which gets me thinking again about Gen and our conversation on the beach about family and children. I guess she isn't wrong that if I ever had a family, I'd have to at least learn how not to kill my kid. I don't have a clue how my parents kept Cooper and me from drowning in the bathtub. Those two could barely stand up straight after ten a.m.

"She's not coming back as long as you're still here," Craig says.

I frown. "Huh?"

"My sister. She left early this morning so she wouldn't run into you, and she won't come home until she knows you're gone." He pauses knowingly. "If you were thinking of waiting for her."

Damn. Somehow, it's even colder coming from this kid. "She told you that?"

He shrugs. "You guys fighting?"

"I'm not." I wish I could make her understand she can have me however she wants. Whatever she needs from me, I'll do it.

"You know, I always kind of looked up to you when I was a kid."

Craig's words catch me off guard. "Oh yeah?"

"Not so much anymore."

Ouch. The kid's full of bullets today. "This unfiltered honesty thing gets a lot less cute when you're old enough to get your ass kicked," I remind him.

He has the decency to blush. "Sorry."

"So what's changed, huh?"

He considers the question for several seconds. Then, with a look of pity that would knock other men out cold, he says, "The bad boy thing gets old."

Well, shit.

It's not every day I get dressed down by a Boy Scout.

Later that night, I hit up one of the usual haunts for a few drinks with Tate, Wyatt, and the guys. After a couple rounds of beers, we drift over to the pool tables and indulge in our favorite pastime: hustling tourists. Eventually they catch on to us, so we start playing for fun. We split into teams, me and Tate versus Wyatt and Jordy. The cash we'd just squeezed out of the tourists sits in a neat pile at the corner of the table. Winners take all.

From the next table, a cute blonde in a pink sundress watches me, while her boyfriend, I presume, is completely oblivious as he stalks around the table sinking shots. I might have been able to work up some enthusiasm about the scenario if Genevieve West didn't have my head in a vise. But since she came back to the Bay, I've had zero interest in hookups with other women. Just one.

"Coop coming?" Tate asks me, shoving the pool cue in my hand for my turn.

I line up my shot and scuff the felt. "Doubt it."

"The wifey doesn't let him out anymore," Wyatt cracks as he easily follows up my scratch by nailing a bank shot.

He's not entirely wrong. Though it isn't necessarily Mackenzie keeping Cooper from drinks with the boys these days, so much as the two of them mind-melding into a single entity that prefers its own company to that of others. They're happy and stupid in their gooey love bubble. For a while, it was a relief when Mac managed to mellow Cooper out, but now their bubble is absorbing the whole house, and it's not so fun anymore.

Or hell, maybe I'm just jealous. Maybe I'm resentful that Coop throws his perfect relationship in my face but does everything in his power to keep me miserable. There was no good reason he and Mac should have gotten together, much less stayed together. But they ignored all of us and made it work. Why can't I have that?

"You're up." Tate smacks me with the cue again.

"Nah, I'm tapping out." I glance toward our table. "Yo, Donovan, take my place."

"Aww, come on." Wyatt taunts me from across the table. "Let me embarrass your ass fair and square."

I reach for my beer and find it empty. "I'm gonna hit the head and then grab the next round."

"Well, you heard the man," Wyatt says, slapping our buddy Donovan on the back. "It's your turn to shoot."

I pay a quick visit to the restroom, drying my hands with a paper towel that I drop in the trash can by the door. I step into the corridor at the same time someone exits the ladies' room. None other than Lauren, Wyatt's ex.

"Evan. Hey," the brunette says.

"Ah, hey." I dutifully lean in for the hug she offers. She and Wyatt might be broken up, but Ren's been part of our crew for years. I can't very well shun her, and I doubt Wyatt would want me to. "How've you been, Ren?"

"Pretty good. Been spending a lot of time in Charleston with my sister." She lifts a slender arm to drag her hand through her glossy hair, drawing my attention to the full sleeve of tats on her skin. Most of the art is courtesy of Wyatt, who did a lot of my own recent ink. "How about you?" she asks.

"Nothing new to report," I say lightly.

"I heard Gen's back in town. We're supposed to grab lunch sometime next week."

"Yeah. She sure is back."

A dimple appears at the left side of Ren's mouth. Her eyes twinkle with amusement. "I'm guessing she didn't come running right back into your arms?"

I smile faintly. "Good guess."

Pensive for a beat, Ren moistens her bottom lip with the tip of her tongue. "We should grab lunch one of these days too. Or better yet, a drink."

My eyebrows shoot up. "You asking me out, Ren? Because you know I can't say yes to that." I might be a total asshole, but Wyatt's one of my best friends. I'd never date his ex.

"I don't want to hook up with you," she answers with a throaty laugh. "Just figured it could be a mutually beneficial arrangement if we went out a couple times." Ren grins. "Our respective exes don't handle jealousy too well."

"No, they don't," I agree. "Still can't do that to Wyatt, though, even if it ain't real."

"Fair enough." She gives my arm a warm squeeze. "See you around, Ev. Say hi to the boys for me."

I watch her saunter away, hips swaying. Women with asses like that are dangerous.

At the bar, I ask the bartender to pour me a shot of bourbon for myself, then line up another round of shots and beer for the guys. The place isn't too crowded tonight. Just the usual faces.

Sports highlights flash on the TVs overhead while '90s rock plays on the sound system. I knock back my bourbon just as I see Billy West grab a seat at the other end of the bar.

I hesitate. I'm not sure he's any more amicable to my situation than Craig was, but I've exhausted all other reasonable means of fixing this thing with Gen. If anyone knows what is going on inside her head, it'll be Billy.

Setting the empty shot glass on the bar, I walk over and grab the stool beside him. "We need to talk," I tell him. "The hell's up with your sister?"

Billy spares me a brief sideways glance. "What'd you do now?"

"Nothing. That's the point."

"So why are you asking me?"

I narrow my eyes. The little shit's two years younger than me, and I still remember all the pranks Gen and I used to pull on him, so I don't much appreciate the attitude he's slinging my way.

"Because she won't answer her damn phone."

"That sounds like a you problem."

Cocky little fucker. "Listen, I know she talks to you. So just tell me what I have to do to get her back, and I'll leave you alone."

Billy slams down his beer bottle and huffs out a sarcastic laugh as he turns to look me dead on. "Why would I want her to take you back? For the last year, I've watched you get drunk like it's your job, hook up with a nonstop parade of college chicks, fight every rich prick you can get your hands on, and do nothing meaningful with your life."

"Are you serious? I co-own a damn business now. Just like your old man. I work for a living. How's that nothing?"

"Right, a business you didn't build. It just got handed to you, same way my dad's business got handed to us. But I don't go around congratulating myself for it."

"Man, fuck you. Not all of us had Mommy and Daddy at

home cooking pancakes every morning. Maybe don't talk about shit you don't understand." I feel remorse the second I mention his mother, but it's too late to take it back. Anyway, I stand by my point. If Gen's brother wants to pass judgment on me, he can save it. I'm not interested in his judgment.

"Gen's finally trying to get her life together," he mutters, slapping some cash on the bar. "And you're doing everything you can to keep her down in the mud with you. That's not how you treat someone you care about."

I have to remind myself that beating the hell out of Gen's little brother is not the way to get in her good graces.

"I do care about her," I say roughly.

"Then here's my advice," he retorts, standing over me. "You want my sister to let you back into her life? Worry about getting your own life together first."

CHAPTER 16

EVAN

Two days later, I wake up at the crack of dawn after another restless night. Rather than laze in bed like a bum, I'm up with the sun to take Daisy out for a walk on the beach, then give her a bath in the driveway to get her looking all shiny and clean. After getting dressed in my nicest outfit that falls between funeral attire and dirtbag, I clip a leash on Daisy and head back to the kitchen for another cup of coffee.

When I find Cooper and Mac eating breakfast on the deck, I pop my head out of the sliding glass door. "Hey. Just so you know, I'm taking Daisy out for a few hours."

"Where?" Cooper grunts with a mouthful of waffles.

"Sit down," Mac tells me. "We made plenty. Have you eaten yet?"

"Nah, I'm good. I picked up a shift volunteering at the seniors' home. The lady on the phone said old folks love dogs, so I'm bringing Daisy."

"Is that like a euphemism for something?" she asks, laughing as she turns to Cooper for the punchline.

My brother looks as bewildered as his girlfriend sounds. "If it is, I don't know what it's code for."

"Alright, gotta run. Oh, by the way," I tell Cooper, "I'm taking your truck." Then I slap the door shut before he can respond.

I can only imagine the conversation they're having in my wake. *Has Evan gone nuts? Obviously he's not volunteering anywhere, right?*

Well, joke's on them, because I certainly fucking am. My last conversation with Gen, followed by my chat with Billy the other night, got me thinking about what "getting my life together" actually looks like. Truth be told, I hadn't thought my life was so scattered to begin with. It's not as if I'm a total deadbeat. I've got a job—my own business, partly. I have a house and a motorcycle. An old Jeep I spend more time fixing up than driving.

Plenty of people I grew up with around here aspired to a lot less. And a lot of people would have put money on me ending up a lot worse. Still, if all that isn't enough for Gen, fine. I can do better. She thinks I can't change? Watch me.

Starting today, I'm hella upstanding. Easing up on the drinking. No more fights. I'm officially on a mission of self-improvement, a complete Good Boy retrofit. Which, according to Google, includes volunteer work.

So bring on the seniors.

At the nursing home, Daisy is psyched at all the new, weird smells. Her little tail excitedly smacks the linoleum floor as she tugs on her leash, anxious to explore, while I check in at the front desk and introduce myself.

A volunteer coordinator named Elaine meets me in the lobby, offering a broad smile in greeting. "Evan! Nice to meet you in person! We always appreciate visitors." She shakes my hand before sinking to one knee to greet Daisy. "And we love having pretty girls around!"

I watch as the middle-aged woman fawns over Daisy, scratching behind her ears and dodging that tongue that just last night got into the garbage again.

This dog doesn't even understand how easy she's got it.

"Yeah, well, we like to give back," I say, then regret how skeezy it sounds coming from me.

Elaine takes us on a tour of the two-story facility. Honestly, it's less creepy than I imagined. I had pictured something at a cross between hospital and asylum, but this place isn't spooky at all. No one is wandering around dead-eyed in a nightshirt muttering to themselves. It simply looks like a condo building with hospital handrails on the walls.

"We underwent a major renovation a few years ago. We have a full-service restaurant that serves three meals every day, plus a café and coffee shop where our residents can grab a snack and sit with friends. Of course, for our less mobile residents, we deliver meals to their rooms."

Elaine proceeds to tell me about activities they organize as we pass one of the community rooms, where the old folks are sitting around easels, painting. Apparently, this is where most of my volunteer hours will be spent.

"Do you have any special skills or talents?" she asks. "Play an instrument, maybe?"

"Uh, no, nothing like that, I'm afraid." I did spend a few months in middle school thinking I might take up the guitar, but that shit's complicated. "I can build stuff, mostly. Just about anything."

"Crafts, then," she says with a placating smile that I choose to ignore. "And of course, our residents enjoy when four-legged friends come by. So we can set up a schedule for that as well."

Down one of the residential halls, Elaine pokes her head in an open door with a quiet knock. "Arlene, may we come in? You have a special visitor."

Arlene, a tiny pixie of a white-haired woman, sits in a recliner watching her television. She waves us in with a frail hand that looks like it might snap off if she moves too quickly. But she's smiling the second her cloudy eyes land on Daisy.

"Arlene, this is Evan and Daisy. They'll be volunteering here," Elaine says. "Arlene is one of our favorite residents. She's going to outlast all of us, isn't that right?"

Then, like shoving a kid into the deep end of the pool to make him figure out how to swim, Elaine abandons Daisy and me to the whims of Arlene and the Weather Channel.

"You better bring the car into the garage, Jerry," Arlene says to me, while petting Daisy, who has hopped up in her lap now. "TV says it's going to rain."

I don't respond at first, confused. But as she keeps chatting up a storm, it quickly becomes evident she thinks I'm someone named Jerry. Her husband, I take it.

I'm clueless about nursing home etiquette, so I'm not sure if I'm allowed to sit on the edge of the old lady's bed. But there's only one chair in the room, and Arlene is sitting in it. So I remain standing, awkwardly sliding my hands in my back pockets.

"Is your brother still up north?" she asks after the weather guy remarks on a line of severe thunderstorms moving up the New England coast. "You should make sure he replaced those gutters like you told him to, Jerry. He doesn't want more leaks like last season."

I nod briefly. "Yeah, I'll tell him."

She goes on like that for more than an hour, and I don't know what to do other than play along. I mean, how are you supposed to respond to someone who probably has dementia? Is it like waking a sleepwalker? Do you wake a sleepwalker? Hell if I know. It seems the kind of thing they should put in a brochure or something. In fact, I'm starting to think Elaine is a terrible volunteer coordinator and that this gig absolutely should come with some training.

"Jerry," Arlene says during a commercial. She's made me change the channel five times in the past five minutes because she never seems to remember what she's been watching, "I think I'd like a bath. Will you help me to the tub?"

"Uhh . . ."

Nope. I'm noping out. I draw the line at stripping little old ladies. Plus, Daisy's starting to get a bit restless, jumping down from Arlene's lap and sniffing around the room.

"Why don't I find someone to come help?" I suggest.

"Oh no, that's not necessary, Jerry. You're all the help I need." Smiling brightly, Arlene starts to stand, then drops back down in her chair, unsteady.

"Here," I say, helping her to her feet. The moment she's upright, she tightly holds on to my arm. "How about we hit that call button and—"

"Arlene, sweetie, where you trying to go?" A big guy in white scrubs walks into the room and pries Arlene out of my arms.

I glance at the newcomer. "She was having trouble getting up, so—"

"Jerry is going to give me a bath," Arlene says happily, walking with the orderly's assistance over to her bed.

"You had a bath this morning," he reminds her as he helps her take off her slippers and get in bed. "How about a nap before lunch, then?"

While he handles her, I get Daisy back on her leash, then follow the orderly out of the room when he gives me the nod.

"She thought I was her husband," I tell him, by way of an explanation.

The orderly grins and shakes his head. "Nah, brother. That old lady's mind is sharp as a tack. She's just trying to get a little frisky with the new guy. She pulls this stunt on all the handsome ones." Guffawing, he gives me a slap on the shoulder. "And she's not the only one. My advice: Trust no one."

Nursing homes are fucked up.

When Elaine finally returns after abandoning me to the wilds, she shows little sympathy for my ordeal. *Comes with the territory* seems to be her attitude; the staff has apparently resigned themselves to the lawlessness. The inmates are running the asylum.

Elaine eventually brings me to a Korean War helicopter pilot named Lloyd. His room is decorated in about a dozen old photographs of him in his helmet and jumpsuit. When we enter, he's in bed grumbling at the newspaper, which he reads with a magnifying glass on an arm attached to the bedside table.

"Lloyd," she says, "this young man would like to spend some time with you, if that's alright."

"Doesn't anyone edit these damn papers anymore? There are two spelling errors on this page alone. When did the newspaper start looking like some lazy kid's homework?" He lifts his gaze only long enough to spot Daisy standing at my side. "Get that thing out of here," he snaps. "I'm allergic."

"You're not allergic to dogs, Lloyd," Elaine tells him with a cadence that suggests this isn't the first argument they've had. "And Daisy is very sweet. I'm sure you two will have a lovely time."

Lloyd huffs and returns to inspecting his newspaper while Elaine leaves me with another pat on the back. It's like some weird handshake, everyone who works here warning me now that I've entered, I can never leave.

"He's harmless," she murmurs from the doorway. "Talk to him about Jessie. He loves to talk about the bird."

"The bird" is a little yellow thing I hadn't noticed in a cage by the window. Elaine ducks into the hallway, leaving me trapped in a tiny room with a crotchety old man who glares at me.

I notice another photo on his wall, and move closer to inspect it. "You met Buddy Holly?"

"What?" Lloyd squints toward the photograph of him and the musician outside a venue, posing beside a bus parked in an alley. "Yes, I knew Charles. Back when music meant something."

"You were friends?"

Daisy, apparently afraid of him, lies on the floor at the foot of the bed.

"I was a roadie. Hauled his gear, that sort of thing." With another huff, Lloyd loudly folds his paper and sets it aside. "Was getting on a train in New York after I got back from Korea when I saw this skinny kid who could barely lift his guitar and all these bags and cases. I offered him a hand."

Lloyd seems to warm up a bit, albeit reluctantly. He talks about traveling the country with Holly, Elvis Presley, and Johnny Cash. Running from the cops and unruly fans. Catching flat tires and getting robbed in the middle of nowhere, at a time before calling AAA from the side of the road was a thing. Lugging guitar amps ten miles on foot to the nearest gas station. Turns out Lloyd's got plenty to say, if I just shut up and let him talk. And in all honesty, I'm enjoying listening to his crazy anecdotes. This guy's *lived*.

Things are going well—he hasn't once asked me to bathe him or called me Sheila—until he asks me to feed his bird and put fresh water in the cage. When I open it up, the bird flies out, which doesn't seem to concern Lloyd at first.

But we both realize too late there's a puppy in the room, and she's been bored silly all afternoon.

Like a slow-motion crash, the parakeet flits over to the dresser. Daisy's ears perk up. She lifts her head, a low growl building in the back of her throat. Alarmed, the bird takes flight. Daisy pounces, snatching the tiny creature out of the air as it explodes in a burst of yellow feathers and disappears.

Goodbye Jessie.

CHAPTER 17

EVAN

Me: *Hey. Just checking in to make sure you're alive.*

Gen: *You've been asking me that question every other day for almost 2 weeks. Still alive. Just been busy with work.*

Me: *Same.*

Gen: *You realize usually when a guy "checks in" at 1 in the morning, it's considered a booty call?*

Me: *Blasphemy! I would never besmirch your purity like that.*

Gen: *Uh-huh.*

Me: *Tbh, I can't sleep.*

Gen: *Same.*

Me: *You good, other than being a busy insomniac?*

Gen: *All good here.*

Me: *Dinner one of these days?*

Me: *Just to catch up?*

It's been six hours since Gen stopped responding to my texts. As I help Mac set the breakfast table outside on the deck, I keep feeling a phantom vibration in my pocket, hoping it's her. But no. Now it's just been six hours, forty-two minutes.

"Grab the napkins, will you?" Mac says, handing me utensils to lay down.

My mind is elsewhere as I duck inside to grab some napkins. I'd thought things were getting better with Gen. We've been texting here and there for the past couple weeks, just random banter or quick hellos. Every time I mention getting together, however, she shuts down and stops responding. I can't get even a foot in the door. She won't go for coffee, won't eat lunch with me—nothing. She's the most infuriating person I've ever known. Worse, she likes it that way.

"So what's your plan for the day?" Cooper asks after we're seated to eat. "Got some orphans to pull out of a burning building, or what?"

Mac passes me the scrambled eggs. "Still doing the nursing home?"

Daisy pokes her head up from under the table to beg for a piece of sausage. When I start to hand her a piece, Mac points a knife at me.

"Don't you dare. That stuff will kill her."

While Mac is preoccupied with chastising me, Cooper slips a chuck to Daisy, and I stifle a grin.

"Anyway, no," I say in response to their badgering. "I'm not allowed back there since our crazed beast ate that dude's bird."

"Wait, what?" Mac's utensils clang on her plate as she drops them. "What the fuck?"

"Well, ate is probably an exaggeration," I relent. "I'm pretty sure most of the bird was intact when Daisy spit it up."

Coop barks out a hysterical laugh, to which Mac shoots him the scary eyes.

"This happened last week?" she shouts. "Why didn't you tell me?"

"I told Coop. Guess I forgot you weren't there." Cooper was falling on the floor cracking up when I told him about the incident with Lloyd. In fact, he'd suggested we keep it on the DL because Mac would flip out. Guess I forgot that part too.

"You didn't think to mention it?" Mac cuts a glare at my brother.

"She's a dog," he says lightly. "It's what they do."

"This isn't over, Hartley," she replies in a voice that says he's not getting his dick sucked anytime soon.

"Anyway, I've got a new gig," I continue just to save Coop from the weight of his impending punishment. "I signed up to be a Big Brother."

Yup, it's happening. I'm hopping on the Big Brothers bandwagon. I tried out a few other volunteer gigs after the nursing home didn't work out, the most recent one being a shift picking up trash on the beach. Which was going well until I was attacked by a homeless dude under the boardwalk. He chased me off by throwing bottles at my head. I swear, nobody had warned me civic responsibility was so treacherous. At any rate, I figured some disadvantaged kid has got to be less dangerous than hobos and handsy old ladies.

"Oh, Christ, no," Coop groans. "You realize you can't just take him to a bar for four hours, right?"

"Fuck off." Just for that, I steal the last pancake. "I'll be a great role model. Teach him all the things adults don't want to tell kids."

"Child endangerment is a crime, Evan." Mac smirks at me. "If the cops find you stumbling out of the Pony Stable with a ten-year-old, you're going to end up in jail."

"As always, I appreciate your support, princess." Their lack of confidence is disappointing if not unexpected. "Anyway, he's fourteen. Plenty old enough to learn how the world works."

"God help that kid," Coop mutters.

I get it. They'd rather keep me in the screwup box than believe I'm evolving. I guess that's not entirely unwarranted, but an ounce or two of faith, a little benefit of the doubt, would be appreciated. They make it sound like I'm gonna kill the poor kid. But how hard can it be? Feed him, water him, turn him in at the end of the day. I mean, hell. I've rented a car before.

Is this really so different?

His name is Riley and he's a typical skinny Bay teenager with shaggy blond hair and a summer tan. I had pictured a little punk-ass like me, some dude with a smart mouth and more attitude than sense, ready to tell me to get bent. In reality, he's a bit shy. Looking at the ground as we wander the boardwalk, because I hadn't thought too much about what there is to do with him that doesn't involve any of the nonsense I was getting up to at his age.

It was weird, if I'm honest, going into the public library to meet him. Like checking out a library book, but a whole damn human. I walked out of there with a person it's my job not to lose or get maimed, and suddenly that seems like a big ask. They didn't even hand me a first aid kit.

"So what are you into, kid?"

"I dunno," he says with a shrug. "Stuff, I guess."

"Stuff like what?"

"Sailing, sometimes. Fishing. And, um, surfing. But I'm not very good. My board's kinda old, so."

He's killing me. He's got his head bowed and hands in his pockets, sweat starting to trickle from under his wispy mop of hair. It's a blistering June day and the boardwalk is swarmed with tourists, all hot and sticky. We're like hot dogs in a sidewalk cart, rolling around in each other's sweat.

"Hey, you hungry?" I ask, because it really is too boiling out here to spend all afternoon walking around.

"Sure, I guess."

Cooper was right—with a lack of any better ideas, I pull Riley into a bar. Well, not exactly a bar. Big Molly's is a kitschy kind of tourist trap, with random tchotchkes on the wall and live music on the weekends. The waitresses run around in skimpy outfits. Turns out, the kid notices. He perks right up when he gets an eyeful of the hostess in a crop top and tiny skirt.

"Hey you," she coos by way of a greeting. "Been awhile."

I flash a grin at her. "Got a table for two?"

Stella leans over the hostess stand, pushing her tits together. "Who's your friend?" She winks at him, which would have been more than enough to give me a boner at that age. It's unfair, torturing the kid like that. "He's cute."

"Riley, this is Stella."

"Hey, sweetie," she says when he can't quite work up a reply. "Come on, I'll get you seated."

"You ever been here before?" I ask him as we settle at a high-top table. A band onstage is playing some early nineties covers. At the bar counter, college guys and dads who escaped while their wives went shopping occupy the old wooden stools.

Riley shakes his head no. "My aunt hates these places."

"So what's the story there?" No one ends up in a program like this if their lives are going totally to plan. "If you want to talk about it, that is."

Another shrug. "I live with my mom's sister. She's an ER nurse, so she works a lot. My mom died when I was little. Cancer."

"Where's your dad?"

He stares at his menu without reading it, flicking the laminated edge with his fingernail. "Went to prison about six years ago. He was out on parole for a while, but then he took off. Got arrested again, I think. My aunt doesn't like to talk about him, so she doesn't really tell me stuff. She thinks it upsets me."

"Does it?"

"I dunno. Sometimes, I guess."

I'm starting to understand why they stuck him with me. "My dad died when I was younger too."

Riley meets my eyes.

"Drunk driving accident," I add. "My mom hasn't been around since then either."

"Did you have to go live somewhere else? Like, in foster care or with another relative?"

"My uncle took care of my brother and me," I explain, and it's not until this very moment that I consider what might have happened to me and Cooper if Levi hadn't been there. Funny how our lives teeter on these rails, riding the edge over a dark unknown. How easy it is to fall off. "Do you like your aunt? You two get along?"

A slight smile erases the gloom from his expression. "She's nice. But she can be kind of a lot sometimes. She worries about me." He sighs quietly. "She thinks I'm depressed."

"Are you?"

"I don't think so? I mean, I don't really have many friends. Don't like being around a lot of people. I'm just, I dunno, quiet."

I get that. Sometimes things happen to us when we're young, and we learn to stay inside ourselves. Especially when we don't know how to talk about what's going on in our heads. It doesn't always mean anything or indicate a bout of depression. Being a teenager is hard enough without real shit getting in the way.

"There's nothing wrong with that," I tell Riley.

"Hey, boys." Our waitress sets down a basket of hush puppies and dipping sauce, along with two tall glasses of water. "How we doing?" The brunette greets me with a wry smile and an arched brow that suggests I better prove I remember her.

Come on now. Give me a little credit here. "Hey, Rox. How's things?"

At that she smiles, satisfied. "Another summer."

"I hear ya."

She gives the kid a once-over. "This guy giving you a hard time, sweetie?"

"No," he says, grinning like he's never seen a pair of fake tits before. "I'm fine."

"Good. What'll you have?"

Riley grabs his menu again and rushes to scan it front and back, realizing he hadn't actually read it.

"What's fresh?" I ask Rox.

"Grouper's good. I'd get it Cajun style."

I glance at Riley. "You like grouper?" It occurs to me he might feel weird about what he should order when some dude he only met today is paying. I would.

"Sure," he says, looking almost relieved.

"Cool. We'll do that."

When she's done taking our order, Riley takes a second to admire her retreating backside before leaning in toward me. "You know her?"

"In a manner of speaking."

"Hey, Evan." Another waitress saunters by. Cass, a short, cute blonde in a tank top she took a pair of scissors to, waves as she passes our table.

"You know a lot of girls here," Riley remarks.

I swallow a laugh at how much he sounds like Mackenzie in that moment. Every time we walk into a place and a girl gives me a nod, Mac rolls her eyes. Like we didn't meet because she was out helping her roommate hunt me down for a one-night stand.

"It's a small town."

"So you've, like, slept with all of them?"

Well, that's more forward than I thought he was capable of. "To some extent or another, yeah, sure."

I realize then his eyes aren't wandering because he's avoiding eye contact with me. As I track his attention around the room, it's clear he's checking out all the teenage tourists, the bored girls perusing their phones while their families sit around tables scarfing down nachos and inhaling two-dollar margaritas. Suddenly, I'm just hoping this kid doesn't ask me to buy him condoms. Not that I wouldn't, but I don't need to get kicked out of another volunteer program because he goes home to tell his aunt I'm trying to get him laid.

"What about you?" I counter. "Got a girlfriend or anything?"

He shakes his head. "Girls think I'm weird. I don't know how to talk to them."

"You're not weird," I assure him. Yes, he's shy, but he doesn't give off any creep vibes. The kid just needs someone to build up his confidence. "Girls can be complicated. You just need to know the signs."

"Signs?"

"When a girl likes you. When she wants you to come talk to her."

"Like what?"

"Well, for one." I scan the room and locate a hot redhead in her early twenties. She's sitting with her girlfriends around a fishbowl of blue liquor with four straws. "When you catch each other's attention and she smiles at you—that means she thinks you're cute."

Riley follows my gaze, his eyes glazing over slightly.

It takes less than two seconds for the redhead to notice me. A mischievous smile curves her full lips. I offer a faint half smile in return.

"Then what?" Riley sounds almost eager now.

"You go introduce yourself. Get her number."

"But how?" he insists, mindlessly popping hush puppies in his mouth. "What do you say to them?"

Me, personally? Not much, really. But I can't tell him to buy her a drink or ask if she wants a ride on his motorcycle. Once I had a driver's license, all I had to do was ask a chick if her parents were home. But that's neither here nor there. Riley is the sensitive type, I'd guess. He needs a different approach.

"Okay," I tell him. "So, if she's alone—you never want to approach a girl standing with her family; dads are a surefire cockblock—but if she's alone, you go up and say hi."

"Hi? That's it? But what do I say after that?"

"Ask her . . ." I mull it over. I don't want the kid to sound like a tool. If I send him out there to get his heart broken, I'm not a very good Big Brother. "Okay, do this. You see a girl you like, she smiles at you. You say hi, introduce yourself, then say something like, what do you like to do at the beach. Then what's her favorite day. Her favorite time of day. And once you get those answers, you take out your phone and tell her you've set a reminder for that day and time to pick her up for a beach date."

Riley studies me with a skeptical grimace. "That seems kinda corny."

"Wow. Okay. Getting heckled by a fourteen-year-old."

He snorts a laugh.

"Look. Chicks like a guy with confidence. They want you to take charge of the situation. Show some game."

He shakes his head, stabbing his straw into his glass of water. "I don't think I can do that."

I ponder some more. How hard can it be to pick up a teenage girl these days? "Right, how 'bout this. You see a girl you like?"

Riley is hesitant, glancing around the restaurant. Beyond the bar, the place is stuffed with the lunch rush. Eventually, his gaze lands on a brunette sitting with her family; she looks to be the youngest of two older sisters. As the girls chat among themselves, the mom grabs her purse from the back of her chair and heads off toward the restrooms.

"Quick, before her mom comes back. You go over there and say to her sisters, 'Hey, I'm Riley, and I'm not very good at this but I'd really like to ask your sister out on a date, and I was hoping you could help me.'"

"I don't know," he says, watching them with trepidation. "What if they laugh at me? Or think I'm a weirdo?"

"They won't. Trust me, they'll think it's cute. Just smile, be natural. You're a good-looking guy, Riley. You've got that sweet-boy face that girls love. Have a little faith in yourself."

For a second or two, I think he's going to psych himself out. He remains glued to his chair. Then, with a deep breath, he gathers his confidence and stands from the table. He takes a couple steps forward before doubling back. "Wait. What do I do if she says yes?"

I smother a laugh. "Get her number and tell her you'll call her tonight."

With a nod, he's off.

Rox comes back with our food just as he's reaching their table, and together we watch him nervously approach the sisters. The girls look uncertain, guarded at first, but when Riley gets a few words out, their faces soften. They smile, amused, looking at their sister. Blushing, she says something in response, which eases the anxiety in Riley's expression. Then he tosses his hair out of his face and hands the girl his phone. They exchange a few more words before he struts back to us and throws his phone on the table like a goddamn hero.

"So?" I demand.

"We're going to play mini golf tomorrow."

I flip my palm up for a high five. "Hell yeah."

Rox's lips twitch wildly, as if she's fighting a rush of laughter. "Be careful with this one," Rox warns Riley, hooking her thumb in my direction. "He'll get you into all sorts of trouble." With a wink, she dashes off again.

I grin at Riley with a strange rush of pride filling my chest. "See, I told you, kid. You got game."

After lunch, we spend a couple hours at the arcade. Turns out I'm kind of a bastard, as far as the whole Big Brother thing goes.

"Some people," Riley says as we're leaving. "*Some people* might find your behavior in poor taste."

"Can't expect life to give you everything you want."

It started at air hockey. Five straight games during which I utterly humiliated him. In the fourth game, it looked like he might've turned it around, going on a pretty good run of scoring, but then he got a bit too pleased with himself and I took him to the cleaners.

"I'm just saying."

"Sounds like whining to me."

"I'm just saying, you wouldn't go to the kids' cancer ward and do victory laps around the room after beating them at Mario Kart."

Next, we played Skee-Ball. I don't know if it's his skinny little arms or lack of trapezius muscles, but I owned him at that too. If he had any cash, I'd have started putting money on those games.

"Who says I wouldn't? What do they have to do all day but hone their skills? I've got a job and responsibilities."

"That's messed up."

I was almost starting to feel bad for him. Even considered taking it easy on the kid. Until he started talking all kinds of smack and challenged me to a Jurassic Park shooting game. At that point, it was an educational imperative—I had to teach the kid some manners.

"You know you're supposed to set a good example for me, right?"

"These are important lessons. Eating shit is the first lesson of adulthood."

"You're terrible at this," he informs me, rolling his eyes.

"You're welcome."

We're making our way down the boardwalk to where I parked my Jeep when a familiar face appears in my line of sight. She's exiting the smoothie place five feet ahead of us and looks over her shoulder to meet my eyes, as if she felt me coming. It always strikes me how good her skin looks under a midday sun.

"You following me now?" Dark sunglasses hide her expression, but I know in the goading tone of her voice she isn't entirely disappointed to see me. Then her attention falls to Riley. "Oh dear. Is this man bothering you?"

"Why does everyone keep saying that to me?" I grumble. "Do I look like I drive a panel van?"

"I'm Riley," the teen says with a shy smile.

"Genevieve, but you can call me Gen." She nods in the direction we'd been heading, asking us to walk with her.

As we fall into step with my drop-dead gorgeous ex-girlfriend, it's as if a switch flips in Riley. His entire demeanor changes as he tips his head toward her. "What do you like to do at the beach, Gen?"

She questions me with a look before answering. "Well, I guess I like to tan and read a book."

"What's your favorite day?"

"Uh . . . Sunday, I suppose." Gen licks her lips, growing more skeptical as the interrogation continues.

"What's your favorite time of day?"

I'm here, watching this happen. Still, I can't believe what I'm seeing. Surreal.

"Sunrise. When it's still quiet." An amused Gen watches Riley pull out his phone and type in a quick note. "What are you writing?"

"There," he says smugly. "I just set a reminder to pick you up for a sunrise date on the beach this weekend."

"Wow." She turns with an arched eyebrow, peering at me above the rim of her sunglasses. "Can I assume this was your doing?"

"They grow up so fast."

Once again, I'm practically bursting with pride. I don't know if Riley is a quick study or if I'm an extraordinary mentor, but I think it's safe to say he's conquered his confidence problem. Although the superpower persuasion of Gen's spectacular rack might have had something to do with it. Kid's been staring so hard I'm worried I might have to take him home cross-eyed.

"I might look young," he tells her. "But I assure you I'm an old soul."

"Oh my God." Gen playfully mashes his face with her palm. "Where'd you find this kid, Evan?"

"I'm his Big Brother."

She scoffs at me, incredulous. "No, seriously. This is Mackenzie's little brother or something, right?"

"Really. I'm giving back to my community."

"Huh."

I'm not sure what to make of her response, but at least she's not telling me to get lost again.

When we come up on Mac's hotel, Gen pauses near the new white-and-green sign with the elegantly scrawled words *The Beacon Hotel*. Sipping her smoothie, she examines the building. There isn't much going on outside anymore, as far as the renovation goes. The façade is all patched up and painted. Most of the work left to do is on the inside. Decorating, installing the mirrors and fixtures, all that tedious stuff. Mac's been getting more anal by the minute about every microscopic detail.

"I've always loved this place," Gen says to no one in particular.

"Is it open yet?" Riley asks curiously.

I shake my head. "Soon. Couple months, I think."

"The woman who owned this place would come to the stone yard sometimes," Gen says, a faraway note in her voice. "She'd hire Dad to do seasonal landscaping. There was something so glamorous about her, even in a place like that. She'd be walking through stone dust and mulch looking like a million bucks. I used to tell my folks I was going to work here someday."

"Mac's hiring," I tell her.

Gen cocks her head at me. "What, seriously?"

"Yeah. Cooper's been giving her a hard time about needing to hurry up and pick some people, or she'll never open." Though I can't see her eyes, I feel the intensity of Gen's interest in the way she presses her lips together. "I could put in a good word, if you're interested."

She hesitates for a beat. Then she nods slowly. "Yeah. Yes. I'd actually really appreciate that. If it's not too much of a thing."

"No sweat." Hell, I'm just happy she's letting me do this for her, rather than making it a whole argument about fending for herself or me getting too involved in her life. "It's done." At that, though, it really is time I bring Riley back to the library. I was warned at least four times that tardiness is frowned upon. "Listen, we gotta go, but I'll talk to Mac and let you know how it goes. Cool?"

"Cool. Thanks again."

She says goodbye to Riley, and we shuffle through an awkward hug that still gets my blood rushing like I haven't touched a woman in months. Something about the smell of sunscreen and her flowery shampoo makes me all stupid, and I can't walk straight. The haze lingers as we walk off in different directions.

Riley and I make it five yards away before something stops me. A nagging sense of money left on the table. This was the longest conversation Gen and I have had in weeks, and I'm just letting her leave? What the hell is wrong with me?

"Give me a sec," I tell Riley. Then I dart off, jogging after Genevieve. "Hey. Fred. Wait up."

She stops, turning to face me. "What's up?"

I let out a hurried breath. "No bullshit, I took what you said seriously. I'm getting my act together."

A groove digs into her forehead. "Is that what this Big Brothers thing is all about?"

"Sort of. I'm reformed," I say earnestly. "And I can prove it to you."

"How's that?"

"I intend to court you."

Gen bites back a laugh, looking away. "Evan."

"I mean it. I'm going to court you. All gentlemanly and shit."

"Is this your latest creative attempt to get me naked?"

I haven't heard a no yet, so I take it as a good sign. "If we do this, sex is off the table. I'm going to prove to you I've changed. Woo you the old-fashioned way."

"Woo me," she echoes.

"Woo you," I confirm.

Twisting her lips as she studies me, Gen considers my offer. Every second she's silent, I know the idea is finding root in her brain. Because she wants me to give her an excuse, to make it okay to say yes. I know her. Better, I know *us*. There's no world in which she can stay away from me. No more than I can tolerate distance from her. Truth is, we've never had any resistance to each other, no chance of severing the immutable connection that always pulls us back together. And because I can't lie to her, she knows when I'm sincere.

"You should know," Gen says, "you wouldn't be my only suitor."

I narrow my eyes. "Baby cop?"

She chides me with a grimace. "Harrison asked me out on another date, and I said yes. You've got some competition."

We have very different concepts of competition, but sure, whatever. If she needs a guy to make me jealous, either as some form of punishment or just to keep things interesting, that's fine by me. It'll make winning all the more satisfying. Because this guy's already been knocked out. He just hasn't hit the ground yet.

I flash the cocky lopsided grin that I know drives her wild. "Bring it, baby."

CHAPTER 18

GENEVIEVE

I'm not sure how it happened. A couple months ago, I was certain coming back to the Bay was a temporary situation. Confident that things would eventually level off with Dad, the house, and the business—he'd find someone to replace me, and everyone would move on from Mom's death. Now, it seems every day I stick around, I'm digging my toes in deeper. Despite my best efforts, my instincts keep me rooted home, and my life in Charleston is slowly becoming blurred with distance.

I wake up to the faint aroma of coffee and the muffled sounds of Billy and Craig arguing over something downstairs. There's a shower running in the hall bathroom, and I hear Jay singing what sounds like a Katy Perry song.

I roll over in bed and strain to make out the words. Oh, that is definitely Katy Perry. I make a mental note to tease him mercilessly at breakfast. Jay crashed here last night after Kellan kicked him out of their apartment because he had a hot date. Who knows where Shane slept. That boy is a walking disaster.

I won't lie. It's good to be home.

On the nightstand, my phone buzzes with an incoming text.

Evan: *Morning, Fred.*

I'd like to say Evan is irrelevant to the roots that are taking hold and tethering me to this town. But since agreeing a few days ago to give him another chance, I've felt nothing but pure relief. My shoulders suddenly feel lighter and unburdened from the effort of avoiding him. I hadn't realized how much it'd hurt, staying away from him.

Me: *Morning.*
Evan: *Good luck.*

The phone rings before I can ponder the meaning of his text.

Wrinkling my forehead, I swipe the screen to answer the call. "Hello?"

"Genevieve? Hey. It's Mackenzie Cabot. Cooper's girlfriend."

My brain snaps to attention. "Oh. Hi. How's it going?"

"Evan told me you were interested in working at the hotel. He gave me some details about your experience, but I figured we should meet in person and have an official interview. How'd you like to come by and talk about the manager position? See if it's something you'd be up for."

Excitement quickens my pulse. "Yes, absolutely."

"Great. If you're not busy, I've got time today."

"Give me thirty minutes."

Once we're off the phone, I throw myself into the shower and forego blow-drying my hair to wrap it in a tight bun. Then I race around my room, digging out a nice outfit that isn't still wrinkled from unpacking and hunting through boxes and under the bed for shoes. I don't bother with much makeup other than some lipstick and mascara. I always do this to myself. Instead of asking for the reasonable time I need, I promise too much and then tie myself in knots to meet my own unreasonable deadline.

Somehow, I manage to get myself out of the house with enough time to make the short drive out to the Hartley house. My mind races over the meager details Mackenzie had provided over the phone, constantly getting stuck on the word "manager." Honestly, I hadn't considered what position I'd aim for when Evan said he'd mention me to Mackenzie. Something supervisory, sure. Operations, maybe. But managing an entire hotel—events, restaurants, catering, a spa—is more than I'm accustomed to.

Then again, I've never been afraid of taking a big leap. Looking down is defeatist. If I want to turn my life around, I might as well aim high right out the gate.

With two minutes to spare, I ring the doorbell.

The front door swings open to reveal a tall, stunning girl with shiny dark hair and big green eyes. I remember catching glimpses of her the night of the bonfire, when Evan threw down with that college guy, but we'd never been properly introduced.

"It's nice to officially meet you," Mackenzie says as she lets me in. She's wearing a striped T-shirt and khaki shorts. The overly casual outfit makes me feel overdressed in my navy linen pants and white button-down shirt with the sleeves rolled up to my elbows.

"Nice to meet you too," I tell her.

She brings me through the house to the back deck, where she has a table set with two glasses and a pitcher of water with lemon.

"The guys have done a lot of work on the place," I remark as we sit down. The short walk inside had revealed new floors and old peeling wallpaper removed. Out here, I note that the siding's been replaced and painted.

"They've been at it for months. Seems like every morning I wake up to a sander or a saw running, and then I go to work and it's the same thing," she says, with an exhausted smile. "I swear to God, when it's all over, I'm going to spend two weeks in an isolation chamber." She pours us a couple glasses of water before relaxing back in her chair. A warm breeze whips across the deck, blowing the wind chimes hanging from the roof.

"I know the feeling," I say wryly.

"Oh, right. The renovation at your dad's house. It must be so hectic over there."

"I'm working most of the day, so it isn't so bad. And when I am home, noise-canceling headphones are my best friend."

"I hope I didn't make you skip work for this," she says, and I wonder if she's thinking I blew off my current job to interview for this one.

"No," I assure her. "My dad gave me the morning off, so I don't start until noon."

With the small talk over, I'm aware that I need to make a good impression here. Evan might have gotten me in the door, but a woman doesn't go out of her way to restore a derelict old hotel just to hand the keys over to some random townie with no sense. She's about to get an uncut dose of Professional Genevieve.

"So," Mackenzie says, "tell me about yourself."

I hand her my résumé, which is admittedly lacking in hotel experience. "I've been working since I was eleven years old. Started out cleaning up and stocking at my dad's hardware store. Worked summer jobs as a hostess, waitress, bartender. Customer service at the stone yard. I even did a summer stint as a deckhand on a sailing yacht."

I tell her about Charleston, where I fudge my title a little. Assistant slash secretary slash adult in the room is basically the same thing as an office manager, right? Wrangling a bunch of real estate agents with massive egos and attention deficit disorders should certainly qualify.

"Now I'm the office manager at the stone yard. I process invoices and payroll, scheduling, ordering. There isn't anything that goes on in that place that I don't keep my finger on. And I see that clients are well cared for, of course."

"I understand you've taken on a lot of responsibility since your mother's passing," Mackenzie tells me, putting my résumé aside after reading it carefully. "I'm very sorry for your loss."

"Thank you."

It's still awkward when someone brings up my mom. Mostly because I've moved on. I've been over it almost since the moment it happened. Yet I get pulled right back in every time someone else pauses to process or acknowledge it. Sucked out of time and transported to the funeral all over again, back to those first days scrambling everyone on the phone.

"It's been a lot to learn, but I've gotten a good handle on things," I say. "I'm a quick study. And I think now is the right time to leave the stone yard and hand the reins off to someone else."

If given his way, my dad would keep me in the office forever. Despite our deal, I know the only way to force his hand is to give him a deadline. I can teach just about anyone else to run the yard for him; he just needs the proper motivation to pick someone.

"I can understand getting thrown into the deep end. Or in my case, jumping. I mean, what business do I have owning a hotel, right?" There's something disarming about her self-awareness, her self-deprecating grin. Mackenzie doesn't take herself too seriously, so it's easy to talk to her like a real person, not just another clone throwing their money around. "I just saw the place and fell in love, you know? It spoke to me. And once my heart was set, there was no talking myself out of it."

"I had the same reaction when I was a kid," I admit. "I don't know how to explain it . . ." I trail off pensively. I can still picture the old brass fixtures, and the palm trees casting shadows on the pool cabanas. "It's a special place. Some buildings, they have character, personality. I'm sure you've seen pictures, but I wish you could have known The Beacon before it closed. It was like a time capsule—entirely unique. I have great memories there."

"Yeah, that's something the previous owner said to me when

I convinced her to let me buy the property. Her only request was that I maintain the original intent as much as possible. The personality, as you put it. Basically, I promised not to go mangling a piece of history." Mackenzie grins. "Hopefully, I've kept that promise. I mean, we've certainly tried. Cooper's exhausted himself tracking down experts to make sure every detail is as close to authentic as possible."

"I'm honestly excited to get a look."

"For me, part of that authenticity is about finding people who know and truly understand what we're trying to recreate. People who care as much about that history as I do, you know? People make the hospitality, after all."

She goes quiet, lingering on what feels like an open question as she sips her water.

Finally, she says, "I do have some other interviews this week, but just so you know, you're comfortably among the top candidates."

"Seriously?" I don't mean to say that out loud and roll my eyes at myself. I offer a sheepish smile. "I mean, thank you. I'm grateful for the opportunity."

Somehow, I'm always surprised when anyone takes me seriously, especially as a matter of trust and responsibility. No matter how well I dress up or maintain good posture, it feels like they all see through me. Like they look at me and see only the screwup teenager running around drunk on the back of a motorcycle.

Nerves dampen my palms. If I get this job, there's no room for mistakes. No spending the night naked on the beach and showing up to work late. If history is any indication, I'm a piece of twine over an open flame. Just a matter of time before I snap. So to get this job—and *keep* this job—the training wheels have to come off this newly self-proclaimed good girl.

As I'm about to make my way out, a golden retriever comes

galloping onto the deck. She's got that gangly look that tells me she's still very young and not in complete control of her limbs. She nudges me with her nose and plops her head in my lap.

"Oh my goodness. Look at this cutie! What's her name?"

"Daisy."

I rub behind Daisy's ears and she makes a happy sound, her brown eyes glazing over. "She's very sweet."

"You want to hang out for a bit? It's about time for her walk. We can take her down to the beach."

I hesitate. Not because Mackenzie isn't perfectly nice, but because I think the interview was pretty great, and the longer I stick around, the more chance I have to screw that up. I'm better in small doses around people who don't know me well. If I'm going to get the job, I'd rather sign the paperwork before my boss figures out I'm a potential disaster.

"Don't worry," she says, apparently discerning my anxiety. "We're both off the clock. Consider this family time."

She winks, and I catch her meaning. A job isn't the only thing we have in common.

"Sure," I agree, and a few minutes later we've got our sunglasses on and are following Daisy as she runs up and down the beach digging for crabs and chasing the waves.

It isn't long before the subject of Evan rises to the surface.

"You two go way back, huh?" Mackenzie says. "It sounds like kind of a complicated history."

"No," I answer, laughing, "not that complicated. A couple teenagers running amok while the town burned in the background. Pretty simple, actually."

Smiling, she picks up a stick and tosses it for Daisy. "That doesn't sound awful, if I'm honest."

"Oh, it wasn't. Especially not when we were drunk, high, naked, or some combination of the three most of the time. It was incredible, even. Until the buzz wore off. Then I looked back at the destruction in my wake and decided I couldn't live with the consequences."

"And that's why you moved?"

"Essentially."

"Evan talked about you a lot while you were gone."

I know she doesn't mean anything by it, but it seems there's no end in sight to being reminded that Evan was one of those consequences. That to fix myself, I had to hurt him. Maybe my decision to leave town was rash—cowardly, in some respect—but looking back, I still think I made the right decision.

"I hit a nerve," Mackenzie says, pausing as we stroll the beach. "I'm sorry. I only meant to say he missed you."

"It's fine. I've made this bed."

"He said you're trying to work things out, though, right?"

Daisy brings her stick to me, pushing her nose into my hand until I accept the stick and fling it down the beach. Her tail furiously slashes through the air as she chases it down.

"He's wooing me," I say with a sigh.

Mackenzie breaks out in a grin. "Oh my God. Please tell me those were his words."

"They were. He's wooing. I'm being wooed." I can't help but laugh. "We never dated in the traditional way, so I guess he's trying to change that. And I figured, what the hell, let's give it a shot."

Ever since he asked me out on the boardwalk, I'd been waiting for the tug of regret, the jolt of dread over this impending date, but it hasn't come. When I moved back home, I convinced myself that I needed to stay away from Evan out of sheer self-preservation, but the more I think on it, the less it makes sense to rest my problems at Evan's feet. He didn't make me drink. He didn't make me blow off school or sneak into abandoned buildings. I did those things because I wanted to, and doing them with him let me pretend I wasn't responsible for myself.

Truth is, we're both different people now. And in all the ways we've changed and grown up, we've also grown closer somehow. He's made the effort. Only seems fair to give it a chance.

"So when's the big date?" Mackenzie asks. "Tonight?"

"Next weekend. And before you ask, I have no idea what he's planning." I groan. "I'm worried there might be a corsage and limo involved."

She hoots in delight. "Please, *please* take a picture for me if that's the case."

"Tonight I'm meeting Alana at the Rip Tide. If you want to come," I hedge. "Our friend Jordy's reggae band is performing."

"Ahh, I can't." She appears genuinely disappointed. "Coop and I are having dinner at his uncle's place."

"Next time, then. Say hi to Levi and Tim for me." I hesitate for a beat. "And thank you again for considering me for this position, Mackenzie."

"Mac," she corrects. "We're dating twins, Genevieve. I feel like that moves us into nickname territory."

"Deal. Mac." I smile. "And you can call me Gen."

"Hey, sorry, I'm late." Alana slides across from me at the table near the small stage of the Rip Tide. Her dark-red hair cascades over one shoulder, appearing a bit tousled.

"Swear to God, if you're late because you were hooking up with Tate—"

"I wasn't," she assures me. Then she rolls her eyes. "And even if I was, you're the last person who should judge. Your love life is a series of bad decisions."

"Ouch." I grin. "But true."

As we laugh, Alana flags down a server and orders a beer. Friday nights are half-price pitchers at the Rip Tide, a deal I would've taken full advantage of not so long ago. But I'm drinking a virgin mai tai, which is damn good if I'm being honest. Who knew the taste of virgin cocktails would start growing on me.

"What's the holdup?" she asks, nodding toward the empty stage. "Weren't they supposed to go on at nine?"

"Technical difficulties." About ten minutes ago, one of Jordy's bandmates came up to the mic to make a vague announcement. Naturally, I'd texted Jordy for more details, and he admitted their steel drum player showed up with a hangover and has been puking backstage since his arrival.

"Technical difficulties?" Alana says knowingly.

"Yeah, as in, Juan is technically having difficulties not projectile-vomiting all the Jägerbombs he inhaled last night."

She gives a loud snicker, before smoothing out her rumpled hair. "Sorry I look like a scrub. I came straight from the club. I was caddying today and it was so windy. I didn't have an elastic, so my hair was blowing all over the place."

I wrinkle my forehead. "I didn't know you were working at the country club again. What happened to the receptionist gig at the *Avalon Bee*?"

"I'm doing both." She rubs her temples, visibly tired. "I'm saving up for a new car because old Betsy's engine is finally threatening to give out for good. So I called my old boss at The Manor and she gave me a few shifts a week over there. I might be landing a better gig, though—some lady at the club approached me about possibly working as her au pair for the rest of the summer. I guess their current one just up and quit."

"An au pair? You realize that's just a fancy word for nanny, right? Also, you hate kids," I remind her, then snicker at the thought of Alana wrangling a bunch of screaming kids into a minivan. She'd kill them in two days, tops.

"Nah, I can tolerate kids. What I *can't* tolerate is caddying for one more pompous jackass. I swear, the group today had four of them and they all took turns offering to buy me expensive shit in exchange for sex." She snorts. "One said he'd settle for a handy in the bathroom, which was sweet of him."

"Gross." I take a sip of my drink. "Speaking of career changes, I had a job interview today with Mackenzie."

"Yeah? How'd that go?"

"Good, I think. She said she'll be in touch once she's done interviewing all the candidates."

After our server drops off Alana's beer, she clinks her bottle against my glass. "Cheers, babe. Glad you're home."

"Glad to be home."

"Did you end up reaching Heidi? Her phone kept going to voicemail when I called."

A sigh slips out. "She's hanging out with my brother tonight. I think they're watching a movie at his place with Kellan serving as third wheel."

"Kinky."

"Please don't ever say the word *kinky* when we're discussing two of my brothers. Thank you."

Alana snorts. "I can't believe she's still dating Jay. No offense, but Heidi eats guys like him for breakfast."

"I know, right? But hey, it seems to be working. I guess opposites really do attract."

We both wince when the screech of microphone feedback pierces through the low murmur of voices in the dive bar. Goodbye, eardrums. Turning to the stage, I see the keyboardist adjusting his mic, while Jordy settles on a stool with his guitar. The other band members take the stage, including a very pale Juan, who staggers toward his drum.

Alana cackles. "Ten bucks says he turns green and runs off the stage after three songs."

"I say he only lasts two."

"Deal."

We're both wrong. Halfway through the first song—a pretty good Bob Marley cover—poor Juan gags, slaps a hand over his mouth, and practically dives backstage. Laughter breaks out in the bar, along with several loud whistles and some applause.

"Looks like we got a bird down," Mase, the smooth-voiced lead singer, drawls into the mic. "But don't you worry, my little pelicans, we're gonna keep chirping without him."

Did I mention Jordy's band is called Three Little Birds? Without fail, every one of their sets involves an obscene amount of bird references and incredibly unfunny fowl puns.

"Hey, girlies," says a familiar voice, and then our friend Lauren sidles up to us. She leans down to smack a kiss on my cheek. "We still on for lunch next week?" she asks me.

"Absolutely. It's been ages since we had a proper catch-up." We've known Ren since grade school, but she's been joined at the hip with Wyatt these past few years. She's one of those chicks who disappears when she has a boyfriend and then comes slinking back whenever they're on a break. Or over for good, which seems to be the case this time.

Still, Ren's good people. She's hilarious and always has your back.

Which is why I'm slightly confused by Alana's reaction to our friend. After a lackluster hello, Alana busies herself by studying the label on her bottle, as if she's never actually read the ingredients in a Corona before and *must* know what they are. Right now.

It doesn't take long to figure out what's what, though.

"I hear you've been spending a lot of time with Wyatt," Ren

says to Alana. Her tone has gone frosty, but she's still got a smile pasted on.

"Well, yeah, we're friends," Alana answers. Her tone has dropped several degrees too.

Ren pauses thoughtfully. "Friends, huh."

"Yes, Ren. We're friends." Alana gives her a pointed look. "So, please, just chill, alright? It's not like we suddenly developed some random friendship after you guys broke up. I've known him since kindergarten."

The brunette nods a few times, briskly. "Uh-huh. I know you guys are friends. But the thing is, you were never the kind of friends who crashed at each other's places or lay on the beach stargazing at two in the fucking morning."

Uh-oh. What on earth has Alana gotten herself into?

I'm the one who's now fascinated with her beverage. My gaze drops to my glass as I pretend I'm seeing ice cubes for the very first time.

Alana quirks up a brow. "You spying on us now, Lauren?"

Ren's jaw tightens. "No. But I was with Danny yesterday, and he said he took a date to the boardwalk the other night and saw you and Wyatt on the beach. And then last week, Shari was driving past your house at like five in the morning and saw Wyatt's truck parked outside. So . . ." Ren trails off deliberately, waiting for Alana to fill in the blanks.

But Ren ought to know better. Alana is not and has never been one to explain herself. She simply stares at Ren as if to say, *are you done?*

On the stage, Mase is singing an original song about a young couple having sex on the beach at dawn while seagulls squawk overhead.

Despite my better sense, I get involved. "Come on, Ren, you

know it's not like that with them." Or is it? Truthfully, I have no idea what Alana's up to. She insists she's not hooking up with Wyatt, but who knows with that one.

"*Do* I know that?" Ren bites out, voicing my own doubts. "Alana sure as shit isn't denying it."

"Because she doesn't feel she needs to defend herself over an accusation so ridiculous," I respond with confidence I'm not sure I should have. "She and Wyatt aren't hooking up. They're friends. Friends go to the beach together. Sometimes they get drunk and crash at each other's houses. Big deal."

"Are you kidding me, Gen? You of all people should be backing me up right now." Ren gapes at me. "You used to cut a bitch for even looking at Evan. There was one time you didn't speak to Steph for days after she kissed him in a game of spin the bottle."

"Well, I was young and stupid back then," I say lightly.

"Oh, really?" she challenges. "So you're saying you wouldn't care if one of your friends was taking moonlit strolls on the beach with Evan?"

"Wouldn't bat an eyelash," I say, shrugging. "He might be my ex, but I don't own him. He's allowed to have friends, and it's perfectly cool if he's friends with my friends."

A smug gleam lights Ren's eyes. "Yeah? Then I guess you won't mind if I ask him to dance."

Ask him to what? But she's already gone, sauntering off toward—

Evan.

He'd just entered the dimly lit bar with Tate and their buddy Chase in tow.

As always, he senses my presence before our gazes even meet. His shoulders tense, chin shifting to the side before his head follows suit. And then those magnetic dark eyes lock onto mine and I can feel the change in the air. The electricity.

I'm helpless to stop the rush of heat that fills my body and tingles between my legs. Evan looks good enough to eat. Dark-green cargo pants encase his long legs. A white band shirt stretches across his broad chest. I squint in the darkness and realize it's one of Jordy's shirts, with the Three Little Birds name and trademark logo scrawled on the front. His hair's swept back from his chiseled face, emphasizing those gorgeous, masculine features. It's infuriating. Why does he have to be so hot?

Ren wasn't making idle threats. Her curvy frame sashays toward my ex-boyfriend, and she takes his hand and gives it a teasing tug. I can't hear what she's saying to him, but it earns her a lopsided smile and a nod of surrender, as Evan allows her to drag him to the dance floor.

"Bitch," I growl under my breath.

Alana barks out a laugh.

"Shut it," I order, pointing a finger at her. "You're the reason she's out there proving a point."

And Ren's definitely making a statement. As the sultry reggae beat thuds in the bar, she loops her arms around Evan's neck and starts moving to the beat.

I breathe through my nose and pretend I don't care that Evan's hands are resting on another woman's hips. In his defense, he seems to be trying to keep at least a foot of distance between their bodies. And he doesn't look very comfortable. But still. He could've said no.

Wearing identical looks of amusement, Tate and Chase wander over to our table. I notice Alana stiffen at Tate's approach. They greet each other with nods, as if they're complete strangers—when we all know they've been sleeping together for months now.

"What's going on there?" Tate nods his blond head toward the dance floor.

"Ren's pissed at me so she's retaliating by pissing off Gen,"

Alana explains, then takes a long swig of beer, draining the rest of the bottle.

"How does that make any sense?" Chase looks confused.

"It doesn't," I grind out through clenched teeth. My fists are clenched too, because Ren's hands are veering dangerously close to Evan's ass. Would I be breaking my good girl vows if I marched over there and dragged her away from him by the hair? Probably.

Evan seeks out my eyes over Ren's shoulder, frowning slightly when he discerns my expression. Yeah, he knows my feelings on this matter. I've never been good at hiding my jealousy.

"Gonna grab drinks," Tate says. He nudges Alana's arm, then gestures to her empty bottle. "Want a refill?"

"Nah. Thanks, though." To my surprise, Alana slides out of her chair. "Gen and I were about to take off. We're meeting Steph."

I don't call her out on the lies. Frankly, I wouldn't mind getting out of here too. Before I do something I'm going to regret. It's taking all my willpower not to rip Ren away from Evan and fuck him right there in front of everyone to stake my claim. And that's terrifying to me. He's not mine anymore. I have no claims on him, and these raw, visceral emotions he evokes in me are too overwhelming.

"Yeah." I stand up and touch Chase's arm. "Would you tell Jordy we had to duck out early, but that he totally crushed it tonight?"

"Sure thing," Chase says easily.

"Alana—" Tate starts, then stops abruptly. His blue eyes cloud over for a second before taking on a careless veil. "Enjoy the rest of your night."

"You too."

Alana and I practically sprint out of the bar. I feel Evan's gaze boring a hole into my back as we flee.

"Are you going to explain what that was all about?" I grumble as we step into the warm night breeze.

Alana just sighs. "I don't want him to think we're together, so every now and then I remind him by being a bitch."

I nod slowly. "Fine. And Wyatt? You going to tell me what the hell is happening there?"

Her expression darkens. "I told you before, there's nothing happening except that he thinks he has a crush on me."

"Maybe he does."

"He doesn't," she says flatly. "We've been friends forever, and he doesn't know what he's fucking talking about."

In other words, *back off*. So I do. I don't press her, and in return she doesn't press me about what's happening between me and Evan. Not that I would have been able to answer that question. My feelings for Evan Hartley have always been far too complicated to articulate.

Alana and I part ways. Ten minutes later, I'm pulling into my driveway at home when my phone buzzes. I fish it out of the cup holder and check the screen.

Evan: *Why'd you run off?*

Sighing, I tap out a quick response.

Me: *Alana wasn't in the mood for Tate.*

The urge to type a follow-up makes my fingers itch. I try to resist it and fail.

Me: *And I wasn't in the mood to watch you rubbing up all over Ren.*

Evan: *Ha! She was rubbing up all over me. I was an innocent bystander.*

Me: *I'm sure it was torture for you.*

Evan: *It was. Whenever there's a chick grinding up on me, my poor dick yells at me and demands to know why that chick isn't you.*

My cheeks feel warm all of a sudden. He's not the most poetic man out there, but he does have a way with words. And those words never fail to turn me on.

Me: *I thought you were reformed. "We're not having sex, yada yada."*

Evan: *I didn't say we were going to have sex. Just that my dick misses you.*

Me: *You still with Ren?*

Evan: *No, she wandered off the moment she realized she didn't have an audience anymore. Just chilling with the boys now.*

There's a short delay. Then:

Evan: *We still on for next weekend?*

This is my chance to back out. To say, "You know what, I changed my mind about the whole wooing thing. Let's just try to be friends."

What I say instead is:

Me: *Yes.*

CHAPTER 19

EVAN

Wyatt taps two fingers on the kitchen table. Cooper also checks after the turn. I'm sitting on a possible jack-high straight, but I've got a fairly good idea that Tate's got the king, and I'm not about to blow my stack to see the river. I check.

"Tate, it's your call, hurry up," Wyatt shouts.

"He checks," Coop says, huffing as he peeks at his cards again, like they've changed since he looked at them twenty seconds ago.

"Yeah, I bet your pair of threes says he checks."

"Then you should have raised," Coop tells Wyatt, getting irritated. "Let's see that king already." At that, Wyatt shakes his head with a knowing smile. Because Coop is a poor sport and it's sort of a running gag at this point.

When we were kids, he'd steal from the bank in Monopoly and throw a fit when he was losing. After numerous tantrums, we started egging him on for fun just to see the fireworks. Really, it's one of the few things that keeps poker interesting when I'm playing my brother. Play with anyone long enough and there ceases to be any mystery left. With twins, it's worse. I might as well be staring at his cards. We can't bluff each other.

"Tate, what the hell?" Wyatt yells. "I'm about to divvy up your chips."

"Coming," he calls from the garage, where we keep the drink coolers.

"I check," Chase says, skipping Tate.

"And dealer checks." Our old high school buddy Luke burns one card off the top of the deck and turns the next faceup on the table. "Queen of clubs. Possible straight, possible royal flush on the board."

"Oh, come on. That's not cool." Tate comes in with his arms full and sets several beers on the kitchen counter. "I was going to raise."

Coop and I smirk at each other across the table. He definitely has the king. We both fold out of turn.

"Yeah, screw you both," Tate says, watching his best hand of the night go belly up.

"Where'd you go? Milwaukee?" Wyatt reaches out an impatient hand for his beer. "Or did you have to brew them yourself?"

"Next time you can get your own damn drink."

It's boys' night at our house, a usual poker game we host every month or so. Enough time for the guys to replenish their wallets after the cash Coop and I took off them the game before. You'd think they'd catch on that the odds are stacked against them. Yet every month, here they are, swimming upstream and right into the bear's mouth.

The rest of the hand quickly plays out, with Tate taking a small pot as everyone either folds or calls. Hardly worth the excellent hand. I almost feel bad for the guy. Almost.

"You gonna have the boat ready for tomorrow?" Danny glances at Luke for an answer, while Tate deals the next hand. Danny's another friend from high school, a tall ginger who works with Tate at the yacht club as a sailing instructor.

"We put it on the water this morning." Luke sighs. "The thing's more duct tape than fiberglass at this point, but it'll float."

"Think you'll try to stay on the race route this time?" Coop glances at his cards, then tosses his chips in for the small blind.

The big blind falls to me this time. Peeping my cards, I luck out with a pair of nines. I can work with that.

"Let me ask you something," Danny says, popping the cap on another beer. "When the teenage girl on the Jet Ski had to tow your sad little dinghy back to the dock, did your balls physically recede back into your body, or just fall off altogether?"

Luke flicks a bottle cap that smacks him between the eyes. "Ask your mom. They were in her mouth last night."

"Dude." Danny deflates, his expression sad. "That's not cool. My dad's in the hospital. He has to have hernia surgery from railing your sister last night."

"Whoa." Luke flinches, staring horrified at Danny. "Too far, man. That's messed up."

"What, how is that different?"

They go on like that, occasionally remembering to call or raise as Tate lays down the flop then the turn. Meanwhile no one is noticing I'm running up on a full house. Easy money.

"I'm racing tomorrow," I say casually, raising the pot again.

"Wait, what?" Cooper arches an eyebrow at me. "In the regatta?"

I shrug while the guys call my bet to see the river. "Yeah. Riley mentioned it sounded like fun, so I put our names in."

"Riley?" Tate asks blankly.

"His Little Brother," Chase supplies.

"You guys have another brother?"

"No, nimrod." Chase shakes his head. "His Little Brother, like that charity thing."

"Where did you get a boat?" Tate demands, dealing out the river card. And there's my flush.

"Weird Pete had one at the yard," I tell him, watching everyone limp into the pot. "Some guy stopped paying rent a few months ago, so it's been sitting around."

"You do realize you don't know anything about sailing, right?" Coop's been paying attention, though, and he quietly folds.

"I watched a couple videos. Anyway, Riley can sail. How hard can it be?"

The regatta is an annual event in the bay. It's a short course, the entrants a fairly even mix of tourists and locals sailing two-man crews on little boats. Some of the guys have competed for years, but this will be my first time. While I warned him we might be lucky to finish at all, Riley seemed stoked on the idea when I brought it up. I figured I ought to start relating to what he's into if I'm going to take this Big Brother thing seriously.

"Welp," Danny says with a self-assured grin. "Good luck with that."

I win the pot with little trouble, the guys all looking at the table like they blacked out for the last ten minutes, uncertain how they let me run away with that one. Poker's as much a game of misdirection as anything else.

"I hope Arlene can come out for the race." It's Cooper's turn to deal. He tosses the cards at us while peering at me sideways. "I'm sure she'd hate to miss your big day."

"Eat me." My cards are trash. Best I can hope for is to pick up a flop pair.

Luke tucks his cards away like they tried to bite him. "Who's Arlene?" he asks.

My brother grins broadly. "Evan's got a stalker."

"Jealous," I answer.

Cooper continues, chuckling to himself. "Old lady from the nursing home got his number somehow and calls him at all hours. She's smitten."

"You should hit that." Tate chucks his empty beer bottle in the garbage can and is rewarded with a glare from Cooper when we hear it shatter. "Old broads put out."

"First, gross," I say, stunned as I find myself with three of a kind when Cooper deals the flop. "Second, I've taken a new vow of abstinence."

Wyatt snorts. "Come again?"

"Not anytime soon," Cooper answers, swallowing a laugh. Child.

"You got the clap or something?" Danny gets some bright idea to steal this pot and splashes it with an overaggressive raise that says he's working on a full house.

"No." I roll my eyes. "Call it a spiritual cleanse."

Tate coughs out a "horseshit" while folding.

"I say Evan doesn't make it one week." Danny throws a ten-dollar bill on the table. Dick.

"I'll take that action," Coop scoops up the bill, adding his own to it. "Anyone say five days?"

"I got five." Tate slaps down his money.

"Wait, does the stranger count?" Wyatt makes a jerking motion in the air with his left hand.

"You offering?" I wink at him.

He flips up his middle finger, then places his ten-dollar bet that I won't last forty-eight hours. My friends are supreme jackasses.

We keep playing. A few beers in now, everyone's playing with one eye closed, fast and loose with their chips. Which is fine by me, as I take nearly three hands in a row.

"So Mac went to pick up Steph for brunch the other day," Cooper says, contemplating his cards. "Said your car was outside in the same place it was parked the night before." He aims the accusation at Tate. "What's up with you and Alana?"

Tate shrugs while pretending to count his chips. "We hook up sometimes. It's not serious. Just great sex."

It's been "not serious, great sex" for a while now. Long enough that some people might start mistaking habit for addiction. And addiction for commitment. Which is to say, if Tate's not careful, he'll find himself settling down whether he realizes it or not. It's uncertain, at this point, whether he's given any thought to the idea beyond the special kind of denial that is friends with benefits. Cooper found himself in a similar trap last year, which damn near split our crew right down the middle when it looked like him and Heidi were headed for war. Thankfully, they called a cease-fire before more damage was done.

Then again, there's a lot to be said for great sex. Gen and I have great sex. Phenomenal, even. The kind of sex that makes a guy forget about promises and good behavior. But for the time being, good behavior is my creed. I made a commitment to Gen, and I want to show her I can be trusted to keep my dick in my pants. It'll be worth it. Eventually. Or so I hope, anyway.

"Of course it's not serious," Wyatt says to Tate. "Alana's just toying with you, bro. Like a lion playing with its dinner. She gets off on it." I don't miss the sharpness to his tone.

Neither does Tate. But rather than confront Wyatt about whatever bug crawled up his ass, Tate throws me under the bus instead. "If you wanna talk about chicks who get off on games, why don't you ask Evan over here about him dirty dancing with your ex last night?"

Asshole. I shoot Tate a glare before turning to reassure Wyatt. "It was only dancing, minus the dirty. Ren's just a friend, you know that."

Luckily, Wyatt nods, unfazed. "Yeah, she's been pulling out all the stops to get me back," he admits. "I'm not surprised to hear she's been flirting with my friends. She likes to make me jealous. Thinks it'll drive me so crazy that I'll get back with her."

Cooper lifts a brow. "But you won't?"

"Not this time," Wyatt replies. He sounds dead serious, and that gives me pause. Wyatt and Lauren's relationship had always followed a similar pattern to mine and Genevieve's. Is he really out for good? His grim expression tells me yes, yes he is.

For a moment I entertain the idea of doing the same—extracting myself from this push-and-pull routine with Gen. Saying goodbye to her, for real.

Just the thought sends a hot knife of agony directly into my heart. Even my pulse speeds up.

Yeah . . .

Not happening.

CHAPTER 20

GENEVIEVE

"Okay, I've got one," Harrison says as we walk past the crews rigging their boats. He's been at this since he picked me up this morning. "Why do they put barcodes on the side of Norwegian ships?"

"Why?"

"So when they return to port, they can be Scandinavian." He beams, so proud of his latest dad joke.

"You should be ashamed of yourself." I don't know where my life took a turn off the misspent youth, coming-of-age CW drama and wound up stranded inside a Hallmark movie, but this must be what blondes feel like every day.

This Sunday morning date is so wholesome it's almost surreal. Harrison brought me out to the marina to watch the regatta. It's a mild, clear, sunny day with a steady breeze—perfect sailing weather. I inhale the scents of ocean air and sugary confections from the carts set up along the boardwalk selling cotton candy and funnel cakes.

"No, wait," he says, laughing happily. "Here's a good one. So one night, there are two ships caught in a storm. A blue ship, and a red ship. Tossed in the wind and rain, the ships can't see each other. Then a rogue wave throws the vessels crashing into each other.

The ships are destroyed. But when the storm clears, what does the moonlight reveal?"

I suppose I'm a glutton for punishment, because as torturously unfunny as his jokes are, I like how excited he gets to tell them. "I don't know, what?"

"The crew was marooned."

Wow. "You talk to your mother with that mouth?"

He just laughs again. He's got those damn khakis on, paired with a tourist-dad button-down shirt. The kind of guy I'd have been making fun of while I sat with my friends smoking weed under the pier. Now here I am, one of the yuppie tools. It doesn't feel as dirty as I'd imagined.

"Have you ever entered this race?" he asks me.

I nod. "A few times, actually. Alana and I placed twice."

"That's awesome."

He insists we stop for lemon slushes, then carries them both because they're melting quick and overflowing a little, and he doesn't want any to drip on my dress. Just another reminder that he's far too nice for someone who once stole a girl's bike to jump it off a collapsed bridge and lost it down the river.

"I took a sailing lesson one time," he confesses as he leads me to a decent viewing position along the railing. "Wound up hanging overboard by my ankle."

"Were you hurt?" I ask, taking back my slush because I'm far less concerned than he is about getting sticky.

"No, just a little bruised." He smiles behind his sunglasses, in that cheerful secrets-of-the-universe way of his that makes me feel bitter and empty. Because people this happy and content must know something the rest of us don't. Either that, or they're faking it. "Lucky for me, there was a resourceful twelve-year-old girl on board who managed to pull me out of the water before I got to experience keelhauling."

It isn't his fault, though, that he makes me feel this way. Harrison is a catch. Well, except that he's a cop, and I'm a fortunate favor or two from being a convict. But the real issue? No matter how hard I try, I can't muster up a sexual attraction to him. Not even a warm, fuzzy, platonic spark. A fact I'm sure isn't lost on him, because for all his small-town charms, he isn't a dope. I've seen the wistfulness that turns to disappointment in his eyes, the slight falter in his smile, at the knowledge that while we get along and have a nice time together, we're not quite a love story. Nevertheless, until I have a reason otherwise, there's no harm in giving this a shot and letting him grow on me. Water and sunlight work wonders on plants, so why not us?

"Sailing's fun, but honestly, it's more work than it's worth," I grumble. "All that running around, pulling, and winding for a few bursts of speed. You spend the whole time making the thing go, you don't get to sit back and enjoy it."

"Sure, but it's romantic. A few ropes and sheets against the forces of nature. Harnessing the wind. Nothing between you and the sea but ingenuity and luck." His tone is animated. "Like the very first navigators who saw the new world as it appeared over the horizon."

"Did you get that out of a movie or something?" I tease.

Harrison offers a contrite grin. "History Channel."

A voice over a loudspeaker announces a ten-minute warning for boats to approach the starting line. On the water, masts tilt and sway, jockeying their way into position.

"Of course," I say, because as terrible as it is, I do appreciate his particular sense of humor. "I bet you stayed up all night watching an eight-part Ken Burns documentary on the history of nautical expedition."

"Actually, it was a program about how Christopher Columbus was an alien."

"Right." I nod, smothering a laugh. "A classic."

I'm finally starting to warm up to this date when I make the mistake of glancing over my shoulder. A familiar face meets my gaze as she leads her four kids away from the fried Oreo stand. Kayla Randall.

Shit. We're both frozen in trepidation. The eye contact lasted too long to blink away and pretend we didn't see each other. The moment has been acknowledged and is now begging for a resolution.

"What's wrong?" Harrison says in concern, noticing my apparent apprehension.

"Nothing." I hand him my lemon slush. "I see someone I need to talk to. Would you mind? I'll just be a minute."

"No problem."

Drawing a breath, I walk toward Kayla, who watches me while she makes a futile attempt to shove napkins in her kids' hands.

"Hi," I say. A wholly inadequate greeting under the circumstances. "Can we talk for a minute?"

Kayla appears rightfully uncomfortable. "I suppose we better." She shifts her feet. "But I've got the kids right now and—"

"I can watch them," comes Harrison's helpful voice. To Kayla's brood he asks, "You guys want to get a closer look at the boats?"

"Ya!" they shout in unison.

God bless this guy. I swear, I've never met anyone so agreeable.

Harrison leads the kids to the railing to watch the boats getting in position. As I'm left alone with Kayla, a familiar nervous sense of anticipation builds in my gut. It's like hanging my toes over the edge of the roof with a backyard full of chanting drunks standing around the swimming pool with their cameras on me. For some people, the fear makes their stomachs weak. But I find fear is a lens. It focuses me, if I aim it right.

"I'm glad you found me," Kayla says before I can arrange my thoughts. We stand in the shadow of a shop awning while she removes her sunglasses. "For a while, I was relieved when you left town."

"I understand. Please know—"

"I'm sorry," she interjects, stunning the words from my lips. "I've had a lot of time to think about that night, and I realize now I overreacted. That I was more angry at having to face the truth than I was with you—which was that Rusty was a bastard."

"Kayla." I want to tell her I was out of my mind for barging into someone's home, drunk and hysterical. That being right didn't make it right. She's kinda stealing my wind here.

"No, the problems were there for a long time. He was emotionally and verbally abusive. But it took you showing up to put that reality into perspective. To make me accept that it was not normal to live the way we were." Grief flickers in her eyes.

"I'm so sorry," I admit. It was an open secret that Randall was a creep and a bad cop, but I had no idea it was so bad at home. In a way, I feel worse now. I feel sorry for Kayla and the kids, and what was surely an ugly aftermath that I invited into their home. "I had no right to barge in like that. The way I behaved that night was . . . I'm so embarrassed."

"No, it's okay."

She squeezes my shoulder, reminding me that for a long time, we were sort of friends. I'd been their babysitter for years. I used to chat with Kayla on the couch after she'd get home from work. I would tell her things I couldn't share with my mom, about boys and school and teenage stuff. She was like an aunt or a big sister.

"I'm glad it was you," Kayla adds. "Things weren't good between me and Rusty for a long time, but my friends were so afraid of, I don't know, pissing him off or getting involved, they didn't want to tell me the truth. And the truth was, I needed to get out of there. I needed to get my kids out of that situation. Because of you, I finally did. And we're much happier for it. Honestly."

It's a relief to hear, although unexpected. I've spent the better part of the last year tied up in knots over the guilt and remorse for how I behaved. I'd uprooted my entire life to get away from the crippling embarrassment. And this whole time, I was hiding from my own shadow.

I can't help but think what might've been different now if I'd stayed. If I had the courage to get myself cleaned up without having to change zip codes. Did I need to remove temptation to get sober, or had I underestimated myself? Had I left to escape my worst instincts, or because I was afraid how everyone would react?

We both glance behind us at the sound of Kayla's kids laughing and squealing in delight. Harrison is probably enthralling them with a magic trick. Some more of his world-renowned comedy stylings.

"He's good with them," she remarks, putting her sunglasses back on.

Of course he is. Harrison has a natural ease with just about everyone, a sincere goodness that disarms people. Especially with kids, who see everything.

She tips her head curiously. "That your new boyfriend?"

"No. It's only been a couple dates."

Watching Harrison with the kids, I suddenly hear Evan's voice in my head. I flash back to the night at our spot, the two of us naked under the stars while he mused about kids and a family. The preposterous notion of Evan as a stay-at-home dad, his motorcycle rusting in the yard. Sure.

Yet as difficult as that image is to conjure, it's not entirely unattractive.

As Kayla and I part with a hug and no hard feelings, the mayor of Avalon Bay takes the mic on a small platform in front of the marina to announce the race participants. I half tune him out, at least until a familiar name greets my ears.

"—and Evan Hartley, sailing with Riley Dalton."

My head jerks up, and I nearly choke on the melted remnants of my lemon slush at the sound of Evan's name. I would think I'm hallucinating if not for Harrison raising an eyebrow at the same time.

Huh.

I wonder if Evan remembers he can't sail.

CHAPTER 21

EVAN

"Mistakes were made."

Riley laughs.

"That much is clear. It may have started when I steered us into another boat coming off the starting line. It may have been when we failed to make the first turn around the buoy. Who's to say, really?"

A hysterical noise escapes his throat, a cross between a snort and a howl. Riley hasn't stopped laughing since we rammed the dock. No, not rammed. We *nudged* the dock. Rammed would suggest a great rate of speed, which I don't think we achieved during the entire race.

Sopping wet, I wring out my T-shirt over the railing of the boardwalk while the trophy presentation kicks off at the other end of the marina.

"Dude," he chokes out between giggles. "We failed miserably."

"Not true," I protest. "There was a high point there when we managed to right the ship and not entirely capsize."

He's still laughing as we make our way to the crowd gathered around the platform, cheering for the winners and politely congratulating all those who placed. I'm just glad we're not getting stuck with a bill for salvaging the boat off the bottom of the bay.

As it turns out, I can't sail for shit. It's hard, actually. So many ropes and pulleys and winches, who the fuck knew. I thought you just put the sail up and steered, but apparently there's such a thing as oversteering, and steering left to go right for some stupid reason. Almost the second the starting gun went off, we were discombobulated. Came in dead last after tipping the boat and nearly going in the drink.

But Riley's still laughing, absolutely stoked on the whole ordeal. Mostly at my suffering, I think, but that's okay. The kid had a great time, which was the whole damn point to begin with.

"There's my guy." His aunt Liz, a petite woman with pretty brown eyes and long hair tied in a low ponytail, finds us among the spectators and gives him a hug. "You have fun?"

"It was a blast," Riley says. "For a minute there, I thought we were goners."

"Oh," she says, covering her alarm with a laugh. "Well, I'm glad you both survived."

"Don't worry. I'm a much better swimmer than I am a sailor. I wouldn't let your kid drown." I say this, of course, shirtless, with a full back of tattoos. Lady probably thinks I look more like Riley's drug dealer than his role model.

"Can I have some money for the hot dog stand?" Riley pleads. "I'm starving."

With an indulgent smile, Riley's aunt hands him a few bucks and sends him off.

"Trust me," I assure her, now concerned that putting a kid's life in mortal peril might reflect poorly on my participation in the program. "He wasn't in any danger. Just a minor mishap."

Liz waves off my concern. "I'm not worried. He hasn't had this much fun in a long time."

I think about the Riley I met that first afternoon—the shy, quiet teen who spent the first couple hours staring at his feet and mumbling to himself. Cut to today, where he's shouting commands at me and taking snarky jabs at my lack of nautical prowess. I don't know if it's what the program had in mind, but I'd call that improvement. For our relationship, at least.

"He's a cool kid. Who knows, maybe he can teach me how to sail and we can try again next year." I surprise myself when it occurs to me what I've just said. I hadn't given much thought to how long this arrangement would last. But now that I give it some consideration, I couldn't imagine Riley and I not being pals a year from now.

"You know, I think you mean that." Liz studies me, and I can't help wondering what she sees. "I do appreciate everything you've done for him. I know it's only been a couple weeks, but you're starting to mean a lot to Riley. You're good for him."

"Yeah, well . . ." I slide my sunglasses on and make another attempt at wringing out my wet shirt. "He's not a total asshole, so . . ."

She laughs at that, letting me off the hook. I've never been great at taking compliments. Being the consummate screwup doesn't often give a lot of reason for praise, so I guess you can say I haven't had much practice. And yet somehow, this kid turns out to be one of the few things I've gotten right. I've seen him several times a week for more than two weeks, and despite all odds, I haven't screwed him up yet.

"I need to get him home so I can head to work," Riley's aunt says. "But I'd like it if you came by for dinner one night. The three of us. Maybe next week?"

The fleeting notion of what would be in some alternate universe if Liz took a shine to me skips through my brain. Until I glance over her shoulder to spot black hair and long, tan legs, and the universe—*this* universe—reminds me there's only one woman for me on this plane.

Gen is strutting down the boardwalk in some girly white dress that gets my blood hot. Because she's trying. She's trying to impress this dweeb, to look the part by dulling herself to his milquetoast sensibilities. She's grinding down the sharp edges that make her everything that's fierce and dangerous and extraordinary, and I won't stand for it.

"Sure," I tell Liz, while my attention remains elsewhere. "Let's do that. Tell Riley bye for me? Just saw a friend I need to say hi to."

I jog through the crowd, dodging sweaty tourists and sunburnt children to catch up to Gen. Then, I slow down and manage to get in front of her and the guy, because now she'll have to notice me and say something, alleviating all guilt of crashing her date for a second time.

"Evan?"

I feign surprise as I turn around. "Oh, hey."

I can sense her rolling her eyes behind those reflective sunglasses. She smirks and shakes her head. "Oh, hey? You get you're terrible at this, right?"

Sometimes I forget I've never been able to put one over on her a day in my life. "Yeah, you know, I'd love to hang around, but I'm kinda busy, so . . ."

"Uh-huh."

With my shirt slung over my shoulder, I nod at Deputy Dolittle in his standard-issue Tommy Bahama. "Nice shirt."

"Stop," Gen warns, though she's still smiling. Because she knows, dude walks around dressed like that, he's asking for it. "What do you want?"

"Hey, there's no hard feelings, right?" I offer my hand to the deputy. "Truce?"

"Sure." He grips my hand with what must be all the force he can muster. I almost feel bad for the guy. Almost. "Bygones."

"Evan . . ." She cocks her head at me, impatient.

"You look nice."

"Don't do that."

I fight a grin. "I can't give you a compliment?"

"You know what I mean." She likes it. The amusement in her voice betrays her words.

"You do look nice." I'll always prefer the real Gen, the girl in a pair of cutoff shorts and a loose tank top over a bikini. Or nothing at all. But that doesn't mean I can't appreciate this little white slinky number that, in the right light, I can all but see through against her tan skin. "Big plans today?"

"We saw your race," the guy says. He could tell me his name a thousand times, and it still wouldn't stick. I could cover my eyes right now and have no idea what the guy looks like. He should have gone into the CIA or something; a dude this incapable of leaving an impression would do well, I imagine.

"It was, um, eventful." Gen tries and fails to pretend she isn't checking me out.

"These things are always so boring," I tell her. "Thought we'd add a little drama."

"Is that what that was? Drama?"

"Rather be last than boring."

Even behind those sunglasses, I feel her dragging her eyes down my bare chest. The way her teeth tug at the inside of her lip conjures all sorts of images in my head. I want to shove my fingers in her hair, put her up against the wall, and make this guy watch her melt against my lips. Whatever ideas she's got about playing the field or making me jealous, we both know he can't kiss her like I can. He'll never know her mouth, her body, the way I do.

"Why don't you join us for lunch?" the chaperone interjects.

Even Gen looks like she'd forgotten he was there. She startles, glancing over at him. "No, you don't have to do that."

"Lunch sounds great," I say cheerfully.

"Seriously?" This time her exasperation is directed at him. "Harrison. We had plans."

Surprisingly, he doesn't budge. "I insist."

Oh, buddy. I don't know what he thinks he's playing at, but there's no scenario where he puts Gen and me in a room together and it goes in his favor.

"Fine. I'm going to the restroom first." She points a finger at my chest. "Behave. And put a shirt on."

Gen leaves us standing outside a tacky gift shop. I'm content to keep my thoughts to myself, but it's Officer Chuckles who speaks up.

"She's a special woman," he starts.

That he talks about her like he knows her at all grates my nerves. "Yep."

"This sounds silly, but even back in high school I had a crush on her."

Back in high school we were making out in the yearbook darkroom while skipping third period.

"I know what this is," he announces, squaring up to me like he just found his balls. "You think you can intimidate me or scare me. Well, I promise it won't work."

"Dude, I don't know you." I remind myself he's a cop, and that I promised both Gen and Cooper I was done picking fights. Still, he's got to know I'm not the guy you test. "But if I were trying to scare you off, I wouldn't be shy or cute about it. I'd just do it."

"What I'm saying is, I like Genevieve. I intend to keep dating her. And nothing you do is going to change that. Keep crashing our dates, if you want. It won't make a difference."

I have to hand it to the guy. Even when putting himself between me and what's mine, he does it with a Boy Scout smile. Almost polite. Civil.

But it doesn't erase the fact that I'd step over his bleeding carcass to get to her. However long it takes for Gen to come back to me, I've already won this fight. He just hasn't figured it out yet.

"Then by all means," I say with a half smile. "Let the best man win."

CHAPTER 22

GENEVIEVE

These days, not much surprises me. For two months now, my life has become a predictable routine of the nine-to-five grind, with the occasional evening where I find a few hours to have a life. That isn't so much a complaint as an observation, because I asked for this. I went to great pains to tame my wilder tides.

But Evan, well, Evan Hartley still manages to surprise me. The weekend after the regatta, he picks me up for our date looking all primped and polished. He's wearing a clean white T-shirt and cargo pants without a single wrinkle in them. He even shaved—an especially rare treat. And where I expected one of his usual hair-brained schemes to get us into trouble on some ill-conceived adventure, we find ourselves sitting down to a late lunch at a modern vegan restaurant overlooking Avalon Beach.

"I have to ask," I say, enjoying the roasted eggplant pasta. "What made you decide on vegan? I can't remember the last time I've seen you eat a vegetable that wasn't wrapped in meat or cooked in animal fat."

As if to prove some point, Evan dabs the corner of his mouth with his napkin. "We're going against the grain, aren't we? I thought that was the whole point."

"I suppose." Not sure I meant we had to apply that philosophy to food, but okay.

"Clean living, Fred." Evan grins as he pops a bite of gnocchi in his mouth, then washes it down with a glass of water. He'd waved away the drink menu when we sat down. "Anyway, after our last dinner—"

"You mean my date you crashed."

"I thought I'd show you I can be civilized."

"You're not funny."

He ponders, then nods to himself. "Yes I am."

It was only a week ago when he barged his way into yet another date with Harrison at the marina, smirking and quite pleased with himself. I might muster up more annoyance if it wasn't so hard to be mad at him. With those eyes that dance with arrogance and mischief. The upturned corners of his lips that hint at secrets and whisper dares. He's impossible.

"You know this isn't what my life is now, right?" I gesture at the elegant table setting. "Dressing up in our parents' clothes, playing adult."

He snickers softly. "Not my parents."

"Or mine, but you know what I mean."

"You looked pretty comfortable in those clothes with him."

And we were having such a nice time.

I swallow a sigh. "Do you really want to talk about Harrison?"

Evan seems to consider this for a second, then dismisses the thought. "No."

"Good. Because I didn't agree to this date because I want you to be more like him. Try to remember that."

This, too, feels familiar—the somewhat adversarial rapport. Arguing for the sake of arguing because we like getting a rise out of each other. Never knowing when to quit. Wrapped up in sexual tension so that our fights become indistinguishable from flirting.

Why do I like it so much?

"Tell me this," he says roughly. "Who are you trying to be?"

Hell if I know. If I had that figured out, I wouldn't still be living at home, afraid to break it to my dad that he needs to move on without me in the family business. I wouldn't be dating one guy who I know is about as close to boyfriend material as anyone gets, while guarding myself from the million bad decisions sitting across the table.

"At the moment, shedding my bad girl reputation, I guess."

He nods slowly. He gets it.

And that's something I appreciate about Evan above all others—I never have to lie to him, or conceal something because I'm embarrassed about what he'd think of the truth. Whether I'm good, bad, or indifferent, he accepts me in all my iterations.

I offer a wry smile. "There're only so many times a girl can break into the waterpark after-hours to tube down the raging rapids before delinquency loses all meaning."

"I hear you. This is probably the longest I've gone without a hangover or a black eye since I was ten." He winks at me, which might as well be an invitation to throw my legs over his shoulders. Gets me every time.

"It's weird, though. Sometimes I'm out with the girls, and it's like I don't know what to do with my hands. If every instinct I have is what was getting me in trouble before, how am I supposed to know what the right ones are? What being good is supposed to look like, you know?"

"You're looking at a guy who Googled *model citizen*, okay? I've narrowed it down to this: Whatever sounds like a good idea, do the opposite."

"I'm serious," I say, flinging a sugar packet at him from the ramekin on the table. "What would you and I do on a normal date?"

"Normal?" He cocks his head at me, grinning.

"Normal for us."

"We wouldn't have left my bedroom," Evan says. Deadpan.

Well, yeah. "After that."

"Hit a bar. A party, maybe. End up in a stolen car doing laps at the old speedway until security chases us out. Getting drunk on top of the lighthouse while you suck me off."

My core clenches at the naughty suggestion. I pretend to be unaffected by hurling another sugar packet at his face. "You've given this some thought."

"Fred, this is all I think about."

He needs to stop doing that. Looking at me like he's starving, with his teeth nipping at his lower lip and those hooded eyes gleaming. It isn't fair, and I shouldn't have to put up with these conditions.

"Well, like you said, we're playing against type now, so . . ." I gulp my virgin cocktail, still expecting the burn of alcohol and left wanting. It seemed like a good idea at the time—trick my brain into believing it's getting what it wants—but the overly sweet concoction feels like sucking down a bottle of straight corn syrup. "What else you got?"

"Alright." He nods briskly, accepting the challenge. "You're on. For the rest of the night, we do the opposite of whatever our instincts tell us."

"You sure about this?" I lean in, elbows on the table. "I don't want to hear about you bailing on the idea . . ."

"I'm serious." He's got that look. A man possessed with a consuming notion. It reminds me of another thing that's always attracted me to Evan. He's shamelessly passionate. Even about the stupidest things. It's endearing. "Prepare yourself for an evening of well-mannered civility, Genevieve West."

I sputter out a laugh. "Hold on to your knickers."

"What do you think?" Evan crouches on the worn green turf beside the imitation Polynesian totem. He lays his putter on the ground, aiming the head of the club at the wooden crate labeled *dynamite*. "Take the left route around the pile of gold doubloons, yeah?"

Bending over beside him, I align my view with his. "I think that patch of old bubble gum stuck at the entrance of the mouse hole is going to give you trouble. The left fork over the ramp is a trickier shot, but once you're there, it's a cleaner descent to the hole."

"Let's go already." Behind us, a shaggy-headed kid grows testy. His friend sighs with loud impatience. "I'd like to get through this game while my clothes still fit."

Evan ignores him. Still evaluating his shot, picking leaves and bits of debris from around his golf ball. "I'm going left. I don't like the look of that turtle on the right." He gets to his feet, adjusts his stance. He takes a practice swing and then another.

"Come on!"

The club smacks the ball, launching it toward the high embankment, up and around the spilled pile of gold doubloons, where it sails straight into the rushing stream and down a waterfall. With a plop, it lands in the pool below, filled with colored golf balls like a hundred painted clams.

"After all that!" the friend heckles, while Shaggy Head guffaws loudly.

"Hey." I round on them, pointing my club. "Get fucked, shitheads."

"Whoa." The boys retreat a step with mocking expressions. "Ma'am, this is a family establishment."

I've got a mind to dangle them over the water feature, because these dudes have been getting on my nerves since the second hole, but Evan throws his arm around my shoulder to hold me back.

"Best behavior," he whispers at my ear. "Remember?"

Right. Nice young ladies don't drown little punk teenagers at the mini-golf course. "I'm cool."

"Get a handle on your chick, bro," Shaggy says.

His friend makes a taunting face. "She's crazy."

That snaps Evan's spine straight. Eyes glittering, he strides up, his fist tight around his club. He backs the kids up into the bushes as they stumble to escape him, expecting a beating.

Instead, Evan grabs a golf ball from the friend's hand and stalks back to me.

"Hey!" the kid complains.

"Consider it an asshole tax," Evan barks over his shoulder. He makes a grand show of sweeping his shoe over the ground to clear the tee for my turn. "My lady."

I fight a smile. "So chivalrous."

Then, knowing better, I hit my shot through the mouse hole, where it travels through an unseen underground passage and spits out from a canon, rather than the apparent turtle's mouth exit, and straight into the hole. Too easy.

Looking back at Evan, I see him twist his lips, cocking his head. "Cold-blooded, Fred."

At the next hole, we place a little wager on the game with the kids behind us after Evan decides to play nice and make friends. The matchup is closer than he'd like, in fact, but my hot hand keeps us up over the boys. In the end, Evan manages a clutch hole-in-one to push us over the top.

"That was decent of you." In the parking lot beside his motorcycle, I crack open a bottle of water. The afternoon is waning into evening, but the sun is still furiously insistent. "Giving the boys their money back."

Leaning against his bike, Evan shrugs one shoulder. "Last thing I need is some irate mom hunting me down for hustling her kid, right?"

"If I didn't know better, I'd almost think you had a good time. Despite the lack of police chasing us."

He straightens, closing the small space between us. His proximity makes it difficult to remember why we aren't getting up to more tactile activities. I want to kiss him. Feel his hands on me. Straddle him over his bike until security chases us away.

"When are you going to accept that I'd be happy watching paint dry with you?" His voice is low, earnest.

"Challenge accepted."

We end up at one of those paint-your-own-pottery places. It also happens to be overrun with a little girl's birthday party. A dozen eight-year-olds run around while a haggard shop girl struggles to keep ceramic horses and knockoff Disney figures on the shelves before they topple into mounds of dust and sharp edges.

At the back of the store, Evan and I pick our table and decide on our canvases.

"I just remembered we've been here before," I inform him, pulling an owl off a shelf. A similar one sits in my bedroom at home.

Evan studies a giraffe. "Are you sure?"

"Yeah, we left homecoming early freshman year and wandered in because you were tripping balls and saw a dragon in the window display, so you wouldn't let us go until you painted a purple dragon."

"Oh, shit," he says, backing away from the animals. "Yeah. I started freaking out because the dragon turned evil, and it was going to burn down the whole town."

I chuckle at the ridiculous memory. Turned out he'd pre-partied a little without me and consumed some pot brownies before the dance.

A sudden shriek rips through the room. The birthday girl in her crown and pink feather boa is red in the face and gesticulating wildly, her mother wide-eyed and horrified as the girl's friends cower in their seats. A tantrum poised to bubble over.

"I want the castle!" The girl fumes.

"You can have the castle, sweetie." The mom places a clearly substandard royal dwelling in front of her petulant offspring with the deliberate motions and sweaty brow of a bomb tech.

"Not that one!" The girl grabs for another child's far superior castle, which the other girl clutches, defiant. "It's my party! I want that one!"

"If I ever have a kid like that," I tell Evan, "I'm leaving it in the woods with a sleeping bag and some granola bars."

"Remind me not to leave you alone with our kids."

Casting a grin over his shoulder, Evan picks a seahorse off the shelf and strides over to the party. He gives the mom a reassuring nod then kneels in front of the angry birthday girl to ask if she'd do him the honor of an original artwork by painting the animal for him. Her bloodshot eyes and feral snarl return to a mostly human expression. She's even smiling.

Evan sits with her, talking and generally maintaining her attention, allowing the mother to take a deep breath and the other girls to go about their projects without fear of reprisal.

A half hour or so later, he rejoins me at our table, now the proud owner of the pink feather boa. Which is oddly fetching on him, for some reason.

"You're some kind of brat whisperer," I say as he takes a seat beside me.

"How do you think we've been friends for so long?"

For that I smear blue paint across his cheek. "Careful. I can do worse than throw pottery."

He flashes a crooked smile. "Don't I know it."

I'd have never thought him capable of wading into such treacherous territory and emerging unscathed. Triumphant, even. Paternal. It does something to me on a primal brain-chemistry level that I'm not entirely ready to unpack.

When this date started, I wasn't convinced we'd know how to be around each other if we weren't drunk, naked, or some variation approaching one or the other. Now, we've been at this a few hours, and I can't say I miss it. Well, I do, but not so much that I can't find enjoyment in the mundane activities of dating. Turns out there's something to be said for normal.

Leaving a while later with my new ceramic fish, we stroll the boardwalk, neither of us ready to go home but understanding the deadline fast approaching. Because once the sun sets, bad ideas come. We're creatures of habit, after all.

"You never told me," he says, reaching to hold my hand. Yet another surprise in this evening of firsts. Not that he's never held my hand before, but this feels different. It's not intentional or leading, but natural. Absent-minded. Like it's the only place our hands belong. "How'd your interview go with Mac?"

"You tell me. Did she say anything?"

"She thinks you're great. I'm more concerned how you feel. If you get the job, you two will be spending a lot of time together. That means Coop too. That means me."

The thought hasn't escaped me. Mac seems cool. It was only one meeting, but we got along well enough. Cooper, on the other hand, might be trickier. Last time we spoke, he was all but trying to run me out of town. Burrowing deeper into his inner circle is likely not going to improve that rift. But that's not what Evan's asking, not really. We both know that.

"If I get the job," I say with a poke to his chest, "that doesn't mean anything about you and me one way or another."

With that cocky grin, he doesn't break stride. "You keep telling yourself that."

Our path is interrupted by a group of old folks walking out of the ice-cream parlor. A couple ladies wave at Evan with disturbingly lewd intent. Meanwhile, a tall, gangly man whose sagging ears are racing his drooping jowls to his shoulders zeroes in on Evan.

"You," he says in a hoarse grumble. "I remember you."

Evan tugs my hand. "We better go."

"Lloyd, come on now." A man in a polo and name tag tries to coax the unruly seniors. "It's time to go."

"I'm not going anywhere." The man's cup of vanilla soft serve splatters to the ground. "That's the son of a bitch who killed my bird."

Um, *what?*

Evan doesn't give me even a second to digest that. As the elderly man launches himself at us, Evan yanks my arm and rockets us forward.

"Run!" he orders.

I'm struggling to keep my balance as Evan drags me behind him, hurtling down the boardwalk. I turn toward the wheezing exclamations at our backs to see Lloyd barreling after us. Unusually spry for a man his age, he's at a dead sprint, dodging food carts and tourists. He's got the devil in his eyes.

"This way," Evan says, pulling me to the left.

We cut down an alley between a couple of bars that leads behind the boardwalk carnival that is set up through much of the summer. We dart between a couple of midway games and through a back door, where we're promptly bombarded by a soundtrack of something I can only describe as trance music overlaid on nursery rhyme melodies with the disconcerting laughter of clowns. It's pitch-black, save for an occasional strobe light that reveals a maze of hanging painted mannequins.

"I always knew this is what I'd see before I died," I say in resignation.

Evan nods solemnly. "There are definitely dead kids walled up in here somewhere."

Catching my breath, I run a hand through my disheveled hair. "So. You killed a man's bird?"

"No, Cooper's Satan dog killed the bird. I strenuously object to any guilt by association."

"Uh-huh. And this happened how?"

Before he can answer, a shard of daylight enters the room from somewhere unseen. We both crouch, hugging the wall to avoid getting caught.

"Who's in here?" a voice shouts from the other side of the room. "We ain't open yet."

Evan puts his finger over his lips.

"You get out here, you hear me?" The angry man's demand is followed by a loud, startling crack of noise. Like a bat hitting a wall or something. "If I gotta hunt you down, I'm gonna turn your insides out."

"Oh my God," I whisper. "We have to get the hell out of here."

We feel around for the door we came through, but it's still dark and disorienting, the music and haunting laughter, and the strobe lights make the whole room appear to stutter. Practically crawling, we creep off in another direction until we find a small alcove. We stop there, listening to our pursuer's heavy footfalls.

Confined, hunted, not making a sound, Evan presses us into

the shadows of the tight corner. With his hands on my hips and his body warm against mine, I almost don't hear the nightmare soundtrack anymore. Just the sound of my own breathing in my ears. My mind trips over random thoughts and sensations. The scent of his shampoo and motorcycle exhaust. His skin. Memories of it on my tongue. His fingers.

"Don't do that," he rasps in my ear.

"What?"

"Remember."

It'd be so easy to grab handfuls of his hair and pull his lips to mine. Let him have me in this funhouse of horrors while we brace to be hacked up by Crazy Willy out there.

"We said we wouldn't," Evan reminds me, reading my mind because we've never needed words to speak to each other. "I'm trying to be a good boy, Fred."

I lick my dry lips. "Just out of curiosity, what would Bad Boy Evan do?" I ask, because apparently I'm into self-torture.

He licks his lips too. "You really want me to answer that?"

No.

Yes.

"Yes," I tell him.

Evan's palms lightly caress my hips, sending a shiver up my spine. "Bad Boy Evan would take his hand and slide it under your skirt."

To punctuate that, one big palm travels south to capture the hem of my pale-green skirt between his fingertips. He doesn't pull it up, though. Just plays with the filmy fabric, while a slight smile lifts the corners of his mouth.

"Yeah?" My voice is hoarse. "And why would he do that?"

"Because he'd want to find out how hot you were for him. How wet." He bunches the fabric between his fingers, giving a teasing tug. "And then, when he felt how bad you wanted it, he'd put his fingers inside you. Wouldn't even need to take your panties off, because Bad Girl Gen doesn't wear 'em."

I almost moan out loud.

"Then, after he made you come, he'd spin you around. Tell you to put your palms flat against the wall." Evan brings his lips close to my ear, eliciting another shiver, a flurry of them this time. "And he'd fuck you from behind until we both forgot our names."

Still smiling, he releases my skirt, which flutters down to my knees. That teasing hand glides back north, this time to cup my chin.

I stare up at him, unable to breathe. Crazy Willy's footsteps have dissipated. And the clown music has all but receded into the background of my brain. All I hear now is the pounding of my heart. My gaze is stuck on Evan's lips. The need to kiss him is powerful enough to make my knees wobble.

Feeling how unsteady I am, he lets out a husky laugh. "But we're not going to do any of that, are we?"

Despite my body screaming *please, please, please* at me, I exhale a slow breath and manage a nod. "No," I agree. "We're not going to do that."

Instead, we check that the coast is clear and then double back the way we came until we find the broken exit sign above the door. We emerge unscathed, but I can't say the same for my libido. My body is throbbing with need that borders on pain. Not putting my hands all over Evan is much, much harder than I thought it would be.

I honestly have no idea how long I'll be able to resist.

CHAPTER 23

EVAN

Come sunrise, I'm on Riley's porch with my phone to my ear. It's the fourth time in ten minutes it's gone to voicemail. I told the kid, *when I say early, I mean it.* So I jump down the steps and round the side of the tiny, pale-blue clapboard house to his bedroom window. I knock on the glass until the groggy teen pushes the blinds aside to rub his eyes at me.

I flash a grin. "Shake a leg, sunshine."

"Time is it?" His voice is muffled behind the window.

"Hurry-up time. Let's go."

When Riley had asked me to take him surfing, I'd warned him that we weren't going to mess around with crowded afternoon beaches. If he wanted to get on the water, he'd have to paddle out with the big boys. That means hitting the waves before breakfast.

I hop in Cooper's truck out front to wait for the kid. A few minutes later, I'm thinking about climbing through his window to drag him out when his aunt knocks on the passenger window.

"Morning," I greet her, turning off the radio. "I didn't wake you, did I? I'm supposed to take Riley surfing."

Wearing a zippered hoodie over a pair of scrubs, Liz glances at my surfboard in the bed of the truck. "Right, he mentioned it last night. You didn't wake me, though. I've got an early shift. He should be out in a minute." She holds up a large tray wrapped in tinfoil. "This is for you. Since we never had that dinner."

"Sorry about that." I slide across the bench seat to take the tray from her and lift up the foil. The homemade pie inside smells terrific. "I've been slammed at work."

"Hope you're not allergic to cherry."

I break off a piece of pie crust to pop in my mouth. Oh fuck, that is delicious. "What if I am?"

She grins. "Eat small bites."

"Ready!" Riley comes jogging out of the house with the screen door snapping shut behind him. He's lugging his board under his arm, with a backpack slung over his shoulder.

"Remember, you need to get some laundry done while I'm at work." Liz moves to let Riley jump in the truck as I slide back to the driver's side. "And taking some bleach to that bathtub wouldn't hurt."

"Yep, okay." He pokes his head out the window to give her a kiss on the cheek. "Call you later."

Smiling, Liz points a finger at me. "Don't drown my nephew."

I smile back. "I'll do my best."

Turns out Riley isn't half bad on a board. He's got good balance and a feel for the rhythm of the water but is just a little rough on technique. Unfortunately, the waves today aren't much worth the effort. We sit on our boards out beyond the breakers, bobbing on the swells. Even when the surfing isn't great, I'd still rather be out here than almost anywhere else.

"How'd you get better?" Riley asks as we watch the occasional intrepid rider attempt to paddle after a minor wave.

The sun at our back slowly climbs the sky, casting long orange streaks across the water. About a dozen other surfers float nearby, spread out, watching the undulating tide and hoping for something to crest.

"I just watched what the other guys did and tried to mimic them. But other than being on the water and getting tossed a lot, the thing that helped me the most was learning to control the board and my body."

"Like how?"

"Well, I swiped a piece of scrap metal pipe from a construction site and put a two-by-four over it. Sort of like a skateboard, you know? And I'd spend hours balancing on it. Learning how to shift my weight to move around. It really helped engage those muscles and train my body."

"So step one: theft. Got it."

I grin at him. "See, this is how you get me in trouble."

One zealous chick turns her board to shore and drives her arms through the water, paddling into position for what amounts to a gentle shove of a wave. Some assholes mockingly whistle after her.

"No worries," Riley says. "You won Liz over a long time ago. I think she's maybe got a little thing for you."

I'd been getting that vibe too. The guy at Big Brothers had even warned that sort of thing wasn't unheard of, but under no circumstances should I entertain the idea—if I was serious about helping my Little. Which isn't to say Liz doesn't have attractive qualities.

"Kind of got my hands full," I tell him.

He eyes me knowingly. "That girl from the boardwalk the other day?"

"Genevieve. We go way back."

Even saying her name gets my heart beating faster and fills me with anticipation. I think about her even a little, and I become impatient for the next time I can see her. I'd spent a year fighting a losing battle against this, driving myself crazy. Now she's here, never more than a few minutes away, and I still barely see her for some reason that I've yet to understand.

"Do you like the guys your aunt dates?" I ask Riley.

He shrugs. "Sometimes. Really, she doesn't get out much because she works all the time."

"What's her type?"

"I don't know." He shakes his head, laughing at me. "Boring dudes, I guess. When she's off work, she just wants to order takeout and watch movies. Relax, you know? I don't think she'd tolerate anyone with too much energy, even if she thinks it seems like a good idea at first. I just want her to have someone nice."

If I wasn't sure it'd set Gen off, I might try and point Liz and that Harrison guy at each other. In another life, maybe.

"I think we ought to do something nice for your aunt," I decide, forcing my brain to a change of topic. "Take her out to dinner or something." Regardless of the skewed Nightingale syndrome emerging here, she's a nice lady who does her best with limited resources. She should get some thanks for that.

"Yeah, she'd like that."

"She's good people." To most kids, moms are a given. They just assume their moms will love and take care of them. Nurture them. Band-Aids and school lunches and all that. Some of us know better. "Don't ever take her for granted."

"You hear from your mom lately?"

I've talked to him about Shelley before, but the question still hits me sideways. Thinking about her puts me in a constant state of whiplash. She sure isn't baking any cherry pies.

"She keeps texting, wanting to get together and reconnect. Make amends, or whatever. I told her I'd think about it, but every time she suggests a time and place to meet, I make up some excuse."

"What are you going to do? Do you want to see her?"

I shrug, scooping a handful of water to douse my hair. Even though it's not over our heads yet, the sun is already at baking temperature. "I don't know how many times I can let her make me the sucker before I haven't got any dignity left."

Riley drags his hands through the water, aimless. "I know it's not exactly the same situation with us. Mine got sick. She didn't leave. But I'd give anything to see her again, to talk to her."

His heart's in the right place, but I wish he hadn't said that. "Yeah, it's really not the same." Because missing his mother doesn't make him feel like an idiot.

He places both hands on his board and gives me a serious look. "I guess what I'm saying is, if your mom died tomorrow, would you regret not speaking to her one more time?"

Riley's words burrow into my brain like a worm eating through an apple. The question festers for hours, days. Until finally, a week later, I'm sitting in a diner in Charleston, placing bets against myself after fifteen minutes whether Shelley is going to stand me up. The pitying eyes of my server aren't giving me great odds as she refills my coffee mug.

"You want anything to eat?" asks the waitress, a middle-aged woman with overgrown roots and too many bracelets.

"No, thanks."

"The pie came in fresh this morning."

Enough with the damn pies. "Nope. I'm good."

Thirty minutes. This is why I didn't tell anyone, least of all Cooper. He would've told me this would happen. After he kicked my ass and took my keys to spare me one more humiliation.

I have no idea when I became the trusting one. The dupe.

I'm about to throw a few bucks on the table just as Shelley

drops into the booth and settles across the table from me. Blown in like a gust of wind.

"Oh, baby, I'm sorry." She pulls her purse off her shoulder and picks up a laminated menu to fan the heat-and-asphalt smell out of her dyed blonde hair. Her energy is hectic and frazzled, always in motion. "One of the girls was late coming back from lunch because she had to pick her kid up, and I couldn't leave on my break until she got back."

"You're late."

She stills. Presses her lips together with a contrite tilt of her head. "I'm sorry. But I'm here now."

Now. This impermanent state between wasn't and won't be.

"What'll you have?" The waitress is back, this time with an accusatory curtness to her tone. This woman's growing on me.

"Coffee, please," Shelley tells her.

The woman walks off with a grimace.

"I'm glad you called me back," Shelley tells me as she keeps fanning herself with the menu. I've never been able to put my finger on it before, but I just figured it out. Her frenetic nature gives me anxiety. Always has. The perpetual motion is so chaotic. Like bees in a glass box. "I've missed you."

I purse my lips for a second. Then I let out a tired breath.

"Yeah, you know what, before we go another ten rounds on this, let me say: You're a bad mom, Shelley. And it's pretty shady how you're pitting Cooper and I against each other." She opens her mouth to object. I stop her with a look. "No, that's exactly what you're doing. You came to me with all your pleas and apologies because you know Cooper won't hear it. You take advantage of the fact that I'm the soft one, but you don't care what that does to your sons. If he knew I was here—I don't know, he might change the locks on me. I'm not kidding."

"That isn't what I want." Any pretense of a sunny disposition fades from her face. "Brothers shouldn't fight."

"No, they shouldn't. And you shouldn't be putting me in this position. And you know what else? Would it have killed you to bake a pie every now and then?"

She blinks. "Huh?"

"I'm just saying," I mutter. "Other moms bake pies for their kids."

She's quiet for a while after the waitress brings her coffee. Staring at the table and folding her napkin into smaller and smaller shapes. She looks different, I can't help but acknowledge. Her eyes are clear. Skin is healthy. Getting sober is a hell of a drug.

Leaning forward on her elbows, she begins in a subdued voice. "I know I've been awful to you boys. Trust me, kid, I know what rock bottom is now. Getting thrown in jail by my own son was kind of an eye-opener."

"Stealing from your own son," I pointedly remind her. "Anyway, he dropped the charges, which was probably more than you deserved."

"I'm not arguing with you." She drops her head, watching her fingers pick at the peeling nail polish on her thumb. "Sitting in that cell knowing that my own kid had me locked up, though . . . Yeah, that was a wake-up call." Hesitant, she lifts her gaze to search mine, probably for some hint that her contrition is landing. "I'm trying here, baby. This is my new leaf. I got a job now. My own place."

"That tree's looking a little bare from where I'm sitting, Mom."

"You're right. We've been here before."

She smiles, all heartsick and hopeful. It's sad and pathetic, and

I hate seeing my own mother so beaten. I don't enjoy kicking her while she's down. But what else is there when she's been down so long, and she's got both hands around my ankle?

"I promise, Evan. I'm ready to be better. I got my shit together. No more of that old stuff. I just want to have a relationship with my sons before I die."

I hate that. It isn't fair, playing the death card on a couple orphans who've already buried one parent in the ground and another in our minds. Still, something strikes a chord with me. Maybe because the two of us have found ourselves on entirely different yet similar journeys of self-improvement. Maybe I'm a sap who will never stop wanting his mother to love him and act like she does. Either way, I can't help feeling she's sincere this time.

"Here's how it is," I say slowly. "I'm not saying no."

Her eyes, dark and daunting like mine, light with relief.

"I'm not saying yes, either. You're gonna have to do more than make promises if you want to be part of my life. That means keeping a steady job and your own place. Sticking around town for a solid year. No running off to Atlantic City or Baton Rouge or wherever else. And I think we should do a monthly dinner." I don't even know why I say that. It just spills out of me. Then I realize I don't hate the idea.

She nods, too eager. It makes me nervous. "I can do that."

"I don't want you coming to me for money. You don't drop by the house to sleep one off. Matter of fact, you don't come by at all. If Cooper sees you, I can't be sure he won't think of a reason to have you arrested again."

She reaches for my hand and squeezes. "You'll see, baby. I'm better now. I haven't even had a drink since you agreed to meet me."

"That's great, Mom. Let me tell you something, though, that

I've started to figure out myself: If the change is going to stick, you have to want it to. That means doing it for yourself, not only because you're trying to impress someone else. Change, or don't. Either way, you're the one who's got to live with the result."

CHAPTER 24

GENEVIEVE

There are few things I love about this town more than a bonfire on the beach. Cool sand and warm flames. The scent of burning pine and salt air. The coastal breeze that carries tiny orange embers into the waves. These things feel like home. And no one does it better than the twins. Summer nights at the Hartley house are a tradition in the Bay—like boardwalk carnivals and hustling Garnet freshmen.

The party is well underway when I arrive. Heidi and Jay are attached at the face. Alana's dancing in the flickering firelight with some roughneck deckhand, while Tate watches from the distance with his fist around a beer bottle like he's thinking about cracking it over the guy's head. Mackenzie, who's sitting beside the fire with Steph, waves when she spots me coming down from the house.

Just a few hours ago, she called to tell me I got the job. I'm officially the new general manager of The Beacon Hotel, which is a little terrifying but a lot exciting. I warned Mac that although I work hard and learn quickly, I don't pretend to know anything about running a hotel, and she reminded me that until a few months ago, she didn't know anything about owning one. Besides, I've never stopped to wonder if the landing might hurt before jumping off a pier or out of a plane. Why start now?

So while I'm not sure Cooper would appreciate seeing me here, I accepted Mac's invitation to the party. My new position doesn't start until the end of the summer, but still. You don't turn down the boss. Or maybe that's an excuse. Maybe the real reason I came tonight is because after I hung up the phone with Mac, there was only one person I couldn't wait to tell. Rather than linger too long on the implication of that instinct, I just got myself in the car and drove over here.

Evan finds me across the flames through the many shadowed faces. He nods for me to come meet him by the folding table and coolers, where they've practically got a whole liquor store stashed.

"Tell me something," he says when I approach. "You get perks, right? Maybe swing a presidential suite with some room service? You and me spend a weekend naked, eating chocolate-covered strawberries in a hot tub?"

"I see Mac already told you."

"Yep. Congratulations, Madam GM." With an elaborate hand motion, Evan presents me with a red Blow Pop.

This asshole is damn sweet sometimes. I hate that he doesn't have to try at all in order to turn my gut to giddy mush. That my nerves never dull to his dark, mischievous eyes and crooked smirk. He throws on any old T-shirt and a pair of jeans splattered with interior paint and plaster, and I get positively slutty.

"Now it feels real," I say with a laugh. "This makes all the fretting worth it."

My brother Billy wanders past us, throwing me the side-eye when he notices how close Evan and I are standing. I give a nod of assurance, making it clear it's all good here, and he keeps walking.

"Let me fix you a drink. I've been working on something special." Evan fills up a cup of ice from the cooler and starts assembling bottles of ingredients.

"I can't."

He waves off my hesitation. "It's non-alcoholic."

Words I never thought I'd hear come out of a Hartley's mouth. Especially this one.

I watch as he caps the shaker and begins vigorously mixing the drink. "Honestly, I was debating not even coming tonight," I confess.

A frown touches his lips. "Because of me?"

"No, because of this—" I gesture at the beer-filled coolers and table laden with booze. "On the drive over, I was trying to convince myself I could have a drink. Just one, you know, to take the edge off. But then, all these worst-case scenarios flashed through my head. One drink turns to two, and suddenly six drinks later, I wake up in a fire engine half submerged in the YMCA pool with the lights still flashing and a llama treading water." And only half of that scenario is hypothetical.

Amused, he pours the drink into the cup of ice. "Gen. You've got to cut yourself some slack. This kind of hypervigilance isn't sustainable. Trust me. If you don't let yourself have a little fun now and then, you're gonna end up burnt out or on a bender. Learn to embrace moderation."

"You get that off a T-shirt?" I ask in amusement.

"Here." He hands me the fruity concoction. "I'll be your chaperone tonight. If you reach for a real drink, I'll smack it out of your hand."

"Is that right?" He must think I'm new here.

"I'm sober tonight," Evan says without a hint of irony. "I plan to stay that way."

Ordinarily, I might laugh in his face. A sober Hartley at a party is like a fish out of water. But taking a good look at him, I note that his eyes are clear and focused. Not a whiff of booze on his breath. Hell, he's serious. If I didn't know him, I might start believing he was sincere about being reformed.

I guess there's only one way to find out.

"Okay," I say, accepting the drink. "But if I wake up on a stolen Jet Ski in the middle of the ocean, surrounded by Coast Guard cutters, you and me are gonna fight."

"Cheers to that." He hoists a bottle of water to clink with my plastic cup.

Turns out Evan can mix a decent virgin cocktail.

"Not for nothing," he says hesitantly. "You know this 'good girl' mission doesn't have to entirely change who you are, right?"

"What does that mean?" I'm somewhat taken aback. Not because Evan might be less than enthusiastic about this new lifestyle, but that there's some genuine distress in his voice I haven't heard before.

"I just think it'd be a shame if you let growing up dull your edges. I'm all for whatever makes you happy," he qualifies. "You don't need to be drinking for me to enjoy your company—you've always been fun no matter what. Lately, though, it seems like the real Gen is slipping away. Becoming a muted version of the incredible, terrifying, vibrant woman you used to be."

"You say that like I'm dying." I won't lie—it hurts a little to hear that from him. The disappointment, the chord of loss. It's like attending my own funeral.

His eyes drop, fingers running over the ridges of the bottle in his hand. "In a sense, maybe it feels that way. All I'm saying . . ." He lifts his attention again to me. A brief, wistful smile is quickly chased off by his typical irreverent grin. "Don't go getting soft on me, Fred."

I've always loved myself best in Evan's eyes. The adoring way he looks at me: part impressed, a little intimidated. But more so, the person he thinks I am. The way he tells it, I'm invincible. Thunder and lightning. Not much scares me, and even less when he's around.

I wash down the thought with another generous sip of my faux cocktail. "Wouldn't dream of it."

There's got to be a way to do both. Straighten out my more destructive tendencies without lobotomizing myself. Somewhere in the world are respectable, functioning adults who've staved off blandness.

Because Evan isn't alone in his concern. I've felt the slow slipping of self too, the image in the mirror becoming less familiar with time. Every morning waking as one person. The day spent tearing myself out and up, clawing through layers like breaking free of my own skin. And I hit my pillow each night as someone else entirely. At some point, I better settle on a persona before I'm not me at all, but another discarded husk on the floor.

"Tell you what," Evan says. "No more serious talk. I've missed the hell out of us. And you deserve to celebrate. So trust me to stop you from falling into old habits, but . . ." His voice roughens. "Not all habits are bad. For tonight, let's just say to hell with it and have a good time."

In other words, let's pretend it's the old days and we're still together. No more rules and boundaries. Feel the moment and let our instincts move us.

It's an attractive offer. And maybe he's caught me in just the right mood to accept.

"Temping . . ." I trail off.

"Oh, come on." He throws his arm over my shoulder and kisses the side of my head. "What's the worst that could happen?"

"Famous last words."

Evan shrugs, hauling me toward the music and dancing couples. "There are worse ways to go."

For a few hours, we are ether. Evan doesn't dance so much as stand there peeling my clothes off with his eyes. I lose my half-empty drink somewhere in the beat. I'm high on sensation. Fabric sticking to my body in the humidity. Sweat down my neck. His hands finding bare skin across my stomach, my shoulders. Lips pressed against my hair, my cheek, under my jaw until they meet my own. Kissing like everyone is watching. Grabbing fistfuls of his shirt and hiking my knee up his leg until I remember where we are.

It's the most fun I've had with my clothes on in a long time, and all we do is everything we've ever done. Laughing with our friends and kicking up sand. Nothing on fire but the burning logs in the pit, and the only flashing lights coming from the flames and cell phone cameras. Lumberjack Jimmy has trotted out his ax-throwing target, and everyone's placing bets as we take turns hurling sharp edges at the upright wooden board. At first glance the concept of mixing medieval weaponry and alcohol might appear like a recipe for a noisy ride to the emergency room, but so far, egos have taken the worst damage tonight.

"You should have a go," I urge Evan. Seeing as he's dead sober, no one's got him beat for aim.

With his arm around my waist as we watch another matchup, Evan strokes his thumb under the hem of my shirt. The seductive touch gets me dizzier than anything from a bottle. "What'll you give me if I win? And feel free to be as lewd as you'd like."

"My respect and admiration," I deadpan, to his utter dejection.

"Mmm-hmm, that's just as good as a blowjob."

When Jimmy asks who's going next, Evan steps up to the lane to take an ax in hand. Someone grabs Cooper to *get a load of this*, and the mass of interested spectators swells. They give him a wide berth, though. Because Evan Hartley with an ax is about as close to death as anyone gets with air in their lungs.

Until the sharp, shrill wail of a siren spooks the crowd. The music cuts out abruptly. Firelight reveals a cop trudging through the sand. He barks orders into a bullhorn, sending those of questionable parole status scattering into the darkness.

"Party's over," he announces. "You have three minutes to clear the premises or be subject to arrest."

For a split second, I hold out some faint hope it's Harrison having a laugh. But then the cop's face is revealed from the shadows.

Deputy Randall.

Of course.

Evan jerks his head at Cooper. Still gripping the ax, Evan struts up to Randall with his brother, shrugging off my weak attempt to stop him. I'm already feeling my pocket for my keys and wondering if Mac will understand when I have to miss a few days of work to skip town and drive Evan over the border.

As if sharing my prophetic vision, Mac comes up to take my arm as we follow our men to the confrontation.

"What's the deal?" Cooper asks, doing his best to control the deep streak of Hartley contempt for law enforcement from seeping into his voice.

"Everyone's got to go," Randall informs the entire crowd.

"This is private property," Evan shoots back with no such restraint. I know without a doubt that right now images of Randall cornering me in a bar and trying to feel me up are spinning in his mind as he holds the smooth wooden ax handle in his fist.

"Your property ends at the grass. This sand here is a public beach, boy."

Evan cocks his head, licking his lips. The madman thrill he gets from tasting his own blood.

"What's the problem?" Cooper takes a step forward to put a bit more of his body between Evan and Randall. "Don't try to tell me you got a noise complaint. All our neighbors are right here."

Without a flinch, Randall spits out a flat response. "You don't have a permit for this bonfire. It's against city code."

"Bullshit." Thin on patience, Evan raises his voice. "People have bonfires all the time. No one's ever needed any damn permit."

"This is harassment," Cooper says.

Looking bored, Randall reaches into his shirt pocket. "My badge number's on the card. Feel free to file a complaint." He flicks it at Cooper, who lets it fall to the sand. "Call it a night, or take a ride with me to the station."

Evan picks up the business card. "Don't want to be litter bugs, do we, deputy?"

With that, the party's over. Meandering toward the house, people begin to disperse. Evan and Cooper retreat, albeit reluctantly, to pack up the drinks. With a regretful shrug, Mac goes to break down the chairs and folding table. Meanwhile, I have no idea where I left my purse. I'm hunting for it, saying goodbye as friends pass me, when I nearly bump into Randall, who's blending into the night in his dark sheriff's uniform.

"That didn't take long." He sneers, arms crossed, that unearned sense of superiority bearing down on me.

"What?" I don't really want a response, so I try to dodge him, but Randall steps into my path.

"Harrison didn't stand a chance, eh? Barely got his foot in the door, and you're already stepping out on him."

"What is that supposed to mean?" He's got me zero to fed up in no time flat. I don't like what he's insinuating, and I'm not about to entertain his garbage on my home turf. We're not in public. Out here, all sorts of things can happen, and no one would say a word.

"Means you're not fooling anyone, sweetheart. Least of all me." Randall leans in, growling words coated in the sickly stench of gas station corn dogs and coffee. "You're still a lying little slut. Out to ruin another man's life."

"I'm sorry." Evan comes striding up beside me, the ax slung with one hand over his shoulder. "I didn't quite catch that." He tilts his ear to Randall. "You'll need to speak up. Say that again?"

"It's fine," I say, grabbing Evan's free wrist. If I was worried about becoming a fugitive before, I'm downright concerned now. "Walk me to my car?"

"Go on, boy." Randall moves his right hand to rest on his gun. The strap on the holster is unbuttoned. "Give me a reason."

Evan flashes a wild smile I've seen a hundred times. Right before he took a running leap off a cliff or unloaded a paintball gun at a police cruiser. It's a smile loaded with the serenity of madness saying, *watch this*.

"Yeah, you see . . ." Evan admires the ax, turning it in hand. "As a respected business owner and upstanding member of my community, I'd never run afoul of a lawman." He flicks his thumbnail across the blade.

It's then I realize this conversation has attracted an audience. A smaller contingent than the aborted party. In fact, with Cooper, Wyatt, Tate, and Billy, the remnants are made up almost exclusively of certified members from the Fuck Around and Find Out Society.

"But you come at me and mine sideways," Evan says, not a hint of humor in his grave tone. "You better come to dance."

For second or two, Randall appears to contemplate the offer. Then, sizing up the opposition, he thinks better of it. He barks a final order into the bullhorn. "Three minutes are up. Clear out."

He doesn't wait for compliance before trudging back through the sand and tall grass to the road and his waiting cruiser. I don't release my breath until I watch the taillights blink red and then disappear.

Following Evan up to the house, I'm still a bit winded by the whole ordeal. Somehow, he's still got the ax, which he tosses on the dresser when we enter his bedroom upstairs. I haven't been in here in a year, and it feels oddly like stepping into a museum of my own life. Memories on every wall.

"What's that look?" he says, pulling off his shirt and tossing it in the hamper. My throat goes dry as my attention is drawn to the lines of his chest, the defined muscles of his abs.

"It still smells the same."

"Hey, I did laundry yesterday."

I roll my eyes, taking a trip around the room. "Not like that. I mean it smells familiar."

"You okay?"

"For a minute there . . ." I'm distracted as I wander the bedroom. He's never been the sentimental type. There are no photographs tacked to the wall. No old concert tickets or souvenirs. Wasn't much into sports either, so none of those little gold men. "I thought you might find a use for that ax. You impressed me back there."

My gaze conducts a final sweep. His room is just a utilitarian composite of some basic furniture, TV, game system, and the contents of his pockets on any given day tossed on the nightstand. Except for one frill on top of his dresser: a decorative glass dish, like something an old lady would put potpourri in, filled with years' worth of Blow Pops.

This jerk is so damn sweet sometimes.

"Which part impressed you?" he asks.

I turn to find him leaning against his bedroom door. Legs crossed, hands shoved in his pockets. Jeans riding low on his hips. Everything about him demands to be consumed. And I'm locked in here with him.

"I admired your restraint." I don't know what to do with my hands now, so I rest them on the edge of his desk, hop up, and sit on them.

"I couldn't remember if we were still playing the opposite game. But I'll go hunt his ass down if we're not."

"No, you did good."

He raises an eyebrow. "How good?"

"Are you leaning against that door because you're afraid I'll leave?"

"Do you want to?"

When Evan looks at me from beneath those thick, dark lashes, all full of memories and hunger, I forget what I'm doing. All the rules and hesitations fly out the window.

"No," I admit.

He pushes off the door and stalks toward me, planting his hands on the desk on either side of me. Reflexively, I open my legs for him to stand between them. I fixate on his mouth. On the warmth radiating from his body and the way my limbs grow restless. When I think he's going to kiss me, he turns his face to brush his lips against my temple instead.

"I've missed you," he says, more a groan than words.

"I'm right here."

My pulse throbs in my neck, in my palms, the phantom echo of my thumping heart resonating across every nerve ending. I'm all but choking on the anticipation of something to happen and uncertain what it should be. Because I made myself a promise. Right now, though, I can't for the life of me think of a good reason to keep it.

With the lightest touch, Evan's hands slide up the outside of each leg, over my knees, thighs. "I've got it bad, Fred." His voice comes out hoarse. "The way I see it, you better send me to a cold shower before this thing gets serious."

I bite my lip to smother a smile. "Serious, huh?"

He grabs my hand and places it on his chest. "As a heart attack."

His skin under my palm is hot to the touch. In the quiet part of my mind, I know he's dangerous. But the rest of it, the loud, screaming voice between my ears, tells me to drag my hands down his chest. To undo the zipper on his jeans, reach into his boxer briefs, and wrap my fingers around his thick, throbbing erection.

Evan sucks in a breath when I stroke him. He looks down, watching me, his abdomen clenching. "Good choice."

Without warning, he draws my hand away and spins me around. I grip the edge of the desk to steady myself as he hastily tugs my shorts down to expose my bare ass. He squeezes my warm flesh with one hand, humming an appreciative sound. I hear a drawer open and shut, followed by the rip of a condom wrapper. His fingers slide between my legs, finding me wet, and then I feel him rub himself against my feverish skin as he leans over to whisper in my ear.

"I don't mind if you want to be loud."

A thrill shoots through me.

He leaves a kiss on my shoulder as he drags his erection along my aching core, before slowly pushing inside me. With one hand on my hip, and the other knotted in my hair to pull my head backward and arch my back, Evan fills me completely. My nails bite the worn desktop as I push back, taking him. The exquisite ache fogs my vision and quickens my pulse.

"Fuck, Gen." He grinds out the words. Lays another kiss at my temple.

I breathe out his name because I can't take the static anticipation a moment longer. I just want him already. I need him to put me out of my misery.

Evan glides his hand up my spine, under my shirt, to unhook my bra and let it slide down my arms. I grab his hand, guide it to my breast. Still, he stubbornly refuses to move.

"Why are you teasing me?" I demand.

"Because I never want this to end." His thumb brushes over my nipple in the most feather light of caresses.

I groan my desperation and buck against him, grinding on his dick.

Chuckling softly, he brings his other hand up and clasps both breasts now. "Better?"

"No," I mumble. "You're still not moving." And the feel of his entire length lodged inside me, completely motionless, is a new form of torment. No oxygen is reaching my lungs. My skin is on fire, and I'm close to self-combusting.

"Breathe." His voice is soft in my ear, his fingers playing with my nipples. "Take a breath, baby."

I manage a shaky inhale, and just as the air fills my lungs, Evan withdraws slowly. I'm mid-exhalation when he slides back in, sending a wave of sensation through my body.

My head drops back on his shoulder, experiencing every inch of him. Pleasure tingles in my nipples and tightens my core as he moves inside me, slow and deliberate. When I can't quell the need alone, I move his right hand between my legs.

"I'm close," I whisper.

"Already?"

"Feels too good." A ragged breath slips out. "Missed having you inside me."

That earns me a satisfied growl. He runs his finger over my clit. Gentle at first, then more insistent when I moan for him. It isn't long before I'm shaking, leaning against him for support as the orgasm sweeps through me.

"You're gorgeous when you come," he rasps against my neck.

As tiny flutters of pleasure continue to dance inside me, Evan bends me over the desk. He takes my hips with both hands and pumps into me with strong, forceful thrusts. Just the right intensity. Having me like it's his last night on Earth.

I twist my head to look at him, floored by the raw need darkening his eyes, the blissed-out haze. When our gazes lock, he stills, groaning through his climax. He runs his hands up my back, soothing my muscles, laying kisses across my sensitive flesh. I'm sated and spent, panting, when he steps away to throw out the condom.

"I'm gonna grab a Gatorade," he says, biting his lip as he stares at me. "Then we're doing that again."

CHAPTER 25

EVAN

"So there's something I need to tell you," Shelley says after our waiter seats us at a table overlooking the water. It was her choice to have dinner at this upscale restaurant, and as I pick up the menu and get a look at the prices, I'm already assuming I'll be the one footing the bill.

More than that, I'm now suspicious as hell, because any time my mother starts a sentence with "there's something I need to tell you," it's usually followed by the confession that she's skipping town again, or she's broke and needs cash. This is only the second time I've seen her since agreeing to give her another chance; last week we had lunch near the budget hotel where she works in housekeeping. She didn't hit me up for money during that meetup, but I shouldn't have presumed it'd be a lasting trend.

Catching my wary expression, she quickly waves a hand to dismiss my concerns. "No, no, it's nothing bad. I promise." But she doesn't elaborate. Her cheeks turn a little pink.

"What is it?" I push, only to be interrupted by our server, who returns to take our drink orders.

Shelley requests a sparkling water. I ask for a pale ale, which could end up being a risky move depending on Shelley's news. This past week, though, I've been testing myself to see if I can live that cheesy motto I gave Gen at the party last week: *Learn to embrace moderation*. I'd never push alcohol on Genevieve when she's hell-bent on sobriety, but, personally, I'd like to be able to have a beer or two at poker night without worrying about taking it too far.

"You know how I've always loved doing my hair and makeup and that kind of stuff?" Shelley shifts awkwardly in her chair, one hand fidgeting with her water glass. "Pretty good at it too."

"Yeah . . . ?" I don't know where she's going with this.

"So, well, I was talking to Raya . . . you know, that coworker I was telling you about last week?"

I nod. "Right. The chick with the psycho toddler who killed their goldfish."

Shelley sputters with laughter. "Evan! I told you, baby, that was an accident. Cassidy's only three. She didn't know fish can't breathe out of water."

"Sounds like something a psychopath would say."

My mom lets out a loud snort that causes the couple in the neighboring table to glare at us with deep frowns. The woman is wearing a string of pearls and a high-necked silk blouse, while the man's rocking a polka-dot ascot. I'm surprised they don't go all out and shush us. They look like shushers.

Shelley and I exchange an eye roll, a moment of shared humor that makes me falter for a beat. This is a whole new mother-son experience for us. I mean, having dinner on the waterfront, exchanging conspiratorial looks about the uptight patrons next to us. Laughing together. It's surreal.

Yet I don't entirely hate it.

"*Anyway*," Shelley says, picking up her glass. She takes a quick sip. "Not sure if I mentioned it before, but Raya has a second job. Works at a hair salon on the weekends. And yesterday, she tells me her salon's opening a second location and is gonna have a bunch of chairs available to rent."

"Chairs?"

"Yeah, that's how it works in the industry. The stylists rent the chair from the salon." She takes a breath. "I think I wanna do it."

I wrinkle my brow. "What? Become a hairdresser?"

Shelley nods earnestly.

"Okay. Don't you need some kind of degree for that? Or a certificate at the very least?"

Her cheeks turn even redder. If I'm reading her right, she looks embarrassed. "I, um, enrolled in cosmetology school. Fees for the first semester are due at the end of the week, and I start next Monday."

"Oh." I nod slowly, waiting for the rest.

I wait for: *But I'm a little short on funds, baby, so can you . . . ?*

Or: *I'm gonna have to quit this housekeeping gig to focus all my attention on school, which means I'll need a place to crash . . . ?*

I stare at her and wait . . . but it doesn't come.

"What?" Shelley's face turns anxious. "What is it, baby? You think it's a bad idea?"

"No. Not at all." I clear my throat and try to paste on an encouraging smile. "It sounds great. It's just . . ."

She gives a knowing look. "You thought I was gonna hit you up for cash."

"Uh. Well. Yes."

Regret flickers through her eyes. "I mean, you have every right to think the worst of me. But let me tell ya, when you're not blowing every paycheck on booze? The savings are out of this world."

I grin wryly. "I bet."

"I've got enough saved up for the first semester," she assures me. "And the classes are at night, so I don't have to quit my gig at the hotel. It's all good, baby. I promise." She picks up her menu. "What looks good? I'm thinking the mussels. My treat, by the way."

Luckily, her head is buried in the menu, so I'm able to wipe the shock from my face before she sees it. Forget surreal—this is downright miraculous. Who is this woman and what has she done with my mother?

I continue to battle my astonishment as we order our meals and proceed to enjoy a really nice dinner. I'm not naïve enough to dive right into the She's Changed camp, but I'm willing to dip in a toe or two. The conversation flows easily. There's no tension, no uncomfortable silences. The only time we come close to one is when she brings up Cooper, but I brush off the subject by saying, "Let's not go there," and we move on.

"You didn't tell me Genevieve is back home," Shelley says, her tone tentative as she watches me devour my surf and turf.

"Yeah," I answer between bites. "She came back for her mom's funeral and stuck around to help Ronan out at the stone yard."

"I was sorry to hear about her momma. I know they weren't close, and God knows Laurie wasn't the easiest woman to get along with, but it can't be easy for Genevieve."

"You know Gen. She's resilient."

Shelley smiles. "Oh, that girl's a fighter." She eyes me from across the table. "You gonna marry her?"

The question catches me so off-guard I choke on a scallop. Coughing wildly, I scramble for my water glass, while the jerk couple at the next table glower at me for the disruption.

"Gee," I croak after I've cleared the obstruction, glowering right back at them. "So sorry to disturb you with my near-death experience."

The woman huffs and honest-to-God clutches her pearls.

My mom is trying not to laugh. "Evan," she warns.

I gulp down some more water before picking up my fork again. "To answer your question," I say, lowering my voice, "I'm pretty sure Gen isn't interested in marrying me."

"Bullsh—nonsense," Shelley corrects herself, shooting a

glance at the judgey table, because God forbid we upset the Pearl Clutcher. "You two are meant to be together. I knew from the second you started dating that you'd get married someday and live happily ever after and all that."

"Uh-huh. I'm sure you knew from the *second* we started dating."

"It's true," she insists. "Ask your uncle. I told Levi my prediction, and he did that thing he does—you know, that half sigh, half grumble—because he knows my predictions always come true." She smiles smugly. "I called it with Levi and Tim, much as he hates to admit it. And I knew it with your brother too, when I met his new girlfriend. Mark my words, he's gonna marry her."

I don't doubt that Cooper and Mac are endgame. But that doesn't mean I'm ready to accept that my mom—who couldn't keep her own marriage together, not to mention all her subsequent relationships—is some kind of love clairvoyant.

"I don't think Gen's as confident as you are in our future," I say ruefully.

Hell, I can barely convince Gen to spend the night, let alone agree to date me again. Since the bonfire, she's been over at my place nearly every night. If I didn't know any better, I'd think she was using me for sex. But it's a lot more than that. She doesn't bail the moment we recover from our respective orgasms. She stays to cuddle. She takes Daisy for walks with me. She even dropped off dinner for me a couple times.

But whenever I push her to define what this is, she clams up. Tells me not to overthink it. So of course, all I do is think about it.

"Then give her confidence," Shelley says with a shrug. "You want her back, yeah?"

"Oh yeah," I sigh.

"Then keep working at it."

BAD GIRL REPUTATION • 235

"Trust me, I'm trying." Now I groan. "But she made it clear she's not looking to be my girlfriend again and that all we're doing is fucking."

"Ahem!" comes an incensed cry. It's Husband Pearl Clutcher. "Is it too much to ask to enjoy our meals without being surrounded by filthy language?"

I open my mouth to retort, but my mother beats me to it.

Eyes gleaming with irritation, she addresses the other table by jabbing a finger toward the man. "Hey, mister, you wanna talk about filth? You've been checking out my rack since the moment I sat down. And you"—she directs that at the wife—"don't think I didn't see you slipping your phone number to that handsome young stud of a waiter when your hubby was in the john."

I snicker into my hand.

"Now, I'm trying to have a conversation with my son, so how 'bout you two Nosy Nellies focus on your own boring lives and mind your own damn business?"

That shuts them both up.

Shelley lifts a brow when she sees me grinning. "What? I might've turned a new leaf, but you can't expect me to always turn the other cheek. Even Jesus had his limits, baby."

I'm feeling oddly giddy as I cross the bridge and drive back to the Bay after dinner with Shelley. I can't lie—that wasn't awful. In fact, I . . . truly had a good time. Who would've thought?

The instinct to tell my brother about it is so strong that I end up veering off the road home, turning left instead of right. No, I can't risk seeing Cooper right now. He'll just ask why I'm in such a good mood, at which point I'll have to lie, and he'll see through the lie because of twin telepathy, and then we'll get in a fight.

So I drive to Gen's house instead. Parking on the curb out

front, I hop off my bike and fish my phone out of my pocket. I shoot off a quick text to Gen.

Me: *I'm standing outside your place like some lovesick stalker. Debating whether to throw rocks at your window or just knock on the front door.*

She responds almost instantly.

Her: *Use the door, you heathen. We're adults now, remember?*

I grin at the phone. True. But this is definitely a first, I reflect, as I tread up the front walk to the door, which swings open before I can ring the bell. I'm met by the sight of Genevieve's dad, who startles when he finds me standing there.

"Evan," he says gruffly, nodding in greeting. His gaze takes in my outfit. "You wearing khakis?"

"Uh. Yeah." I shove my hands in the pockets of said khakis. "I had a thing in the city."

He nods again. "Gen's upstairs. I was just heading out to meet your uncle for a beer, actually."

"Oh, nice. Tell him I said hey."

"Renos are looking great," Gen's dad adds, gesturing in the vague direction of inside. "The new kitchen cabinets turned out nice."

"Thanks." I feel a little burst of pride, because I installed those cabinets myself.

"Anyway." Ronan eyes me again. "Glad you and Gen are getting along again." He claps my shoulder before striding off toward the pickup truck in the driveway.

I let myself in, half expecting one of Gen's million brothers to intercept me, but the house is quiet as I head for the stairs. Last time I was here, the place was jam-packed with mourners and reverberating with hushed conversation. Tonight, all I hear are the creaks and groans of the old house, including the very loud protest of the second step from the top when I walk over it. Gen and I always made sure to skip over it whenever we snuck in after curfew, but tonight there's no need for stealth.

Gen's lying on her side reading a book when I enter her room. My gaze feasts on her sexy body and the curtain of black hair cascading over one shoulder. She looks up at my entrance.

"Are you wearing khakis?" she demands.

"Yup." I throw myself on the bed, causing her paperback to bounce on the mattress.

She grabs it before it falls over the edge. "Jerk."

Grinning, I clasp both hands behind my neck and get comfortable. Gen smiles in amusement as she watches me kick off my shoes and stretch out my legs. I'm too damn big for this bed, my feet hanging off the end.

"You're in a good mood," she remarks.

"I am," I agree.

"Are you going to elaborate?"

"Had dinner with Shelley tonight."

"You did?" Gen sounds surprised. "You didn't mention anything about it when we spoke this morning. Was it a last-minute thing?"

"Not really."

"So why didn't you tell me?" When I shrug, she pokes me in the rib. Hard. "Evan."

I glance over at her. She's sitting cross-legged beside me, her astute blue eyes studying my face. "I don't know. I guess I didn't say anything just in case she bailed."

Gen nods in understanding. "Ah. That's why you keep telling me about these meetings after the fact. You don't want to get your hopes up beforehand."

She gets it.

"Honestly?" I say quietly. "Every time I drive to Charleston to see her, I've given it fifty-fifty odds on whether she'll show." A lump forms in my throat. "So far she hasn't missed a date."

Gen moves closer to curl up beside me, resting her palm on my abdomen. The sweet scent of her hair wafts up to my nose. "I'm glad. And I hope to God she keeps it up. My mom's gone, but yours still has a chance to redeem herself."

I wrap my arm around her shoulder and plant a kiss atop her head. "I ran into your dad at the front door, by the way. He was happy to see me."

"Uh-huh."

"Face it, Fred. Your dad's always loved me."

"There's no accounting for taste."

"He said he's glad you and I are getting along again." I slide my hand down to lightly pinch her ass. "So, the way I see it, all that's left to do now is make it official."

"Or . . ."

She trails off enticingly and rolls over—directly on top of me. I'm semi-hard almost instantly, and her tiny smile tells me she notices.

"We can quit talking and take advantage of this empty house," she finishes, and then she's lifting my shirt up and kissing my chest, and my brain short-circuits.

A groan slips out when she undoes the button of my khakis.

"Gen," I protest, because I know she's trying to distract me with sex. And it's working.

She peers up at me with big, innocent eyes. "It's okay, baby. I don't mind if you want to be loud."

She's throwing my own words back at me, uttered the night of the bonfire before I spent hours making her gasp and moan and scream. I was relentless in my seduction that night. But now it's my turn to be weak and helpless, to fight for control as she leaves a trail of hot kisses along my stomach on her way down south.

When she takes my cock in her mouth, I give up on resisting. There's no better feeling in the world than having Gen swallow me up. She curls one delicate hand around my shaft and sucks me deep, while her other hand strokes my chest, her nails scraping along my sensitized flesh.

I give an upward thrust, pleasure gathering inside me, pulse quickening with each languid swipe of her tongue. And as I tangle my fingers in her hair and rock against her wet, eager mouth, I tell myself that we can talk after. Later. When my heart isn't hammering against my ribs, and my balls aren't drawn tight with need.

But we never get around to having that talk.

CHAPTER 26

EVAN

Weeks later, I lie in my bed while Gen is getting dressed. It's past noon, the two of us having slept in after staying up late with Mac and Cooper in a Mario Kart death match that damn near came to blows. Girls are such sore losers.

"I told you I should have gone home last night," she grumbles.

"You see how screwed up this is," I answer, watching as she shimmies a tiny pair of cutoff shorts up her long, tan legs. I'm still here with a semi and she's running off to *him*.

"And if you'd let me go home last night, we wouldn't be having this conversation." She ties her hair up in a ponytail and walks over to sift through the sheets for her phone.

"Stay."

Gen lifts her head to glare at me. "Stop it."

"I'm serious. Blow him off and let me go down on you instead."

"Isn't your Little Brother coming over for a barbecue today?"

"Yeah, in like an hour. Think of all the orgasms I can give you until then."

She finds her phone tucked under my back and snatches it.

I blink innocently. "How'd that get there?"

Gen rolls her eyes before straightening up and hunting for her shirt. "You knew this was the deal. Stop acting like I changed the rules."

The deal being that for the last several weeks, Gen and I have been going at it like it's the end of the world, while she's still dating Deputy Dumbfuck. Now she's jumping out of my bed and right into his car. How is this happening?

"Guess I thought there may have been some implied amendments to that deal after you begged me to spank you last night, but sure."

She pauses, after pulling her top on, to direct a frown my way. "And if you want to keep those spanking privileges, mind your mouth."

For no good reason, an unbidden image of her going down on the dweeb in his cruiser flashes behind my eyes. My dick goes soft as I shake the thought. This is why I don't ask. Very little could stop me from running up on him at the gas station and flicking a lit match his way.

And yet . . . "Are you sleeping with him?" I find myself blurting out.

Gen looks at me, tilting her head with sympathy as she comes to sit on the edge of the bed. She brushes her lips over mine in a fleeting caress. "No."

At least there's that.

"We haven't even kissed."

Relief floods my chest. "So then what are you getting out of it?"

With a frustrated sigh, she stands and grabs her keys from the nightstand. "Let's not, okay?"

"I'm serious." I sit up. "What are you getting out of it?"

She doesn't answer, and that's when I realize she doesn't have to. I already *know* the answer. We both do. There's only one reason she's continuing to date Harrison despite the fact they haven't so much as kissed—it's her way of keeping that final bit of distance between us. Keeping me at arm's length.

Now I'm the one sighing in frustration. "What's it going to take to make this official between us? I'm done messing around."

"Done, huh?"

"You know what I mean." I know this chick well enough to understand an ultimatum is the quickest way to drive her away. And that's the last thing I want to do.

We might've had a rocky start when she first moved back to the Bay, but the path is smooth now. It's as if all the bad parts of us, the fighting and jealousy and chasing highs—it's morphed into something else. Something softer. Don't get me wrong, the passion's still there. The soul-deep need to be together, to lay ourselves completely bare and raw, is stronger than ever. But there's something different about us now. About her. About me.

"I want us back together for real," I tell her. "What's the holdup?"

Gen leans against my dresser and stares at the floor. The summer's almost over, and still this question hangs between us. All this time I thought we were of the same mind, moving in the same direction—together. Now, every second she spends deciding what not to say, the fracture gets wider.

"You still don't trust me," I answer for her. My tone is grim.

"I do trust you."

"Not enough." Frustration jams in my throat. "What do I have to do to prove myself?"

"It's hard," she says, anguish drawing lines across her face. "I have a lifetime of instinct about you that says there's no way Evan Hartley gave himself a complete personality makeover in one summer. Yeah, you didn't chase Randall off with an ax and you're not getting wasted every night, but I guess I'm still hesitant to believe you've changed. Feels too easy."

"Has it occurred to you there's something more important to me in this room than drinking and fighting?"

"I know you want this to work." Most of the agitation leaves her voice. "But you're not the only one I have doubts about. Every day I question whether I can trust myself. How much I've really changed. Put the two of us back together, and maybe we realize this condition is temporary and we end up right back in our old roles."

I go to her, holding her. Because right here, the two of us, is the only thing that's ever made sense to me. And whatever she tells herself, I know she feels it too.

"Trust me, baby. Give us a chance to be good for each other. How am I ever going to convince you we can if you won't try?"

Her phone buzzes in her pocket. She gives me a contrite shrug as I release her to answer it.

"Trina," she says, wrinkling her forehead.

I haven't heard that name in a while. Trina went to high school with us, though she was more a friend of the girls in our crew than of Cooper or me. If I remember right, she moved not long after graduation. But her and Gen used to be tight. Two peas in a chaos pod.

"She's in town for the weekend," she reads aloud. "Wants to grab a drink." Gen swipes her finger across the screen to delete the text, then shoves the phone back in her pocket.

"You should go."

She lets out a sarcastic laugh. "Pass. Last time she came home for a visit, I got piss-drunk and stormed into Deputy Randall's house in the middle of the night to scream at his wife about what a creep she married."

"Oh."

"Yeah."

An idea springs to my mind. "Go anyway."

Her skeptical gaze says there'd better be more to that suggestion. And as I roll it over in my head, the plan starts to make more sense. Maybe the thing she needs to finally trust herself is the only thing she fears more than me. The thing that drove her out of town in the first place.

"Treat it as a test," I explain. "If you can behave yourself around the girl who once slipped acid to the girls' volleyball coach in the middle of a match, I'd say you conquered your demons."

Sure, it might be a little hairbrained, but I'm desperate here. One way or another, I need to get Gen on my side. The longer we stay trapped in relationship limbo, the more she gets used to the idea of us not being a couple. And the further away she slips.

"A test," she echoes dubiously.

I nod. "The final exam to your journey of reform. Show yourself you can spend an evening with Trina and not burn anything down."

Hesitation lingers on her gorgeous face, but at least she's not shooting down the idea outright. "I'll think on it," she finally says. Then, to my chagrin, she heads out my bedroom door. "Talk to you later. Harrison's waiting."

Riley shows up around one o'clock with a rack of marinated ribs and another homemade pie courtesy of Aunt Liz. God bless that woman. I lead him out to the back deck, my mouth watering as I inhale the aroma of meat and pastry. My two favorite things.

"How's your week been?" I ask him as we prep the barbecue.

He shrugs. "Meh."

"You looking forward to school starting in a few weeks?"

"What do you think?"

I grin. "You're right. Dumb question." I always hated it too, watching with dread as the calendar neared closer and closer to September.

"But," he says, brightening slightly, "Hailey's family is coming back and they'll be here till Labor Day."

"Hailey . . . That's the girl whose number you got at Big Molly's, right?" Riley went out with her a few times over the summer, but every time I asked for details, he'd clammed up.

Today, he's a bit more forthcoming. "Yeah. We've been texting since she went back home." He shoves his hands in the pockets of his board shorts, then removes them and starts fidgeting with a pair of metal tongs.

"What's going on? You're acting all bouncy."

"Bouncy?"

"Fidgety. Whatever. Are you nervous about seeing her, is that it?"

"Sorta?"

"But you guys have already gone out before," I remind him. "What's there to be nervous about?"

"We played mini golf and went to the movies a couple times. Oh, and ice cream on the boardwalk. So, like, four times. But we never—" He stops abruptly.

I narrow my eyes at him, but he avoids my gaze. He's antsy again, now pretending to check the temperature on the barbecue like some grilling expert, when we both know he's never grilled anything a day in his life.

"You never what?" Then it dawns on me. I stifle a curse. "Aw man, nope, don't tell me. I don't need to hear about how you're planning on having sex. Your aunt would murder—"

"Jeez!" he yelps. "We're not having sex, you idiot."

I'm swamped with relief, although a tad intrigued by the genuine shock on his face, as if he can't fathom the idea of sleeping with the chick. Riley's fourteen, the age I lost my virginity, but I suppose not everyone is an early bloomer like I was.

"I just wanna kiss her," he adds, the confession coming out as an embarrassed mumble.

"Oh. *Oh.* Okay." Kissing? I can handle a chat about kissing. There's no way Aunt Liz can be mad at me for that, right? "Well. Judging by your tomato face, I take it you've never done it before?"

He awkwardly jerks his head from side to side, a reluctant *no*.

"Dude, you don't need to be embarrassed. Lots of guys your age haven't kissed anyone." I lean against the railing of the deck, slanting my head. "So what do you want to know? How much tongue is too much tongue? Whether to grab her boobs when you do it?"

He squawks out a laugh, but some of the blush has left his face. Relaxing, he wanders over to stand beside me. The mouth-watering smell of the ribs cooking on the grill floats toward us.

"I'm just, like, not sure how to go for it. Like, do I say something beforehand?" He rubs his forehead with the back of his hand. "What if I lean in and she's not ready for it, and our heads smash together and I break her nose?"

I choke down a laugh, because I know he wouldn't appreciate being laughed at during such a sensitive topic. "I'm almost certain that won't happen. But yeah, you don't want to just go for it while she's mid-sentence or anything. There's a thing called consent. So, read the moment, you know? Wait for a lull in the conversation, gauge her expression and look for the signals."

"What signals?"

"Like, if she's licking her lips, it usually means she's thinking about kissing you. If she's staring at your mouth, also a good sign. Actually, that's the way in," I tell him, pushing away from the railing and heading for the cooler near the door. "Alright, listen up. This is what you gotta do."

He trails after me, accepting the soda I hand him. For myself I get a beer, twisting off the cap and tossing it in the plastic bucket on the deck. I return to the wooden railing and hop up to sit atop it.

"So at the end of the date," I continue, "or in the middle, or whenever you gather up the courage to do it, this is what you do—you stare at her lips. For like five seconds."

Riley sputters out a laugh. "That's so creepy!"

"It's really not. Stare at her lips until she gets all awkward and says, *why are you looking at me like that?* Or some variation of that question." When he opens his mouth to protest, I interject, "Trust me, she'll say it. And when she does, you say, *because I really want to kiss you right now—can I?* So now she's prepared, right? And based on her response, you go from there."

"What if her response is no?"

"Then you handle the rejection like a man, tell her you had a great summer with her, and wish her luck on her future endeavors."

I can't help but marvel at the sheer maturity I'm exuding. If only Gen were here to see it.

"But for what it's worth, a chick doesn't go out with someone four times if she's not interested," I assure him.

"Truth," Cooper's voice echoes from the sliding door. "For once, my brother's not talking out of his ass."

Riley's gaze snaps to the door. His jaw falling open, he glances at Cooper, then me, then Coop again, and finally me. "Holy shit, you didn't tell me you guys were identical," he accuses.

I roll my eyes. "I said we were twins. Figured you'd extrapolate from there."

Grinning, Coop extends a hand toward my Little Brother. "Hey, I'm Cooper. It's nice to finally meet you."

Riley's still blinking like an owl, astounded at our twinship. "Wow. It's scary how alike you look. If you weren't wearing different clothes, I don't think I'd be able to tell you apart."

"Not many people can," I say with a shrug.

"What about girls? Like, your girlfriends? Did they ever get you guys mixed up?" He's utterly fascinated.

"Sometimes," Coop answers as he grabs a beer for himself. He strides toward the barbecue, lifts the lid, and groans happily. "Oh man, those ribs look amazing." He turns back to Riley. "Serious girlfriends usually know the difference, though. My girl says she can tell us apart by our footsteps."

"I don't believe that for a second," I crack, sipping my beer. Yes, Mac can tell us apart, but from the sounds we make while we walk? I call bullshit.

Coop flashes a smug smile. "It's true."

Beyond his shoulder, I glimpse Mac through the open sliding doors. She just entered the kitchen and is removing items from the fridge. Then she starts preparing a sandwich at the counter, her back to us.

I slide off the railing. "I request permission to test that theory."

Cooper follows my gaze, smirks, and nods magnanimously. "Go for it."

Utilizing the stealth mode I'd perfected after years of sneaking in and out of houses and girls' bedrooms, I creep into the kitchen. Mac is focused on arranging cheese slices on her bread, singing softly to herself. Only when I'm close enough that she won't have much time to turn around, I walk normally and come up behind her.

Wrapping both hands around her waist, I nuzzle her neck and speak in my perfect, uncanny Cooper voice. "Hey, babe, your ass looks good enough to eat in those shorts."

An outraged cry fills the kitchen as she spins around and tries to knee me in the groin. "What the fuck, Evan! Why?"

Luckily, I capture her knee with both hands before it connects with the family jewels. Then I dart backward and raise my hands in surrender. From the deck, loud laughter greets my ears.

"Told you!" Cooper calls out.

"What is *wrong* with you!" Mac huffs.

"It was just an experiment," I protest, keeping my distance. "Question, though. How did you know it was me?"

"Your footsteps," she growls. "You walk like it's a game."

"What does that even mean?"

"Evan, please get out of my sight before I punch you in your stupid face."

I go back outside with a defeated sag to my shoulders. "She says I walk like it's a game," I inform my brother, who nods as if that makes any goddamn sense.

Riley, as usual, is in hysterics. Seems like all I do is make this kid bust out in laughter.

But maybe that's a good thing.

It ends up being a good day. Good food, good company, good everything. Even Cooper is in high spirits. He doesn't get on my case about Gen or whatever else disappoints him about me, not even once. He's, dare I say it, downright chipper. He and Mac face off against me and Riley in a game of beach volleyball, and when Liz comes to pick Riley up around four o'clock, he looks bummed to leave.

But in my life, "good" is a fleeting concept. Which is why I'm not surprised when later, while I'm on the beach with Mac and Cooper watching Daisy chase seagulls, I'm faced with a new dilemma.

Shelley's blowing up my phone about random stuff in between trying to set up another date. I usually don't spend much time on my phone, so answering the barrage of texts has Cooper eyeing me in suspicion. Normally I'd just turn it off and ignore the messages until later, but I've found Shelley gets impatient. If I don't answer, she goes into a panic spiral, thinking I've blown her off.

I'm worried she might impulsively drive out here, and I can't have that.

It's still weird, spending time with her like a normal mom-and-son duo. Talking about our days and pop culture. All the while delicately trying to avoid mention of Cooper to stave off the inevitable question of when he might join us at one of our meetups. I hate lying to my brother, but Cooper's a long way from ready to know about any of this.

Playing with Daisy, he shouts something at me about pizza for dinner. I nod absently, while Shelley is telling me there's a stray cat hanging around outside her work, and she's gotten it in her head she's going to take it home. Which makes me think she probably should have had to practice with a pet before having twins, but what the hell do I know?

A chewed-up, sandy tennis ball suddenly lands in my lap. Then a blur of golden fur is flying at my face. Daisy barrels into me to snatch the ball before running away again.

"Hey! What the hell?" I sputter.

Cooper stands over me, all puffed up and bothered. "You talking to Gen?"

Not this again. "No. Fuck off."

"You've been hunched over that thing ever since Riley left. Who is it?"

"Since when do you care?"

"Leave him alone," shouts Mac, who's still tossing the ball with Daisy at the tide line.

Cooper does the opposite—he yanks the phone from my hand. Instantly, I'm on my feet, wrestling him for it.

"Why are you such a drama queen?" I get one hand on the phone before he sweeps my leg and we end up rolling around in the sand.

"Grow up," Cooper grunts back. He digs his elbow into my

kidney, still reaching for the phone while we toss around. "What are you hiding?"

"Come on, quit it." Mac stands over us now with Daisy barking like she's waiting to get tagged in.

Fed up, I throw sand in his face and climb to my feet, brushing myself off. I shrug in response to Mac's looks of exasperation.

"He started it."

She rolls her eyes.

"You're up to something." Shaking sand out of his hair, Cooper stands up and snarls at me like he's ready for round two. "What is it?"

"Eat shit."

"Quit it, will you?" Mac, ever the peacemaker, utterly fails to get through to him. "You're both being ridiculous."

I don't particularly care that Coop's suspicious or annoyed. It's whatever. But he's got this perpetual sense of entitlement to know and have an opinion on everything I do—and I'm so over it. Over him acting out his hang-ups on me. My twin brother playing a poor approximation of a father I never asked for.

"Can we move on?" Mac says in frustration, glancing between the two of us. "Please?"

But it's too late now. I'm pissed, and the only thing that will make me feel better is rubbing it in his self-righteous face. "It's Shelley."

Cooper comes up short. His face is expressionless for a moment, as if he isn't sure he heard me right. Then he smirks, shaking his head. "Right."

I throw my phone at him.

He looks at the screen, then at me. All humor and disbelief has been replaced by cold, quiet rage. "Your brain fall out of your head?"

"She's getting better."

"Jesus Christ, Evan. You get how stupid you sound?"

Rather than answer, I glance at Mac. "This is why I didn't tell him."

When I turn back, Cooper's up in my face, all but standing on my toes. "That woman was ready to run off with our life savings and you just, what, go crawling back to Mommy the first chance you get?"

I set my jaw and back away from him. "I didn't ask you to like it. She's my mother. And I'm not kidding—she's making a real effort, man. She has a steady job, her own apartment. She enrolled in beauty school to get her hairdressing certificate. Hasn't had so much as a sip of booze in months."

"Months? You've been doing this behind my back for *months*? And you actually believe her crap?"

I swallow a tired sigh. "She's trying, Coop."

"You're pathetic." When he spits out the words, it's like he's had them sitting in his mouth for twenty years. "The time for getting over your mommy issues was when you stopped sleeping with a night-light."

"Dude, I'm not the one flying off the handle at the mention of her."

"Look at what you're doing." He advances on me, and I take another step back, only because I was just praising my self-restraint to Gen earlier. "One drunk, deadbeat woman walks out on you, so you go fall in love with another one. Man, you can't hang on to either one of them, and you never will."

My fist itches to put a dent in Cooper's face. He can say what he wants about our mother. He's earned his anger the honest way. But no one talks like that about Gen while I'm around.

"Because you're my blood, I'm going to pretend I didn't hear that," I tell him, my voice tight with restraint. "But if you feel like you got too many teeth in your mouth, go ahead and try that shit again."

"Hey, hey." Mac wedges herself between us and manages to walk Coop back a couple paces, though his glare still says he's thinking about my offer. "Both of you take it down a notch." She puts both hands on Cooper's chest until he drops his gaze to hers. A few breaths later, she's got his attention. "I know you don't want to hear this, but maybe give Evan the benefit of the doubt."

"We tried that last time." He flicks his gaze to me. "How'd that turn out?"

"Okay," she says quietly. "But this is now. If Evan says Shelley's making an effort, why not trust him? You could go have a look for yourself. If you'd be open to meeting her."

He tears away from Mac. "Oh, fuck off. Both of you. This ganging up stuff isn't cute most of the time, but about this?" Cooper levels Mac with a withering glare. "Mind your goddamn business."

At that, he storms off, marching back up to the house.

Unfortunately, this isn't the first time he's lost his cool over Shelley, and it's not likely to be the last. Mac has more experience with his tantrums than she should. Which is to say, she isn't fazed.

"I'll work on him," she promises me with a sad smile before going after him.

Well. No one walked away bloody. We might call that a success, under the circumstances.

I don't hold out much hope for Mac's mission, though. Cooper's been burned one too many times, so I can't say his reaction is entirely unwarranted. In our family history, Shelley's done more wrong than right, the worst of it practiced on Coop, as he was always the one trying to protect me from her latest betrayal. His self-imposed, older-by-three-minutes big brother complex insisted it was his job to shield me from the awful truth: that our mom was unreliable at best and downright malicious at worst.

So I get it. Because now it feels like I've betrayed him, thrown all the brothering back in his face to take her side. But the thing is, while he reached his tolerance for her a long time ago, I've still got some left. And I have to believe people can change. I *need* to believe it.

Otherwise, what the hell am I doing with my life?

CHAPTER 27

GENEVIEVE

Trina is a piece of work. We met in detention in the sixth grade and became fast friends. She enjoyed skipping class and smoking cigarettes in the baseball dugout as much as I did, so really, it was inevitable that we'd cross paths. And while I have more good memories of Trina than bad, I'm still nervous when I walk into the bar to meet her. Even when we were kids, she always had an infectious quality about her. Like she was having so much fun, you wanted in on whatever she was getting up to. Insatiable and alluring.

Evan's right, though. If I can survive Trina's temptations, I'll most definitely be cured.

"Damn it, Gen."

Winding through the crowded high-top tables, I turn at the familiar voice. Trina sits at a table against the wall, an empty highball and a bottle of beer in front of her. She hops to her feet and gives me a tight hug.

"I hoped you'd gotten hideous since the last time I saw you," she says, brushing my hair off my shoulder. "Would it have killed you to sprout some heinous zits for the occasion?"

"My bad," I laugh.

"Sit down, slag." She looks over my shoulder and waves for a waitress. "Catch me up. What the hell have you been up to?"

We didn't really talk after I left Avalon Bay. As I did with most of this town, I quit cold turkey. Other than some texts here and there, I'd kept my distance, even muting her on social media so I couldn't be tempted by her exploits.

"As it turns out, I start a new job soon. Cooper's girlfriend is reopening The Beacon Hotel. I'm the new manager."

"For real?" She's incredulous at first. Then, apparently realizing there isn't a punchline coming, she throws back a swig of her beer. "That means the next time I come to town, you're hooking me up with a room. I think me and my dear mother have exceeded our quota of quality time."

I grin. "Didn't you get in last night?"

"Exactly." Her eyes widen. "Shit, I'm sorry. I heard about your mom. You okay?"

It seems like ages ago now, though it's only been a few months. The reminders of Mom are fewer and further between. "Yeah," I say honestly. "I'm good. Thank you."

"I'd have been at the funeral if I'd known. But I only heard recently."

I don't think she means them to, but the words come out like an accusation. She'd have been there if I'd bothered to tell her, is the subtext. If I hadn't all but ghosted her a year ago. But that's probably my own guilt talking.

"It's fine, really. Was mostly a family thing. She didn't want a big fuss." Least of all from her kids.

Trina gets a menacing glint in her eye as she sips her drink. "You seeing much of Evan lately?"

I swallow a sigh. For just one night, can't something be about anything but him? My head's been on backwards since I came back to town. I'm my favorite self when I'm with him—and also my worst. Everything at both extremes wrapped up in this volatile cocktail we become.

"Sometimes, I guess. I don't know. It's complicated."

"You've been using that same line since we were fifteen."

And I don't feel much better equipped than I was then.

"So what's up?" With another mouthful of beer, she plasters on her usual irreverence when she reads the heaviness closing in. "You back for good now?"

"Looks that way." It's strange. I don't remember making the decision to stay. It just snuck up on me, the ties reattaching overnight while I slept. "Dad's selling the house, so I need to find a new place soon."

"I've given some thought to sticking around too."

I snort a laugh. "Why?"

Trina always hated this town. Or rather, the people. She loved her friends fiercely, the few she kept. Beyond that, she'd have lit a match and never looked back. Or so I thought.

We're briefly interrupted when the waitress finally makes it to our table. She looks young and flustered, a new hire struggling through the waning weeks of the summer crush. I order a club soda and ignore Trina's judgmental eyebrow.

"I don't know. . . . This place is a drag," she says. "But it's home, I guess." There's something in the way her gaze drifts to the soggy coaster, the way her fingernail picks at the corners, that suggests a deeper explanation.

"How are things?" I ask carefully. "LA not agreeing with you these days?"

"Eh, you know me. I've got a four-second attention span. I think maybe I've seen and done everything worth doing in that city."

Only from Trina would I believe that. "You still working at the dispensary?" The least surprising part of her West Coast move was getting a job doing stuff that, around here, still gets you thrown in jail.

"Sometimes. Also bartending a little. And this guy I know, he's a photographer, I help him out now and then, too."

"This guy . . ." I watch as she dodges eye contact. "Is that a thing?"

"Sometimes."

The conundrum of Trina is a bitter one. Few others I know manage to suck as much out of every minute of their lives as she does—eyes open and arms wide, try anything once, twice as much—and yet, at the same time, be so utterly unfulfilled. There's a hole in the bottom of her soul, where everything good leaks out and all the worst, thickest, blackest muck clings to the sides.

"He's an artist," she says by way of an explanation. "His work is important to him."

Which is the kind of thing people say when they're making excuses for why their needs aren't being met.

"Anyway, I didn't tell him I was coming here. Probably still hasn't noticed my stuff is gone."

A wave of sympathy swells in my chest. I felt like that for a long time. I kept grasping for anything at all to satisfy me, whether it was good for me or not. How could I know unless I found out for myself, though? It takes a lot of trial and error to realize all the good advice we ignored along the way.

When our drinks arrive, she drains the last of her previous beer and gets a start on the next. "Enough chat," she announces, running a hand through her hair. She's wearing it shorter these days, which gives her even more of a tough girl vibe. "I'm bored with myself."

"Okay. How shall we entertain ourselves?"

"If I remember right, you owe me a rematch. Rack 'em up, West."

I follow her to the pool table, where we split two games and call it a draw. From there, we barhop down the boardwalk, with Trina ingesting a quantity of shots and beers that would kill a man twice her size.

It's a relief, actually. A taste of the old life without the accompanying blackout. And it's incredible the things you notice when you're not wasted. Like the guy who hits on Trina at the second bar. She thinks he's twenty-five, but really, he's pushing forty with a spray tan, Botox, and a tan line from his missing wedding ring. Still, he's good for a couple drinks before she instigates him up to the karaoke mic for shits and giggles, as if he's her personal court jester. I'd feel bad for the dude if I wasn't sure there's a kid at home somewhere, whose college fund will be a little lighter after this midlife crisis.

"He was not forty," she insists too loudly when I inform her, as we trudge down the boardwalk in search of our next venue. "It was the lighting!"

"Babe, he had white chest hairs."

Trina shudders, a tremble of revulsion that vibrates through each limb. She makes a dry gagging noise while I howl with laughter.

"No," she moans.

"Yes," I confirm between giggles.

"Well, where were you? Tell a girl next time. Throw up some hand signals or something."

"What's sign language for pendulous, sagging testicles?"

Now we're both doubling over in hysterics.

The boardwalk at night is a drag strip of lights and music. Shops with neon signs and bright window displays. People pouring out of bars with the competing soundtracks mingling in the humid salt air. Patio restaurants bursting with tourists and souvenir cups. Every dozen steps or so, a young guy is barking about two-for-one drinks or free cover.

"Live music," one of them says, shoving his arm out to give Trina a pale green flyer for the music venue around the corner. "No cover before midnight."

"Are you in a band?" A flicker of interest brightens her eyes.

Trina has this way about her. Flirtatious in a vaguely threatening manner. It's hysterical when she's had a little to drink. When she's had a lot, it's not dissimilar to a lit firecracker that's stalled. You stand there. Waiting. Watching. Certain the moment you try to intervene, it'll explode and take your fingers and eyebrows with it.

"Uh, yeah," he says, hiding his fear behind an alert smile. Some guys like the hot, scary ones, and some have a sense of self-preservation. "I play bass."

He's cute, in a Disney Channel punk rock sort of way. The kid who grew up with parents that encouraged his creative endeavors and put out a plate of fresh-baked cookies while he did home-work. I'll never understand the well-adjusted.

"Oh." Trina's carnivorous grin flattens to a grimace. "Well, no one's perfect."

We take the invitation, nonetheless, if only because it's the closest restroom that doesn't require a purchase in advance. To-gether, Trina and I stand in line down a dingy hallway covered in framed concert photographs and graffiti. It smells of cheap liquor, mildew, and perfume-scented sweat.

"You realize you've probably jinxed that poor guy, right?" I tell her.

"Please."

"Seriously. You just put ten years of bad mojo on him. What if he was supposed to become the next great American bassist? Now he's going to end up vacuuming baseboards at the Spit Shine car wash."

"The world needs bass players," she says. "But I can't be re-sponsible for their misplaced notions of fuckability."

"Paul McCartney played bass."

"That's like saying Santa is fuckable. That's nasty, Gen."

Six women stumble out of the single-toilet restroom, sloppy and laughing. Trina and I take our turn. She splashes water on her face while I pee.

After we've both finished up and washed our hands, Trina pulls a small compact out of her purse. Under it is a little plastic baggie of white powder. She dips her finger in to gather some in her nail and snort it up her nose. Takes another up the other nostril, then spreads the excess on her teeth, sucking them dry.

"Want a bump?" She offers the compact to me.

"I'm good."

Cocaine was never my vice. I smoked plenty and drank like a sailor. Dropped acid every now and then. But I was never tempted by the harder stuff.

"Oh, come on." She tries shoving it at me. "I haven't said anything all night, but your sobriety is starting to become a buzzkill."

I shrug. "I think you've got enough buzz for both of us."

Big saucer eyes plead with me. "Just one little hit. Then I'll shut up."

"But then who's going to stop you from going home with some middle-aged car salesman?"

"You make a good point, West." Backing off, she snaps the compact shut and drops it in her purse.

To each their own. Trina gets no judgment from me. We all have our coping mechanisms, and I'm in no position to fault anyone for theirs. Just not my bag.

"So this straight-edge thing," she muses as we exit the restroom and scout a good table for the show. "You serious about that?"

We spot a two-seater high-top beside the stage and make a beeline to snag it.

I nod slowly. "Yeah, I think so."

I'm rather proud of myself, in fact. A whole night together, and I've yet to hop on a table or steal a pedicab. I'm still having a good time, not once missing a drink. That's progress.

Lifting a flask from her purse, Trina nods. "Cheers to that, then. May your liver bring you many years of health and prosperity."

Hell, if Trina can accept the new me, maybe there's hope yet. Maybe I really can make this change stick, and I'm not simply fooling myself.

Our party swells during the concert. A group of friends we went to high school with wander by our table and pull up a few stools. Some, like Colby and Debra, I hadn't seen in years. When the second act of the night turns out to be a '90s one-hit-wonder cover band, the entire place goes bonkers, everyone singing slurred, slightly wrong lyrics at the tops of our lungs. We're all breathless and hoarse by the time Trina and the rest of the group go outside to the smoking patio, while I babysit her purse at the bar and order a very big glass of ice water. I pull out my phone to find a missed text from Evan earlier in the night.

Evan: *You haven't asked for bail yet. Good sign?*

I have to admit, he was right. Meeting up with Trina turned out to be an affirming experience. Hardly the catastrophe I'd worked it up to be in my head. But I'm definitely not going to tell him that. Evan doesn't need any ego stroking from me.

Me: *We're on 95 with a one-eyed bounty hunter and his pet wolverine hot on our trail. Send snacks.*

When I feel a hand tap me on the shoulder, I'm impressed

Evan managed to track us down. But then I turn around and am met with the dark, pleated polyester of a sheriff's deputy uniform and the potbelly of Rusty Randall.

"Genevieve West." He grabs my wrist and roughly jerks it behind my back. "You're under arrest."

My jaw drops. "Seriously? For what?"

I'm pulled off my stool, struggling to find my feet. People around us retreat, some taking out their phones to record. Camera flashes blind me while my brain stutters to understand what's happening.

"Possession of a controlled substance." He wrenches my other arm behind my back, where metal cuffs bite into my skin. Deputy Randall grabs Trina's purse, picking through it, until he pulls out the compact and opens it to reveal the baggie of cocaine.

"That's not even my purse!" I shout, my head spinning with the instinct to run or fight or . . . something. I look desperately at the door to the smoking patio.

Wrapping his hand around my biceps, he leans close to my ear and whispers, "Should've left town while you had the chance."

CHAPTER 28

GENEVIEVE

Outside, I'm pushed up against the side of Randall's car, my face to the window, while he runs his fat, sweaty hands down my arms, ribs, and legs.

"You're just loving this," I say through gritted teeth. "Pervert."

He takes my phone, keys, and ID from my pockets and throws them on the roof of the car with Trina's purse. "Know what your problem is, Genevieve? You don't appreciate discretion."

"The hell does that mean?"

"It was only a matter of time before you screwed up again." His fingers comb through my hair as though I've got some needles and maybe a bowie knife stashed in there. "I told you, I've got eyes everywhere."

"Then your snitches are even dumber than you are."

He chuckles cruelly. "Yet you're the one in cuffs."

As he finishes patting me down, I'm trying to figure out how someone would have known about the coke. The person Trina bought it from in town? A lucky guess? Either option feels equally unlikely. But then, who knows the shady deals Randall's cut? The man is as corrupt as they come.

It occurs to me, then, that at any point in the night when Trina and I were separated—while one of us went to the bar for another round or to the restroom alone—she might have done a bump in front of any number of witnesses. It only takes one of them to have seen us together.

He grabs a plastic bag from the trunk of his cruiser and throws my stuff and Trina's purse inside. Then, with a sick grin, he opens the rear door and pushes my head down to shove me into the backseat.

"Sorry about the smell," he chirps. "Haven't had a chance to clean it out after the last guy threw up."

As long as I live, I'll remember his sadistic smile as he slams the door shut. And if it's the last thing I do, I'll get to wipe it off his smug face.

At the sheriff's office, I sit in a plastic chair against a wall down a narrow hallway with the drunk and disorderlies, prostitutes, and other pissed off victims of tonight's dragnet.

"Hey!" The frat boy with a bloody nose at the end of the row shouts at a passing deputy. "Hey! You get my dad on the phone. Hear me? My dad's gonna kick your ass."

"Man, shut up." A few chairs down, the townie with a black eye stares up at the ceiling. "No one cares about your stupid daddy."

"You're so dead. Every one of you idiots are so dead." The frat boy rattles around in his chair, and I realize they have him cuffed to it. "When my dad gets down here, you'll all be sorry."

"Dude," the townie says. "I'm already sorry now. If I have to keep listening to this pussy whine, someone just hand me a gun. I'll pistol-whip myself."

I'm tired, hungry, and I've had to pee since the moment Randall tossed me in the cruiser. My foot bounces with the anxiety of waiting. My mind runs a mile a minute, picturing Trina walking inside to find me and her purse gone, and wondering if she's figured out what's happened. I ponder the chances she'll have gotten in touch with my dad or one of my brothers, considering her phone is likely sitting in an evidence locker right now. Then I realize, if she *has* figured it out, she's not coming back for me. She's getting the hell out of the state before the cops pull her driver's license out of that purse and go looking for her too.

"You're doing fine." The woman in a sequin tank top and miniskirt has an almost Zen-like quality about her as she sits beside me, utterly relaxed. "Don't worry. It's not as scary as it looks on TV."

"When do we get to call someone? We get a phone call, right?"

Ironically, as many times as I've gotten myself in and out of trouble, I've never sat in this police station before. Given my previous lifestyle, I probably should have made a greater effort to understand the finer details of the criminal justice system.

In response, the woman tilts her head back and closes her eyes. "Get comfortable, sweetie. This could take a while."

"A while" is an understatement. It takes more than an hour just to get fingerprinted. Another hour for photographs. Another hour of waiting some more. It feels like every deputy in the station comes by to leer at me, each one with a look of amusement or smug satisfaction. I recognize some of them who'd wagged their fingers and sneered at me when I was in high school. They leave me with a visceral sense of the powerlessness of incarceration, and I'm only sitting in a well-lit hallway. Within these walls, they have all the power and we have none. We're guilty degenerates because they say so. Unworthy of respect or basic human decency. It's enough to radicalize even the softest suburbanite.

There's another hour of paperwork and more sitting around before we're finally placed in holding cells. Men and women separated. My wrists are sore and bruised when I take a seat on a bench beside a sleeping homeless woman. In the corner, a blonde tourist, probably about my age, cries silently into her hands, while her friend sits beside her looking bored. The metal toilet-sink combo on the far wall smells like every bar bathroom in the Bay flushes into it, curing me of any thoughts of having to go.

Sometime in the middle of the night, my name snaps me out of my meditation on the stains on the floor.

I glance toward the iron bars and almost burst into tears. It's Harrison. In uniform.

Because this night hasn't been mortifying enough.

Reluctantly, I go meet him at the front of the cell. "This is fitting, huh? Like a blind date game show reveal."

"I heard you were here and came as soon as I could." The poor guy appears genuine in his concern. "You alright? Anyone mistreating you?"

I don't know if he's asking about the people inside this cell or out. "I'm fine, given the circumstances." I smile wryly. "Don't suppose you want to accidentally drop a key and walk away."

"Okay," he says, his voice lowering to a stage whisper. "But you need to make it look convincing so I can tell them you over-powered me when I tried to stop you."

"Seriously, though. How does this work? I have money. If you can post my bail or whatever, I'll pay you back. They haven't even let me call someone yet."

He looks away with a sigh of frustration. "The sheriff's out of town at some family thing, so no one's in a big hurry to push papers."

Meaning any hope I had that Sheriff Nixon might realize I'm in here, and at least let my dad know, is right out the window. It wasn't a sure thing, but Hal Nixon and Dad play in a monthly poker game and have gotten chummy over the past couple years. I thought maybe, if I was extremely lucky, Nixon would let me plead my case that this whole thing is a misunderstanding blown sideways by a vindictive asshole.

"Can't post bail until they file the arrest," Harrison continues. "I don't know what the holdup is on phone calls. I'll see about that."

"I didn't do it." I look him square in the eye. "This is Randall again. You saw him. He's got a vendetta."

"We'll get this straightened out." Conflict and indecision contort his face.

Not that I'm feeling especially magnanimous, given my current situation, but I've had some time for deep contemplation lately, and I can appreciate that the fragile worldview of a rookie cop is perhaps a bit shaken when confronted with such blatant shitfuckery. These are his people, after all.

My tone softens. "It was sweet of you to check on me. Even if it was just to confirm I'm stuck here."

His tense posture relaxes. "I'm sorry. I feel like there's more I should do, but I really don't hold a lot of cards here."

"Tell you what," I say, sticking my hand through the bars to hold his. "When they give me the chair, I want you to be the one to throw the switch."

"Jesus." Harrison coughs out a disturbed laugh. "You're something else."

Which is a nice way of saying I'm better in small doses. "Yeah. I get that a lot."

"I'm going to see what I can find out. I'll try to make it back if I can. You want me to call anyone for you?"

I shake my head. As much as I want out of here, it'll be worse if Dad gets the call from Harrison instead of me. Besides, I've just gotten used to the smell in here.

"Go on, Deputy. Get out of here."

With a last regretful nod, he walks away.

Harrison never does find his way back. Instead, it's a sleepless night and an impatient morning before I'm allowed to make a phone call.

"Dad . . ." The embarrassment I feel when he answers, knowing what I have to say to him—I've had all night to agonize over it, and it's still worse than I anticipated. "Listen, I'm at the sheriff's office."

"Are you okay? What happened?" Dad's concern ripples over the line.

I hate this. Standing at a phone on the wall with a line behind me, I etch nervous patterns into the chipping paint with my thumbnail. My stomach churns queasily as I force myself to say the words.

"I was arrested."

He's quiet while I rush to explain. That the purse wasn't mine. That Randall's got it out for me. And the more I talk, the angrier I get. All of this started when I wouldn't accept the sexual advances of a married man with a badge. For so long, I felt guilty for wrecking that family with my drunken intrusion, but it hits me now that I didn't do that to him. *He* did. He set this entire year-long chain of events in motion because he's a sick, petty person. I should have kicked him in the scrotum when I had the chance.

"I swear, Dad. It wasn't mine. I'll take a drug test. Anything." My heart clenches tight against my rib cage. "I promise you. This isn't like before."

There's a long silence after I've stopped talking, during which I start to panic. What if he's had it with my shit, and this is one time too many? What if he leaves me in here to learn a lesson he should have taught me a long time ago? Gives up on his worthless, wayward daughter who was going to run out on him and the family business anyway.

"You sure you're okay?" he asks gruffly.

"Yeah, I'm okay."

"Alright, good. Hang tight, kiddo. I'm on my way."

It's only minutes before a deputy calls my name and opens the cell. As he escorts me from the holding area and through the bullpen of desks, I'm relieved that Randall isn't skulking around somewhere waiting for me. After our first run-in when I returned to the Bay, I understood that he had an ax to grind. When he showed up to hassle Harrison and I after our date, I prepared myself that he would become a perpetual annoyance. But this was a drastic escalation. And who knows what else is in store for me? This time, he throws me behind bars. Next time, maybe he isn't satisfied with conventional means of retribution. I'd hate to see what happens when he decides to be creative.

The deputy opens an office door and points me inside, where the sheriff is sitting in a polo shirt behind his desk. My father stands from his chair and gives me a tight nod.

"Good?" he says.

"Fine." As fine as I can be, anyway. When I notice the paper bag and cup of coffee sitting on the corner of the desk, I quirk a brow. "That for me?"

"Yeah, I brought you something," Dad says. "Figured you might be hungry."

I tear into the bag and practically inhale the two greasy sausage-and-egg sandwiches. I don't taste any of it when I wash it down with hot black coffee, but I feel better immediately. The exhausted haze has been chased away, my belly no longer fighting itself. Though now I really need to pee.

"Let me say," Sheriff Nixon speaks up, "I'm sorry about this whole mix-up."

That's a start.

"I had a look at the purse," he continues. "The ID, credit cards, and other personal items clearly all belong to a young lady named Katrina Chetnik."

I look to my father. "That's what I tried to tell him."

Dad nods, then narrows his eyes at the man behind the desk. "Sitting next to a purse at a crowded bar ain't a crime. Correct?"

"No, it isn't." To the sheriff's credit, he looks irritated with the whole scenario too. Annoyed to have been dragged down here on a Sunday to clear this mess up. "We'll make an effort to locate the owner."

Meaning Trina's problems are just beginning. But I can't say I care much about that. After spending a night in jail, I'm not about to run interference for her. She knew the risks. In hindsight, it was shitty of her to leave me sitting there with her coke in the first place.

There's a sharp knock on the door. A moment later, Rusty Randall enters. Apparently called in from home, he's dressed in a T-shirt and jeans, and I do take some small joy in the idea he was woken by an urgent call telling him the boss said *get your ass down here.*

Randall appraises me, then my father. Nothing about the scene appears to jostle him in the slightest. With his hands on his hips, he stands in the center of the room. "You needed to see me, sir?"

"Rusty, we'll be sending Ms. West home with our sincere apologies for her trouble. You can take care of the paperwork. I'll want to see a report on my desk by EOB."

"Fine," he says, voice tight.

"Anything you'd like to say?" the sheriff prompts, cocking his head.

Randall doesn't so much as blink in my direction. "I acted on probable cause for the arrest. My actions were entirely appropriate.

Of course, I respect your decision, and will handle that paperwork at once."

Coward.

But we both know he'd sooner wax his legs than apologize or admit he was wrong. Doesn't make much difference to me, though, because I couldn't care less what that man thinks.

"Ronan," Sheriff Nixon says, "go and get her home. And Ms. West . . ." He regards me for a moment. "I don't imagine I'll see you in here again."

I'm not sure how much I should read into his remark. Whether he means he'll see to it there aren't any further dirty arrests, or that he expects I've been scared straight. Either way, no, I don't believe we'll be seeing much more of each other. Not if I can help it.

"Not a chance," I agree.

Despite having my name cleared, the ride home only exacerbates my shame. I might have been wrongfully arrested, but my dad still had to call the sheriff first thing in the morning to get his only daughter out of jail. It was humiliating for me, so I suspect it was no picnic for him, either.

"I'm sorry," I say, cautiously studying his profile.

He doesn't respond, intensifying my guilt.

"I get that what I do reflects on you and the business. And even though the drugs weren't mine, and I wasn't using, I still placed myself in that situation. I knew Trina had the coke and I should have walked away. 'Cause let's be honest, a couple years ago, it wouldn't have been unheard of that the purse would have been mine."

"First of all," he says. "I'm not mad."

He watches the road as his jaw works, like he's trying to arrange his thoughts.

"Sure, you've made some mistakes. A couple years is a long time, though, and you're not that girl anymore." His voice softens. "I'd have gone down there no matter what you told me. You're my daughter, Genevieve." Dad glances at me. "But let's be clear. I had no doubt you were telling the truth. Don't think I haven't noticed the changes you've made. They matter."

Emotion clogs my throat. It suddenly occurs to me that I've spent so much time trying to convince myself I was for real, I missed when other people started to believe it. My dad. My friends. Evan.

I speak through the lump threatening to choke me. "I didn't want you to think this was me acting out or backsliding. That because of Mom or whatever . . ." The thought dies on my tongue. He doesn't acknowledge the mention of her, which I immediately regret. "But that's not the case at all. I'm trying so hard to be a better person, to take myself more seriously and have others do the same. I would never jeopardize that, especially now that I've got a new job starting soon."

Dad nods slowly. "Right. I don't know if I said this when you told me about the hotel, but . . . I'm proud of you, kiddo. This could end up being a big career for you."

"That's the plan." I give him a faint smile. "And no, you didn't say anything about being proud. If I recall correctly, you said 'congratulations' and then kind of grumbled about how Shane will make a terrible office manager."

He chuckles sheepishly. "I don't like change."

"Who does?" I shrug, adding, "Don't worry, we're not going to let Shane anywhere near that office. I already promised I'll help you interview candidates. We'll find an even better office manager than me."

"Doubt it," Dad says gruffly, and damned if that doesn't make my heart expand with pride. My throat closes up a little too.

"Hey, at least my replacement won't have a rap sheet," I say to lighten the mood.

"What's the deal with Rusty, anyway?" my father asks, glancing over suspiciously. "He have it out for you for some reason?"

Sighing, I tell him the truth. Most of it, anyway; there are still some things I won't repeat in front of my father. But he gets the gist. How Randall accosted me in the bar. How anger and too much to drink drove me into his living room to traumatize his family. The threats and run-ins since then.

"He blames me for destroying his family," I admit. "To some extent, I did too."

"That man did it to himself." Dad's features are cold and unforgiving. Randall's not going to want to bump into him in a dark alley anytime soon.

We ride in silence for a while. I don't interrupt what feels like his attempt to process all the information I just gave him. At which point I realize we're taking the long way home. My palms go damp. I guess this is the talk we've been putting off since I returned home.

"You're the most like your mother," he says suddenly. His eyes remain squarely on the road. "I know you two didn't get along. But I swear you're the spitting image of her when she was younger. She was a wild thing, back then."

I settle back in my seat, staring out the window at the little passing houses. Flickering, blurry images of my mother come to mind. They get fuzzier with every passing day, the details fading.

"Having a family changed her. I think I changed her first, if I'm honest. I've been wondering a lot lately, you know, if I broke her spirit—wanting to have a big family."

My gaze flies to his. "I don't understand."

"She was this energetic, lively woman when I met her. And

little by little, she dimmed. I don't even know how much she noticed until the light was all but gone."

"I always figured it was us." My voice cracks slightly. "I assumed she didn't like us, that maybe we didn't turn out the way she hoped."

Dad takes a deep breath, which he expels in a gust. "Your mom suffered a rough bout of postpartum depression after Kellan. Then we found out she was pregnant with Shane, and that seemed to help some. For a little while. Truth is, I don't know if she wanted so many kids because I did, or if she hoped the next one might snap her out of it. The next one would come along and fix her." He glances at me, full of remorse and sadness. "When she had Craig, something changed. The depression didn't come. Whatever hormones or chemicals are supposed to kick in that help women bond with the infant—well, it finally happened. And that only made her feel guiltier. She'd tried so damn hard to bond with the rest of you and was constantly fighting the depression, the dark thoughts, and then with Craig it was suddenly easy, and—"

He exhales a ragged breath, gaze still fixed on the road ahead. By the time he speaks again, I'm holding my breath. On pins and needles.

"Christ, Gen, you have no idea how much it ripped her apart, having that easy relationship with him when her relationships with the rest of you were so difficult. Her greatest fear was being a bad mom, and it crippled her. She couldn't get past the idea she was screwing you kids up. I don't know everything that went on in Laurie's head, but you've got to understand it wasn't her fault. Whatever it is, you know. The chemicals in her brain or whatever. She hated herself the most."

My eyes feel hot, stinging. I never thought about it that way. It wasn't something we talked about in our family. It felt like she hated us, so that was the truth we believed. Or I did, at least. Not once did it occur to me it was an illness, something she was incapable of controlling and even ashamed of. It must have felt so much easier for her to stop trying, to back away from the fear of breaking her kids. But, God, how much we all suffered for it.

Nothing changes our childhood, the years lost without a mother. The pain and torment of growing up believing that the act of being born, a decision we had no part in, was the reason she hated us. But Dad's pained confession, this new, sad piece of knowledge, changes a lot of how I feel about her now. How I look back on her.

And how I look at myself.

CHAPTER 29

EVAN

There's something in the air. I've got a crew at a storm-damaged house we're renovating for a flipper, and since lunch, the guys have been acting weird. I keep catching furtive glances and whispered conversations. People going silent when I walk into a room, yet feeling their eyes, everywhere, watching me. It's creepy is what it is. The scene before the pod people turn in unison and descend to assimilate their hapless target. Swear to God, if anything tries to probe me or vomit down my throat, I'm swinging a sledgehammer and aiming for nut sacks.

In the second-floor master bath, I catch my shift chief, Alex, hunched over a phone with the guy who's supposed to be installing the new tub.

"Grady, I'm pretty sure you billed us for something like thirty hours of overtime on that Poppy Hill job," I say loudly, and the tub guy startles and drops his phone into his pocket. "How do you figure Levi's gonna react when I tell him you're up here standing around on your phone with your dick in your hand?"

"I got you, boss. No problems. Gonna have all this . . ." Grady gestures at the tub, sink, and toilet left to install. "Gonna get it wrapped by today. Don't worry."

Amazing how agreeable people become when your name is on their paychecks.

To my shift chief, a young guy I vouched for to get this job, I give a nod to follow me down the hall. Alex and I step into one of the empty bedrooms, where I narrow my eyes. "What the hell is going on with everyone today?"

He hesitates to answer, taking off his baseball cap to scratch his head and then adjust and readjust it, hoping perhaps I might forget my question in the meantime. It sets my teeth on edge.

"What is it, for chrissake?" I demand.

"Yeah, um, so . . ." Oh, for the love of God. "Well, word is Genevieve got arrested. For like cocaine or something."

"What?" A cold tide rushes through my limbs. "When?"

"Last night. I mean, the rumor is she was caught moving a kilo of coke to an undercover agent on the boardwalk, but that's just talk. The way I heard it from my cousin who was working barback last night, some cop came in and found drugs in her purse, only she was telling him it wasn't her purse. Anyway, that girl Trina was looking for her a little while after that."

Damn it.

"We weren't sure you heard," Alex continues. "So the guys—"

"Yeah, fine." I wave him off. "Just get back to work. And tell them to put their damn phones away. Nobody's getting overtime for screwing around."

Trina.

Of course.

I should have seen this coming. I know as well as anyone the shit that girl gets up to. Anger burns my throat, most of it self-directed. What part of driving Gen toward her did I think would end any other way? Especially with Deputy Randall skulking around trying to pin something on Gen. If I'd given even a single thought to Genevieve's best interest instead of my own, I would've seen this coming.

Fuck.

No wonder she ran away from me. This turn of events was so predictable, Gen tried everything short of beating me back with a baseball bat to keep me away from her. And as it turns out, with all my efforts to prove she was overreacting and that nothing bad would come of us being together, I proved her right the first chance I got. I was so wrapped up in pleading my case, changing her mind, that I didn't give a single thought to the repercussions if it went badly.

What kind of asshole is so damn selfish?

This isn't a minor consequence either. Gen was cuffed. Probably perp walked out of the bar in front of half the town and a hundred tourists. Paraded through the police station and degraded by the same jerks who've been telling her she was no good her whole life. She must have been tearing out of her skin.

And I put her there.

I spent all this time trying to convince her that I'd be good for her and make her life better. What a goddamn joke.

It's hours before I can leave the jobsite to see Gen. Throughout the day I agonized over whether to call her, but eventually decided having this conversation over the phone was more insulting than waiting to do it in person. Or maybe I'm a coward who hoped the delay would help me figure out what to say to her.

As I'm pulling up to her house, I'm still at a loss.

Gen's little brother Craig answers the door. With a knowing look that says *good luck*, he nods upstairs.

"She's in her room."

I knock a couple times, then let myself in when there's no answer. Gen's asleep on her bed in pajamas and a bathrobe, hair still wet. The largest part of me wants to leave. Let her sleep. The longer I can put this off, the more time I have to come up with something sufficient to say. But then she opens her eyes to find me standing in the doorway.

"Sorry," she says drowsily, gathering herself to sit up against her headboard. "I didn't get much sleep in the clink."

"I can go. Come back later."

"No. Stay." She draws her knees up to make room for me. "I take it the whole town knows by now?"

She doesn't look so bad, all things considered. A bit groggy and pale from exhaustion, but otherwise unscathed. It doesn't help the lump of guilt stuck in my throat, though.

"You okay? He try anything with you?" Because throwing a Molotov cocktail through Randall's bedroom window might go a long way to improving my mood.

She shakes her head. "It was fine. Not much worse than the DMV, honestly."

"That's what you've got? A night in the slammer and you're doing '90s sitcom humor?"

A weak smile curves her lips. It breaks my fucking heart. "I'm thinking about touring the prison circuit with some new material."

"Have you heard from Trina?"

"Nope." Gen shrugs. "I wish her well. If she's smart, she's well into Mexico by now."

When I open my mouth to speak again, she cuts me off.

"Can we not talk about it? Later, fine. Right now, I don't want to think about it anymore. It's been a long day."

"Yeah, of course."

Taking my hand, she pulls me to sit beside her against the headboard. "Hey, I never said this, but the house looks great. You guys did a stellar job on the renovations. I'm almost sad it's over."

"I am gonna miss you wandering around the house in skimpy silk nighties, watching me work up a sweat."

Gen snorts. "You have an active imagination."

"Oh, were you not there for that? Must have been some other leggy brunette with nice tits."

Her elbow jabs my ribs. "I meant now that it's over, Dad's going to put the house on the market. This won't be my room for much longer. And the place is so nice now, it's a shame to leave."

"A lot of good memories in this room." Climbing in her window after everyone's gone to bed. Sneaking her out of it.

"Kellan and Shane tried smoking some old pot they found hidden under the floorboards in Shane's closet." This time when she laughs, it reaches her eyes. The sound is comforting and debilitating all at once. "They were throwing up for hours. Shane swore he was going blind."

I want to laugh with her and reminisce about all the stuff we got away with in this house. Every time we held our breath under the covers having sex while her entire family slept a few feet away. Constantly in fear for my life that one of her brothers would barge in and break my dick off if he found me on top of her.

But all I can think about is that if circumstances were different, she might've been facing serious jail time because of me.

Only now does it occur to me that some of those memories—running from cops or whoever we pissed off that night, stumbling in drunk at fifteen, getting high and blowing off class—aren't as cute as they seemed in high school.

"Dad wants me to look at houses with him. With Mom gone, he's feeling a little overwhelmed with the decisions."

The words barely reach my ears. A thought spiral drops like a heavy blanket on top of me, my mind weighted with all the ways I haven't conceived of yet that I'll ruin this girl. She was happy when she came back. Maybe not right away, thanks to the funeral and everything. But when I compare the person who showed up at that first bonfire to the person sitting next to me now? She looks burnt out. Dried up. A couple months around me and I've already sucked the life out of her.

And no matter what I do to think my way out of this, I come

back to one undeniable conclusion: I did this to her. And if given the chance, I'll do it again.

"Actually, a couple days ago I drove by a house on Mallard. That blue one with the palms. It's a newer home. I looked it up on—"

"Gen." I launch to my feet. "Look, you were right."

"Huh?"

Agitated now, I pace the room. How do I do this? I don't want to come off as an asshole, but maybe it's well too late for that.

"Evan?" Her voice ripples with worry.

"I should have listened to you."

Fuck, why didn't I listen? She gave me a dozen opportunities to respect her wishes and keep my distance. I ignored every one of her warnings and went straight off a cliff. Slowly, I turn to face her, all the guilt and regret bubbling up and spilling over. What did she ever do to deserve me?

"I'm sorry, Fred."

Alarm grows in her expression. "About what?"

"You were right. This can't work. You and me."

"Evan." A wary look of disbelief sucks the color from her face. "This is because of last night? You didn't put the coke in Trina's purse. You didn't sic Randall on me. None of that is your fault."

"But I talked you into going. That's on me." My voice rises of its own volition. It feels like I don't have control of my own mind. The frustration running away with me. The anger at myself that I let this happen. "I'm no good for you. I'm sorry it took me so long to figure that out." I swallow. It hurts to do so. "You need to stay the hell away from me."

"You don't mean that." Gen jumps off the bed. "I get that you feel responsible, but it was not your fault."

"Don't do that." I pull myself away when she reaches for my arm. "You've been making excuses for me my whole life."

She rolls her head in frustration, huffing out a breath. "That's not what I'm doing. I was only nervous about going out with Trina because I didn't think I could resist getting trashed around her. You had more faith in me, and you were right. I didn't drink at all last night. She offered me some of her coke, and I didn't take it. The rest of the night was my choice. I stuck around. I let her leave her purse with me. At any point I could have said no and gone home." Fight flashes across her face. "You've been taking bullets for me *my* whole life. But I'm all grown up now, Evan. I don't need a martyr."

I appreciate what she's trying to do, but I can't let her. This is how habits start. She forgives me this time, and the next. And the next. Until inch by inch, she backslides into all the self-destructive patterns she's worked so hard to break. She always was the best part of us.

I love her. I'd rather never see her again than be the reason she hates herself.

"You should stick it out with your cop," I tell her, my voice cracking slightly before hardening with resolve. "He's a decent guy, and he'll bend over backward to make you happy. Better influence than I'll ever be."

"Evan."

I watch the realization cement in her eyes. Watch as she grasps for some lever to pull to make this stop. Then I turn my back on her.

"Evan!"

I'm out the door and down the stairs. Practically running to my bike. I have to get out of here before I lose my nerve. I know she's looking at me from her bedroom window when I speed away from the curb. The ache begins before I've reached the end of the block. By the time I get home, I can't feel anything. Not sure I'm even awake.

It's dark when I take a seat on the back deck later. Clouds block the stars and make the sky feel small and too close. The cricket songs and katydids roar inside my skull. This is shell shock. I'm not fully present in the aftermath.

A cold beer lands in my lap. Beside me, Cooper pulls up a chair. "You check on Genevieve?" he asks.

I twist open my beer and take a swig. I don't taste a thing. "Think I broke up with her," I mumble.

He stares at the side of my face. "You okay?"

"Sure."

Turns out I could've saved everyone all sorts of grief if I'd listened to both of them. Coop doesn't know his head from his asshole where Gen is concerned, but as much as I hate his second-guessing, he does know me.

"I'm sorry," he tells me.

"She's not a bad girl." People have always given her a hard time for the crime of trying to enjoy her life. Maybe it's because her lust for it sparked envy, longing. Most people are too afraid to truly experience their lives. They're passengers or passive observers to a world happening around them. But not Gen.

"I know," Coop says.

When she left a year ago, it never really ended. Nothing was said. She was gone, but we remained frozen in place. Even after it'd been months and everyone told me to take the hint, I couldn't let go of where we'd left off. It was only ever a matter of time before she came home and we picked up again. Except it didn't happen that way. She changed. And though I hadn't noticed, so did I. We tried to shove ourselves back together, fill in the same blank spaces, but we don't fit the same way we used to.

"You love her?"

My throat closes up to the point of suffocation. "More than anything in the world."

She's the one. The only one. But it's not enough.

Cooper lets out a breath. "I am sorry. Whatever my beef is with Gen, you're my brother. I don't like seeing you hurting."

He and I have been through a lot with each other this past year. Finding one reason or another to be at odds. It's exhausting, honestly. And lonely. Nights like this remind me that whatever else happens, it's just the two of us.

"We've got to do a better job of being brothers," I say quietly. "I know this thing with Mom gets you mad, but do we have to come to blows about it every time her name comes up? Man, I don't want to keep this stuff from you. I don't like lying about where I am or sneaking away to take phone calls so you can't hear me. I feel like I'm tiptoeing around my own house."

"Yeah, I get it." Coop takes another swig of his beer, then turns the bottle between his palms while the breeze kicks up and blows in salt air from the beach. "I've spent so long being mad at her, I guess I wanted you to be upset at her with me. Kinda lonely out in the cold."

"I'm not trying to leave you out in the cold. I knew you weren't ready to let her back in. That's cool. I told her not to expect anything. Hell, I warned her you'd tell the FBI she had Jimmy Hoffa buried in her backyard if she came around here."

He coughs out a stiff laugh. "Not a bad idea. You know, if needed."

"Anyway, I didn't ask you to see her because I know how bad she messed you up last time. I'd wanted you to give her a chance and she'd betrayed you. Both of us. Yeah, I was worried she'd make me a sucker again. Still am. I'm not sure that feeling goes away when it comes to Shelley. This is just something I need to do. For me."

"I was thinking." His attention is drawn to his lap, where he picks at the melting label from the sweaty bottle. "Maybe I'd be willing to consider meeting up with her."

"Seriously?"

"Oh, what the hell." Cooper downs the last of his beer. "As long as you and Mac are there. What's the worst that can happen?"

I wouldn't have put money on such a dramatic change of heart. I doubt it was anything I said; more likely Mac worked on him. But it's all the same to me either way. We don't have much of a family left. It got even smaller today. I'm just here trying to cobble together as much as I can out of the bits and pieces. If we can stop fighting about this one thing, it'll go a long way.

"I'll set it up."

"Telling you now, though," he warns. "If she comes looking for a kidney, I'm giving her one of yours."

CHAPTER 30

GENEVIEVE

I've been sitting on the floor in the same place I landed when Evan walked out. Staring at the patterns in the carpet, the scuffs on the wall, trying to understand what just happened. I crawl back into bed, turn the light out, and hug the blankets tight around my shoulders with the scene playing through my mind. His cold detachment. The way, even when our eyes met, he seemed to look through me. Untouchable.

Did he actually break up with me? Yesterday I would've said he wasn't capable of such a cruel and sudden turn.

My memory of the conversation we just had is fragmented, as though I wasn't entirely present for it. Now I'm sewing clips together and still can't fathom how I ended up alone in the dark with an ache tearing at my chest.

It was one thing when I left last year. He was still here. The way we think of home as permanent. Safe in a memory. Unmovable.

Then I came back, and I thought I could keep him there. Perfect and preserved. Always the boy with more daring than sense. If I didn't let myself take him seriously or see him as a whole complex person, I wouldn't have to answer the hard questions about what these feelings were and what to do with them. What happens when the party girl and the bad boy grow up.

Now he's stolen that possibility from me, made the hard choice for us both. Except I wasn't ready. Time ran out and I'm left sitting here alone.

Why'd he do this to me? Make me care about him all over again, test every boundary and knock down every wall, if only to walk away now?

It hurts, damn it.

More than I thought it could.

And my mind won't stop running over what-ifs and if onlys. What if I hadn't been so obstinate at the start? If I hadn't set up quite so many hurdles to a relationship? If only I'd been more open, would we have had this all figured out by now?

I don't know.

None of it helps me sleep. I'm still staring at the ceiling well after one in the morning. And that's when a noise outside startles me.

I'm not sure what it is at first. A passing car with the radio on? The neighbors? For the briefest moment, my pulse lurches with the thought it might be Evan climbing his way up.

Suddenly something smashes against my bedroom window.

Loud and piercing. I'm frozen in panic for a second before I turn on my bedside lamp and run to the window. There I see the foaming liquid sheeting down the windowpane and the brown shards of glass littering the sill. A beer bottle, from the looks of it.

"You fucking slut bitch!"

Below, Rusty Randall stands unsteady on my front lawn, his outline barely visible in the outer edge of the streetlamp's glow. He staggers, shouting almost incoherently except for every other word or so.

"Bitch ex-wife . . ." He growls something about "*won't let me see my damn kids*" and "*my own damn house.*"

On the bed, my phone lights up, and I make a mad dash for it.

Kayla: *I know it's late but I wanted to warn you. Rusty was here. He's drunk and angry. Stay away if you see him.*

Kayla's house is just down the street. A quick walk on his belligerence tour. One more stop on the midnight grievance stroll. Tonight, of all nights, I'm not interested in entertaining his rage.

Luckily, I don't have to.

"What the hell was that?" Craig barges into my room rubbing crust out of his eyes as he comes to stand beside me at the window. "Is that the one who arrested you?"

"You did this!" Randall shouts again. "You fucking bitch!"

Craig and I both turn our heads when we hear the stairs creak followed by the front door opening. The floodlights from the front porch pop on, lighting Randall on the front lawn. A second later, our dad walks out in shorts and a T-shirt with a pump-action shotgun in his hands.

"Oh, shit. Dad's pissed," Craig breathes.

He's not the only one. More footsteps follow, down the stairs and out the door. Then Billy, Shane, and Jay walk out to stand behind our father. Six-foot-five Jay has a baseball bat slung over his shoulder. I didn't even know he and Shane were here tonight. Kellan must've kicked them out again for a chick.

Randall drunkenly grumbles at Dad. I can't hear them well, but by the gesticulations, I catch the gist.

"I don't care about a badge," Dad says, raising his voice. "You get the hell off my property."

When Randall doesn't move quick enough, Dad pumps the shotgun to reiterate his demand.

That gets Randall backpedaling, growling along the way to his car. The Fuck Around and Find Out Society remains undefeated.

Craig and I make our way out to the porch in time to see his taillights pass.

"That guy's a real weirdo," Jay says, strutting in like he just chased off the British Army single-handedly with his Louisville Slugger.

"Should have put one in his ass," Shane laughs as Dad comes in and safely stows the shotgun.

"He's driving drunk," Craig pipes up. "We should tell the sheriff."

"I'll call him," Dad says before glancing at me. "You okay, kiddo?"

"Yeah, good." I flick on the living room lights, and we all congregate on the sofas.

"We were watching upstairs," Craig tells them, a big dumb grin on his face. "I thought for sure you were going to shoot that guy."

Dad leans against the back of his recliner, grimacing.

I fight a rush of guilt-tinged anger. "I'm so sorry, Dad. I had no idea he'd show up here. Kayla texted me after he was already out there to tell me he'd been by her place too. Guess she wouldn't let him in."

"Uh-huh." After a beat, he walks around to sit in the big leather chair. "I think I'm gonna stay up for a little while. Make sure that numbskull doesn't get any dumb ideas."

"What's that guy's deal?" Craig searches all of us for an answer. "I mean, something happened, right?"

Billy meets my gaze.

It was bad enough having that conversation with my father. No way I'm rehashing it for my youngest brother.

"You knuckleheads get on back to bed," Dad tells the boys.

"I can't sleep now." Shane all but bounces at the end of the sofa. "I'm hyped. I'll stay up too. Sit on the front porch with the shotgun in case he comes back."

Jay rolls his eyes, then gives me a sympathetic nod. "Let's go."

"Oh, come on." Craig huffs at being dismissed. "I never get to hear the good stuff. Gen?"

He searches me for support or permission, but I just shrug and say, "I'll tell you when you're older."

He flips up his middle finger. "Aw, you're no fun."

Jay yanks Craig by the arm and then wrangles the others, pushing Billy and Shane up the stairs, while cooing, "Bedtime, kiddos." Which gets him more middle fingers and a "fuck off" from Billy.

I remain with Dad, watching him cautiously. To his credit, he'd remained remarkably cordial out there, given that a deranged man was screaming obscenities at his daughter and hurling bottles against the house. While his clenched fists and white knuckles suggest he'd like to reach for the shotgun again, he gives up only a threatening throat clearing as he reaches for his phone.

"I'm going to have a talk with the sheriff." Dad rises from his recliner to kiss the top of my head. "Go to bed, kiddo. I'm taking care of it."

Sometimes, a girl just needs her dad. As far as they go, mine's pretty alright.

CHAPTER 31

EVAN

I dream about her. One of those half-awake meanderings of the mind after my eyes have blinked open a couple times to clench shut again against the spill of sunlight across my face. It's not so much a dream as a memory of something that never happened, indistinct and evaporating before I can consciously hold on to it. But we're together, and when my brain finally rocks me awake, I'm reminded there's no sleeping this one off. I let her go. And dreams are all I have left.

Rolling over, I grab my phone from the nightstand to check the time. The screen is full of texts from Gen. It takes me a minute to get up to speed, not understanding what I'm reading because I'm seeing it in reverse order. Only the most recent show up first, so I scroll up to read them properly.

Gen: *Randall showed up here last night.*
Gen: *Screaming on my front lawn.*
Gen: *Threw a beer bottle at my window.*

That one slaps any lingering grogginess from my head.

Gen: *Dad chased him off with a shotgun.*
Gen: *Please, we need to talk.*

I'm out of bed and throwing on the first shirt and pair of shorts I find.

Gen: *I wouldn't ask if it wasn't important.*
Gen: *Things have changed. Meet me at our spot as soon as you get this. You owe me that much.*

Already, I'm regretting how I went at her yesterday, especially considering everything she'd already been through. I could have done it better. Gently. Now she sounds like she's afraid I'd ignore her, and that's never what I wanted. Distance, yeah. Enough for both of us to get used to the idea of living our own lives. So she could get on with hers without interference from me. But thinking she'd have to beg for my help when she's in trouble? That's an awful feeling.

I'm out the door only minutes later, peeling out of the drive-way on my motorcycle. When I arrive at the narrow path that cuts through the trees to the hidden beach, Gen is already there, wearing a pair of cutoffs and a loose red T-shirt. She's on a blanket just above the tide line, staring at the waves.

"Hey," I say, announcing myself as I approach. "You okay? What happened?"

She doesn't stand, but encourages me to sit. "I'm fine. Good thing we didn't have any loose pavers lying around or we might have had you out installing new windows."

"I'm serious." I search her face, but she seems okay. Just a little tired. "Your messages sounded—"

"Right." She ducks her head. "Sorry. Didn't mean to scare you."

"It's fine." When Gen won't look at me, I bow to meet her eyes. "I mean it, it's cool. You need me, I'm here. No problem."

After a breath, her shoulders relax. Her finger draws aimless patterns in the sand as she explains what exactly went on last night. Finding the ranting lunatic in her yard. Ronan West walking out to meet him like Dirty Harry.

"So then Dad called the sheriff and told him to get his ass down to the station. They brought me in at the crack of dawn to fill out a petition for a restraining order. We hung around for a while making a formal police report while Sheriff Nixon had Randall brought in. He was arrested for drunk driving, and they put him on leave." A glint of vindication lights her expression. "They have to do a whole internal investigation thing, but Dad says he's getting canned."

"Good." It's about time. I get why it didn't go that way in the first place, but at least something's finally being done about that guy. Hopefully, it brings Gen some peace of mind. "Do you see now that none of his problems were your fault?"

She slides me a sarcastic side-eye. "Yeah."

"Feel better?"

"If this keeps him away, sure. I'm honestly tired of thinking about him."

"He's gotten more of your time than he deserved."

"Exactly."

I'm glad she told me, and I'm relieved that she's alright. If I'd heard about it through the rumor mill, I would've been making a pass by Randall's house, and then there'd be nobody to talk some sense into me. Anyway, she deserves to catch a break. This thing's had a hold of her for more than a year.

As much as I want to, I don't know, console her, keep her company, the longer we sit here, the less I know what to say or how to act. I basically dumped her last night, so I can't imagine she wants me here any longer than necessary.

"Yeah, so I'll head out." I climb to my feet. "Leave you be."

She jumps up after me. "I'm not done. I didn't call you out here just to tell you about Randall."

My heart clenches. I'm not sure I can go another round about us today. Last night was brutal. Even now, I'm not sure how I managed to walk out of there without losing my nerve. If we have to rehash the whole argument, I can't be certain my resolve will hold. I've never been good at saying no to her.

"I stopped for coffee with Harrison on the way here."

Well, then. There it is.

I swallow the hysterical laughter that bubbles in my throat. Was I really just thinking she'd come here asking me back when I all but shoved her at another man yesterday? Idiot. Gen's got everything going for her. She doesn't need my dumb ass making things harder. But this is good, actually. It takes all the wishful thinking and foolish notions right off the table.

"He's a stand-up guy," I tell her.

"He is."

"Still a doofus." Alright, maybe I can't help myself. "But he's nice, polite. Probably sorts his laundry according to the care instructions, so you won't have to worry about him shrinking your clothes."

Gen smirks, biting her lip as she turns her head. "You are so weird sometimes."

"Your kids are going to be short, though. He's got kind of an odd-shaped head too. That might be hereditary. You should probably put them in karate or something. Get them into boxing. With a cranium like that, they're gonna need to know how to defend themselves."

Exasperated, she shakes her head. "Will you stop?" Still, she's beaming. "I told him I couldn't see him anymore."

Our gazes lock. "Why would you do that?"

"Because." Gen's smile is so infectious, I can't help but mimic her. "I told him I was in love with Evan Hartley."

I can feel my heartbeat in my face. Yet somehow I still manage to play it cool. "That's so strange, 'cause I know that guy."

"Uh-huh." There's a bizarre gleam in her eyes that's almost got me frightened. "Took me a little while, but as it turns out, I've been in love with him for a long time."

Part of me wants to throw her over my shoulder and toss caution to the wind, but we ended up here for a reason.

"What about Trina's coke? You spent the night in jail because of me," I remind her. "If Randall hadn't been the one who arrested you, or your dad wasn't friends with the sheriff, maybe the whole thing doesn't go away so easy."

"No, see." She holds one finger in the air. "I've decided I reject your premise."

She's so cute sometimes. "Really?"

"Indeed." She nods sharply. "I already told you, I'm glad I went out with Trina. You said I needed to see that I could go out and have a good time without losing control. And I did. I proved a lot to myself that night. Like I said before, nothing about how it ended was your fault."

When my expression reveals I'm less than convinced, she digs in.

"You and I could go back to single digits trying to take the blame for everything that ever happened to either of us. It's a zero-sum game. None of it is useful."

"It worries me that you're starting to make sense," I say, smothering a grin.

"I had to convince myself I'd really changed. To me, that night shows I have. And I did it with you in my life. You know what else? You've changed too. For most of the time I've known you, you've had this chip on your shoulder. Fighting the whole world on a thousand fronts, always ready to throw a punch before it threw one at you. I don't see that anymore. Like it or not, Evan, you've mellowed in your old age."

"Jesus . . ." I grab my chest. "Right for the heart, Fred."

She shrugs at me. "It's called growth. Get over it."

I don't know where this new energy is coming from, but I don't hate it. She's alive, happy. Glowing with that old fire and verve. Like she could turn sand to glass with a wink.

"We've grown as a couple," she continues. "But I'm hoping we can grow a little more."

This feels like being blindfolded, as if she's walking me around in the dark and I'm following her, a little terrified and expectant. She's up to something. Something both terrible and exciting. It's like that first time watching her take a running leap off the pier, but this time she's got me by the hand.

"I've been sitting here for a while. And I was thinking . . ." Gen steps closer and puts her hands against my chest. My muscles quiver beneath her palms. We both know what her touch does to me. "I think you should probably marry me."

My mouth goes dry. "That right?"

"Make a whole bunch of babies."

"An entire bunch?" I can't feel my fingers. The sounds of the ocean turn to a sharp ringing in my ears as my chest expands with a rush of pure, unfiltered joy.

"I'll run Mackenzie's hotel, and you can be the stay-at-home dad raising our seven kids."

Going quiet for a beat, Gen looks up at me through thick lashes. Then she holds out a red Blow Pop.

"If you want," she says impishly, though her expression conveys utter sincerity, "this is me asking."

I'm not even sure if I'm still standing. But I'm not a moron, either. "Yeah, I want."

Fingers tugging my shirt, she leans up to press her lips to mine. I'm still half stunned for a few seconds before my brain reboots and I wrap my arms around her, kissing her deeply. This amazing, absurd woman who has no idea what she's getting herself into.

"You're going to get sick of how much I love you," I tell her, brushing her hair off her shoulders. "Totally disgusted with it."

"I'll take that bet." She tips her head to smile at me, then tries to kiss me again.

"Listen." I hold her still. "Don't get me wrong, I love this plan. Whatever you had for breakfast, let's stick with that. But what about . . ." Hell, I don't know how to say it. "You know, your dad. And your brothers. I'm pretty sure they have a hole dug somewhere with my name on it."

"What about your brother?" she counters. "Who cares. They'll come around or they won't. You're what I want. The only thing I've ever asked for. I think I'm kind of entitled at this point."

"Well, I have a feeling Cooper will come around sooner than you think."

For the first time in my life, I can picture my future more than a few days out. A sense of family and security. Permanence. Me and Gen, married and blissfully happy. I'm catching glimpses of what waking up to someone feels like, knowing they aren't rushing to sneak out with their shoes in their hands.

"Seriously. We're doing this?" I ask roughly. "Because if you think you had to come up with some grand gesture to get me back, you could have just shown me your tits. I would've caved right away. No question." I chew on the inside of my cheek. "I don't want you to think we need to get married to prove this is real."

She flashes a cocky grin. "Trust me, I've known I've had you whipped since seventh grade."

"See." With my arms around her, I slide my hands into her back pockets to grab her ass. "You think that's an insult, but I don't mind a bit. My masculinity is entirely intact. I'd follow this ass anywhere."

This time when she tries to kiss me, I let her. She does me in when she bites my lip. By then, I've got no sense left. Instead, I wrap my arms under her thighs to lift her up around my hips as we kiss.

How did I ever think I could live without this? Her skin under my palms. Her taste on my tongue. The way my heart beats almost painfully fast when she weaves her fingers into my hair and pulls. *This woman.*

As Gen begins to breathe harder, sliding her tongue in my mouth to tangle with mine, I shove my hand up her shirt to grab a handful of her breast. She arches into my hand, grinding herself on me. I'm hard and pushing against the zipper of my shorts as she scrapes her teeth against the stubble on my chin and runs her tongue down my neck.

"Wait." She lowers her legs to stand. "Get in the backseat of my car."

I stare at her. "You know, if a cop comes by, this time we'll both end up spending a night in jail."

"Maybe. But I'll take my chances." She plants a sweet kiss on my cheek. "Gotta be a bad girl some of the time, right?"

Good enough for me. Because I'll take her any way I can.

Forever.

EPILOGUE

GENEVIEVE

I've got my head in the twins' linen closet looking for an outdoor tablecloth when I'm jolted by a pair of arms coming around me from behind. Evan's lips brush my neck. His hands travel up my ribs, under my shirt, to sneak their way past my bra and cup my breasts. I feel his erection pressing against my ass.

"I want you," he breathes.

"So you keep saying." This is the fourth time this afternoon he's cornered me somewhere around the house to make his intentions clear. "Dinner will be ready soon."

One hand slides down my stomach and into my shorts. "I want to eat now."

A hot shiver rolls through me. He isn't playing fair. Since we made the engagement official, we can't keep our hands off each other. Evan's new favorite game—which I've been less than sincere about deterring—is seeing how close he can get to outright seducing me in public before I call a time-out.

So far, pretty damn close.

"Have I mentioned I love you?" he whispers, his fingers slipping between my thighs. "Especially this part."

"Especially?" I yank his hand free and turn to face him, eyebrow raised.

"Equally. I meant equally. As I love all the . . ." His eyes drag over my body. "Parts of you."

"Just for that"—I reach under my shirt and unclasp my strapless bra, letting it drop to the floor—"I'm not wearing a bra to dinner."

"Whoops." Mac appears around the corner of the hallway. She pauses, then spins on her heel. "Carry on. Not even here."

With a devilish grin, Evan bends down and picks up my bra. He shoves it in his back pocket. "I'm keeping this."

Among the stranger things he's done, this is up there. "Why?"

"You'll find out."

Far too happy with himself, he saunters off.

Once I've found the tablecloth, I head back to the kitchen where Mac is placing trays of food on a larger serving tray to carry outside. I toss the cloth at Evan and order him to go set the table on the deck.

"So what's the score?" Mac asks me.

"Honestly, I've lost count." I spoon the potato salad into a big bowl then pull the roasted carrots out of the oven.

We're having an al fresco buffet-style dinner tonight. Several of our friends, along with Riley and his aunt, are already outside milling about. Steph keeps joking that it's our engagement dinner, but it's really not. More of a spur-of-the-moment suggestion on the part of Evan, whose impulsive tendencies haven't completely abated.

He bumps into me while pulling utensils out of a drawer. "I'm winning."

"I'm gonna say this again—" Cooper announces, coming to stand in the middle of the kitchen.

"Coop, stop." Mac rolls her eyes as she picks up a tray laden with various salads.

"No, I'd like to reiterate. If I find out anyone but me is having sex on my bed, I'm setting theirs on fire in the backyard."

"Dude." Evan laughs at him. "Seriously, what makes you think I'd want to blow a load in your room? I've heard what you get up to in there."

For that, he gets a swift smack to the arm from Mac.

"Just so you know," Cooper shoots back as Evan is picking a cucumber spear off the cutting board to pop in his mouth. "I've had sex with her on that counter. So enjoy."

"Jesus." Evan shudders. "I know you confuse me with a mirror, but we don't actually share a dick, man. Keep it to yourself."

Lately, most of the ribbing has come at our expense. Just a little good-natured teasing about our newly engaged bliss. That we're too young to get married and, before we know it, we'll both be bored with each other and drowning in baby diapers. Still, it doesn't faze us. Like Evan told Cooper when we announced it, we know we're forever. We've always known.

As Mac and Evan drift onto the back deck, I set my oven mitts on the counter and give Cooper a sidelong glance. He cocks a brow when he notices. "What?" he says defensively.

My answering smile is saccharine. "Still haven't gotten my apology for the day."

"Fuck's sake. Are you seriously going to hold me to that?"

"Sure am."

A few days ago, Cooper and I took a walk on the beach and had a long overdue chat. And it didn't even take any urging from Evan or Mackenzie. My future brother-in-law and I were mature enough to know we needed to squash the beef. So I apologized for being a bad influence on Evan in the past, while Cooper apologized for confronting me outside my place of business and telling me what a horrible person I was. He then offered me the privilege of his friendship again, to which I'd laughed and informed him if he wanted the privilege of *my* friendship, he would need to apologize to me every day until the wedding. Whenever that'll be. We're on Day Four now, and I'm having a blast.

"Fine." Cooper lets out an annoyed breath. "I'm sorry for telling you to fuck off and saying we weren't friends."

"Thanks, Coop." I walk over to ruffle his hair. "Appreciate it."

Mac returns to witness the exchange, laughing under her breath. "Cut him some slack, Gen. He promised to be nice from now on."

I think it over. "Fine. I release you from your apology obligations," I tell Cooper.

He rolls his eyes and heads outside to assist his brother.

"Need some help?" Alana appears at the open sliding door, uncharacteristically eager to help out. She practically grabs the potato salad bowl from my hand.

I stare at her. "Why are you being weird?"

Beside me, Mac peers past Alana's shoulder toward the deck. "She's avoiding Wyatt," Mac supplies. "He's glaring daggers at us right now."

I don't know whether to laugh or sigh. Whereas my love life finally straightened itself out, Alana's seems to be growing ever more complicated. "What did you do to him this time?" I ask her.

She scowls at me. "Nothing."

Mac lifts a brow.

"Fine." Alana huffs. "I'm getting my left wrist inked for my birthday next week. So I had a tattoo designed."

I'm confused. "And?"

"By someone other than Wyatt."

I gasp. "No!"

Even Mac, who's only lived in the Bay for a year or so, grasps the implications of that. Wyatt is the best artist in town. Going to anybody else for a tat is sacrilege.

"I'm allowed to use someone else," Alana argues. "Preferably someone who doesn't think they're in love with me."

"Guess you can't go to Tate either, then," Mac cracks, and she and I giggle.

Alana's mouth twists in another scowl. She swiftly sets down the potato salad. "You know what? I'm not helping anymore. I hate you both."

She stomps off, leaving us laughing in her wake. Through the sliding door, I see her march past Wyatt to join Steph and Heidi on the other side of the deck, where she tries to camouflage into the railing.

"Oh, the tangled webs we weave," Mac remarks, still chuckling.

We step outside and start arranging the serving dishes on the table. Another folding table has an array of drinks, and a few coolers of beer sit on the floor nearby. Cooper goes to check the meat he's grilling on the barbecue, while Evan wanders out with a stack of napkins and places them next to the pile of utensils.

"Where's Riley?" he asks, glancing around.

I nod toward the yard below, where Riley and Tate are on the sand engaged in an animated conversation about sailing. Riley's aunt Liz stands a few feet away, checking her phone.

"He told me he has a crush on a girl in his biology class," I whisper to Evan, nodding at his surrogate baby brother.

"Oh, Becky? Yeah, I know all about her."

"Becky? No, he said her name was Addison." My jaw drops. "Oh my God. He's turning into a little player."

Evan grins proudly. "Good. Let him play the field a bit. He's too young to settle down."

I sigh, about to offer a comeback, when a flash of movement catches my peripheral vision. I turn toward it and suck in a breath.

"What the hell," I hiss at Evan.

He's still all smiles. "Harrison!" he calls to the khaki-and-polo-clad deputy who approaches the deck from the side of the Hartley house. "Glad you could make it!"

He invited *Harrison*? And he's actually calling him by his proper name instead of some passive-aggressive taunt?

"Evan," I growl softly. "What have you done?"

"Chill, baby," he whispers back. "Just think of me as the love fairy. Spreading all the love around."

What in the actual fuck. I've barely registered the absurdity of the remark before Evan is gone, sauntering down the steps toward the new arrival. I find my footing and hurry after him, prepared to do damage control. Just how much of it will be required? Undetermined.

I reach them in time to witness Evan clap Harrison on the shoulder and say, "Been wanting to introduce you two for ages."

You two?

I blink in surprise as my crazy fiancé ushers Harrison over to Riley's aunt and starts making introductions. Harrison and Aunt Liz? That's just . . . genius, I realize. As my initial surprise wanes, it occurs to me that this might be the greatest matchmaking scheme in history. I'm almost disappointed I didn't think of it first.

"Liz is, like, the best nurse ever," Evan is raving. "At least that's what I hear in all my nursing circles."

I choke down a laugh and add to the pitch. "Harrison once carried a gator down from a roof with his bare hands," I inform Liz.

Evan's brows raise. "Seriously? Dude. I need to hear this story—"

"Another time," I chirp, latching a hand onto his arm. "We need to finish bringing the food out first. 'Scuse us."

With that, we leave a slightly dazed Harrison and an amused-looking Liz to their own devices.

"Damn, Mr. Love Fairy," I murmur as we return to the kitchen. "That was some good thinking. They're the perfect match."

Evan nods vigorously. "Right?"

I'm grabbing the last of the condiments from the fridge when the doorbell rings.

"I'll get it," he says before darting off.

I set down the ketchup and mustard bottles, then wipe my hands and go to see who's at the door.

Standing in the doorway is Shelley Hartley. I haven't seen Evan's mother in . . . I don't know how many years. She looks good, though. Like she's taking care of herself. Her hair is no longer dyed blonde, but her natural dark brown. Her skin looks healthy, and her jeans and tank top actually cover all the important bits.

Last time I asked Evan about her, he'd said he wasn't quite ready to spring her on me. Until now, it seems.

"I baked a pie." She holds up a tin wrapped in foil. Then her smile falters. "Okay, that's a lie. I bought it at the grocery store and rewrapped it. But it's a start, right?"

Evan is clearly trying not to laugh. "That's great, Mom." He gives her a kiss on the cheek and invites her in. "We appreciate it."

Cooper's standing in the living room as she enters. He offers to take the pie from her. While he doesn't entirely manage a smile or a kiss for his mother, he gives her a nod. "Thank you," he says brusquely. "That was thoughtful."

By the relief on her face, it's more than Shelley hoped for.

"Mom. You remember Genevieve." Evan coaxes me forward.

"Of course I do. And oh my goodness, you've gotten so gorgeous." She pulls me into a tight hug. "Evan told me about the engagement. I'm so happy for you two," she gushes, holding me out with her hands on my arms. She glances at her son with an oddly smug smile. "See, baby? Didn't I tell you? My love predictions always come true." She turns back to me. "I always liked you two together. Even when you were little. I said, he's going to marry that girl someday, if he knows what's good for him."

I get a tad choked up. "That's really sweet."

"Man, your kids," she exclaims, eyes huge. "Such beautiful kids you two are gonna have. I can't even."

Shelley is already planning playdates with her grandkids before we've even set a date for the wedding. Not that we're stalling, but with the grand opening at The Beacon coming up, scheduling is a nightmare.

Anyway, I think my dad is still in denial about the whole thing. A little upset that I asked Evan to marry me without talking to him first—and a lot scared that his only daughter isn't five years old anymore. Bad enough he's losing Craig to college next week. Billy and Jay insist he'll work his way through the grief process in time for the wedding. Well, that's if Evan survives the ritual hazing Shane and Kellan have promised to execute until he cracks or goes into hiding. But I have faith Evan can hold his own. One way or another, we're mashing these families together, and consequences be damned. Kicking and screaming if need be.

After the greetings, we all go outside and start loading up our plates. It's a super-casual affair. Harrison and Liz seem to have hit it off, so busy talking and smiling that they're ignoring their food. Heidi and a few others gather at the railing to eat standing. Riley scarfs down hot dogs and coleslaw on the deck steps.

Meanwhile, the twins sit at the table, with me and Mac at their sides and their mom sitting across from them. Evan squeezes my hand under the table. He'd been anxious the past couple days. Tense. I hadn't understood why, but now, seeing the contentment in his eyes, I realize this is a big moment for him. Having Shelley and her boys at the same table has been a long time coming. Despite the different roads we've taken to get here—and because of them—we've all found our second chances.

A cool breeze wafts over the deck and flutters our napkins. The season's changing in the Bay, summer's almost over. My arms break out in goosebumps, and a tiny shiver travels down my spine. It's then I realize my shirt feels a bit drafty. I glance up to see Evan's smug grin and remember I'm not wearing a bra. At my first dinner with his mother. And my nipples are hard.

Evan draws a tick mark in the air.

I walked right into this one. "So it's going to be like that, huh?" I grumble under my breath.

He pulls my hand up to kiss my knuckles. "Always."

ACKNOWLEDGMENTS

Some stories are harder to write than others, and some are an absolute joy to put down on the page. This book falls into the latter category—I loved every second of writing *Bad Girl Reputation* and breathing life into Genevieve and Evan. Their story is one of redemption, forgiveness, second chances, and the difficulties that come with shedding your past and trying to be a better, healthier version of yourself. I'm so thankful for everyone who helped me shape the Avalon Bay world and bring this book into your hands:

My editor Eileen Rothschild and the SMP all-stars: Lisa Bonvissuto, Christa Desir, Beatrice Jason, Alyssa Gammello, and Jonathan Bush for another incredible cover.

Kimberly Brower, agent extraordinaire and fellow *Felicity* fanatic.

Ann-Marie and Lori at Get Red PR for helping spread the word about this book and the Avalon Bay series.

Every single reader, reviewer, blogger, Instagrammer, Tweeter, Booktokker, and supporter of my books. I couldn't do this job without you, and I'm forever grateful to you.

And to all the former bad girls out there, know that second chances and new beginnings are always within your reach.

ABOUT THE AUTHOR

Amanda Nicole White

A *New York Times, USA Today,* and *Wall Street Journal* bestselling author, ELLE KENNEDY grew up in the suburbs of Toronto, Ontario, and is the author of more than forty romantic suspense and contemporary romance novels, including the international bestselling Off-Campus and Briar U series.